GARTHOWEN

A Story of a Welsh Homestead

ALLEN RAINE

1ˢᵗ WORLD
LIBRARY
Literary Society

Garthowen

Allen Raine

© 1st World Library, 2009
PO Box 2211
Fairfield, IA 52556
www.1stworldlibrary.com
First Edition

LCCN: 2009923324

Softcover ISBN: 978-1-4218-8801-9
Hardcover ISBN: 978-1-4218-8900-9
eBook ISBN: 978-1-4218-8702-9

Purchase *"Garthowen"*
as a traditional bound book at:
www.1stWorldLibrary.com/purchase.asp?ISBN=978-1-4218-8801-9

1st World Library is a literary, educational organization
dedicated to:

- Creating a free internet library of downloadable ebooks

- Hosting writing competitions and offering book publishing
scholarships.

Interested in more 1st World Library books? contact:
literacy@1stworldlibrary.com
Check us out at: www.1stworldlibrary.com

1st World Library Literary Society

Giving Back to the World

"If you want to work on the core problem, it's early school literacy."

- James Barksdale, former CEO of Netscape

"No skill is more crucial to the future of a child, or to a democratic and prosperous society, than literacy."

- Los Angeles Times

"Literacy... means far more than learning how to read and write... The aim is to transmit... knowledge and promote social participation."

- UNESCO

"Literacy is not a luxury, it is a right and a responsibility. If our world is to meet the challenges of the twenty-first century we must harness the energy and creativity of all our citizens."

- President Bill Clinton

"Parents should be encouraged to read to their children, and teachers should be equipped with all available techniques for teaching literacy, so the varying needs and capacities of individual kids can be taken into account."

- Hugh Mackay

CONTENTS

I. A Turn of the Road 9

II. "Garthowen" 16

III. Morva of the Moor 33

IV. The Old Bible 45

V. The Sea Maiden 54

VI. Gethin's Presents 65

VII. The Broom Girl 76

VIII. Garthowen Slopes 87

IX. The North Star 100

X. The Cynos 111

XI. Unrest 124

XII. Sara's Vision 135

XIII. The Bird Flutters 147

XIV. Dr. Owen 158

XV. Gwenda's Prospects 175

XVI. Isderi 187

XVII. Gwenda at Garthowen 201

XVIII. Sara.. 219

XIX. The "Sciet" 230

XX. Love's Pilgrimage...242

XXI. The Mate of the "Gwenllian".........................255

XXII. Gethin's Story 270

XXIII. Turned Out! 281

XXIV. A Dance on the Cliffs..................................301

CHAPTER I

A TURN OF THE ROAD

It was a typical July day in a large seaport town of South Wales. There had been refreshing showers in the morning, giving place to a murky haze through which the late afternoon sun shone red and round. The small kitchen of No. 2 Bryn Street was insufferably hot, in spite of the wide-open door and window. A good fire burnt in the grate, however, for it was near tea-time, and Mrs. Parry knew that some of her lodgers would soon be coming in for their tea. One had already arrived, and, sitting on the settle in the chimney corner, was holding an animated conversation with his landlady, who stood before him, one hand akimbo on her side, the other brandishing a toasting fork. Her beady black eyes, her brick-red cheeks and hanks of coarse hair, were not beautiful to look upon, though to-day they were at their best, for the harsh voice was softened, and there was a humid gentleness in the eyes not habitual to them. Her companion was a young man about twenty-three years of age, dark, almost swarthy of hue, tanned by the suns and storms of foreign seas and many lands, As he sat there in the shade of the settle one caught a glance of black eyes and a gleam of white teeth, but the easy, lounging attitude did not show to advantage the splendid build of Gethin Owens. One of his large brown fists, resting on the rough deal table, was covered with tattooed hieroglyphics, an anchor, a mermaid, and a heart, of course! Anyone conversant with the Welsh language would have divined at once, by the long-drawn intonation of the first words in every remark, that the subject of conversation was one of sad or tender interest.

"Well, indeed," said Mrs. Parry, "the-r-e's missing you I'll be, Gethin! We are coming from the same place, you see, and you are knowing all about me, and I about you, and that I supp-o-s-e is making me feel more like a mother to you than to the other lodgers."

"Well, you *have* been like a mother to me, mending my clothes and watching me so sharp with the drink. Dei anwl! I don't think I ever took a glass with a friend without you finding me out, and calling me names. 'Drunken blackguard!' you called me one night, when as sure as I'm here I had only had a bottle of gingerpop in Jim Jones's shop," and he laughed boisterously.

"Well, well," said Mrs. Parry, "if I wronged you then, be bound you deserved the blame some other time, and 'twas for your own good I was telling you, my boy. Indeed, I wish I was going home with you to the old neighbourhood. The-r-e's glad they'll be to see you at Garthowen."

"Well, I don't know how my father will receive me," said her companion thoughtfully. "Ann and Will I am not afraid of, but the old man—he was very angry with me."

"What *did* you do long ago to make him so angry, Gethin? I have heard Tom Powell and Jim Bowen blaming him very much for being so hard to his eldest son; they said he was always more fond of Will than you, and was often beating you."

"Halt!" said Gethin, bringing his fist down so heavily on the table that the tea-things jingled, "not a word against the old man—the best father that ever walked, and I was the worst boy on Garthowen slopes, driving the chickens into the water, shooing the geese over the hedges, riding the horses full pelt down the stony roads, setting fire to the gorse bushes, mitching from school, and making the boys laugh in chapel; no wonder the old man turned me away."

"But all boys are naughty boys," said Mrs. Parry, "and that wasn't enough reason for sending you from home, and shutting the door against you."

"No," said Gethin, "but I did more than that; I could not do a worse thing than I did to displease the old man. I was fond of scribbling my name everywhere. 'Gethin Owens' was on all the gateposts, and on the saddles and bridles, and once I painted 'G. O.' with green paint on the white mare's haunch. There was a squall when that was found out, but it was nothing to the storm that burst upon me when I wrote something in my mother's big Bible. As true as I am here, I don't remember what I wrote, but I know it was something about the devil, and I signed it 'Gethin Owens,' and a big 'Amen' after it. Poor old man, he was shocking angry, and he wouldn't listen to no excuse; so after a good thrashing I went away, Ann ran after me with my little bundle, and the tears streaming down her face, but I didn't cry—only when I came upon little Morva Lloyd sitting on the hillside. She put her arms round my neck and tried to keep me back, but I dragged myself away, and my tears were falling like rain then, and all the way down to Abersethin as long as I could hear Morva crying and calling out 'Gethin! Gethin!'"

"There's glad she'll be to see you."

"Well, I dunno. She was used to be very fond of me; she

couldn't bear Will because he was teazing her, but I was like a slave to her. 'I want some shells to play,' sez she sometimes, and there I was off to the shore, hunting about for shells for her. 'Take me a ride,' sez she, and up on my shoulder I would hoist her, as happy as a king, with her two little feet in my hands, and her little fat hands ketching tight in my hair, and there's galloping over the slopes we were, me snorting and prancing, and she laughing all the time like the swallows when they are flying."

They were interrupted by a clatter of heavy shoes and a chorus of boisterous voices, as three sailors came in loudly calling for their tea.

"Hello, Gethin! not gone? Hast changed thy mind?"

"Not a bit of it," said Gethin, pointing to his bag of clothes. "I have been a long time making up my mind, but it's Garthowen and the cows and the cawl for me this time and no mistake."

"And Morva," said Jim Bowen, with a smile, in which lurked a suspicion of a sneer. "Thee may say what thee likes about the old man, and the cows, and the cawl, but I know thee, Gethin Owens! Ever since I told thee what a fine lass Morva Lloyd has grown thee'st been hankering after Garthowen slopes."

There was a general laugh, in which Gethin joined good-humouredly, standing and stretching himself with a yawn. The evening sun fell full upon him, showing a form of sinewy strength, and a handsome manly face. His dark skin and the small gold rings in his ears, so much affected by Welsh sailors, gave him a foreign look, which rather added to the attractiveness of his personal appearance.

Allen Raine

When the tea had been partaken of, with a running accompaniment of broad jokes and loud laughter, the three sailors went out, leaving Gethin still sitting on the settle. This was Mrs. Parry's hour of peace—when her consumptive son came home from his loitering in the sunshine to join her at her own quiet "cup of tea," while her rough husband was still engaged amongst the shipping in the docks.

"Well, what'll I say to Nani Graig?" said Gethin.

"Oh, poor mother, my love, and tell her if it wasn't for my boy Tom I'd soon be home with her again, for I'll never live with John Parry when my boy is gone."

"He's not going for many a long year," said Gethin, slapping the boy on the back, his more sensitive nature shrinking from such plain speaking.

But Tom was used to it, and smiled, shuffling uneasily under the slap.

"What you got bulging out in your bag like that?" he asked.

"Oh, presents for them at Garthowen; will I show them to you?" said the sailor awkwardly, as he untied the mouth of the canvas bag. "Here's a tie for my father, and a hymn-book for Ann, and here's a knife for Will, and a pocket-book for Gwilym Morris, the preacher who is lodging with them. And here," he said, opening a gaily-painted box, "is something for little Morva," and he gently laid on the table a necklace of iridescent shells which fell in three graduated rows.

"Oh! there's pretty!" said Mrs. Parry, and while she held the shining shells in the red of the sun, again the doorway was darkened by the entrance of two noisy, gaudily-dressed girls, who came flouncing up to the table.

"Hello! Bella Lewis and Polly Jones, is it you? Where you come from so early?" said Mrs. Parry.

"Come to see me, of course!" suggested the sailor.

"Come to see you and stop you going," said one of the girls. "Gethin Owens, you *are* more of a skulk than I took you for, though you are rather shirky in your ways, if this is true what I hear about you."

"What?" said Gethin, replacing the necklace in the box.

"That you are going home for good, going to turn farmer and say good-bye to the shipping and the docks." And as she spoke she laid her hand on the box which Gethin was closing, and drew out its contents. There was a greedy glitter in her bold eyes as she asked, "Who's that for?" and she clasped it round her own neck, while Gethin's dark face flushed.

"Couldn't look better than there," he answered gallantly, "so you keep it, to remember me," and tying up his canvas bag he bade them all a hurried good-bye.

Mrs. Parry followed him to the doorway with regretful farewells, for she was losing a friend who had not only paid her well, but had been kind to her delicate boy, and whose strong fist had often decided in her favour a fight with her brutal husband.

"There you now," she said, in a confidential whisper and with a nudge on Gethin's canvas bag, "there you are now; fool that you are! giving such a thing as that to Bella Lewis! What did you pay for it, Gethin? Shall I have it if I can get it from her? Why did you give it to her? you said 'twas for little Morva—"

Allen Raine

"Yes, it was," he said; "but d'ye think, woman, I would give it to Morva after being on Bella Lewis's neck? No! that's why I am running away in such a hurry, to buy her another, d'ye see, and Dei anwl, I must make haste or else I'll be late on board. Good-bye, good-bye."

Mrs. Parry looked after him almost tenderly, but called out once more:

"Shall I have it if I can get it?"

"Yes, yes," shouted Gethin in return, and as he made his way through the grimy, unsavoury street, he chuckled as he pictured the impending scrimmage.

CHAPTER II

"GARTHOWEN"

Along the slope of a bare brown hill, which turned one scarped precipitous side to the sea, and the other, more smooth and undulating, towards a fair scene of inland beauty, straggled the little hamlet of Pont-y-fro. Jos Hughes's shop was the very last house in the village, the road beyond it merging into the rushy moor, and dwindling into a stony track, down which a streamlet trickled from the peat bog above. The house had stood in the same place for two hundred years, and Jos Hughes looked as if he too had lived there for the same length of time. His quaintly cut blue cloth coat adorned with large brass buttons, his knee breeches of corduroy, and grey blue stockings, looking well in keeping with his dwelling, but very out of place behind a counter. His brown wrinkled face and ruddy cheeks were like a shrivelled apple, his shrewd inquisitive eyes peered out through a pair of large brass-rimmed spectacles, and, to judge by his expression, the view they got of the world in general was not satisfactory.

It was a day of brilliant sunshine and intense heat, but through the open shop door the sea wind came in with refreshing coolness. Behind the counter Jos Hughes measured and weighed lazily, throwing in with his short weight a compliment,

Allen Raine

or a screw of peppermints, as the case required.

"Who is this coming up in the dust?" he mumbled.

"'Tis Morva of the moor," said a woman standing in the doorway and shading her eyes with her hand. "What does she want, I wonder? There's a merry lass she is!"

"Oh! day or night, sun or snow don't matter to her," said Jos Hughes.

At this moment the subject of their remarks entered the shop, and, sitting on a sack of maize, let her arms fall on her lap. She was quickly followed by a large black sheep dog, who bounded in and, placing his fore-paws on the counter, with tongue hanging out, looked at Jos Hughes intently.

"Down, Tudor!" said the girl, and he sprang on a sack of peas beside her.

The mountain wind blowing in through the open doorway touzled the little curls that were so unruly in Morva's hair; it was neither gold nor ebony, but, looking at its rich tints, one was irresistibly reminded of the ripe corn in harvest fields, while the blue eyes were like the corn flowers in their vivid colouring.

"How are they at Garthowen?" asked Fani "bakkare."

"Oh! they are all well there," answered the girl, panting and fanning herself with her sun-bonnet, "except the white calf, and he is better."

"There's hot it is!" said Fani, taking up her basket of groceries.

"Oh! 'tis hot!" said the girl, "but there's a lovely wind from the sea."

"What are you wanting to-day, Morva?" said Jos.

"A ball of red worsted for Ann, and an ounce of 'bacco for 'n'wncwl Ebben, and oh! a ha'porth of sweets for Tudor."

The dog wagged his tail approvingly as Jos reached down from the shelf a bottle of pink lollipops, for, though a wild country dog, he had depraved tastes in the matter of sweets.

"There's serious you all look! what's the matter with you?" said the girl, looking smilingly round.

"Nothing is the matter as I know," said Fani, "only there's always plenty of trouble flying about. We can't be all so free from care as you, always laughing or singing or something."

"Indeed I wish we could," said Madlen, a pale girl who was bending over a box of knitting pins, looking round curiously and rather sadly; "I wish the whole world could be like you, Morva."

Morva snatched the girl's listless hand in her own warm firm grasp, and pressed it sympathetically, for she knew Madlen's secret sorrow.

"Wait another year or two," said Fani, "we'll talk to you then! Wait till your husband comes home drunk from 'The Black Horse!'"

"And wait till you put all your money into a shop and then find it doesn't pay you," said Jos.

Madlen said nothing, but Morva knew that in her heart she

Allen Raine

was thinking, "Wait until your lover proves false to you!" and she gave her hand another squeeze.

"Well, indeed!" she said springing up, "what are you all talking about? I won't put all my money in a shop, and I won't marry a drunkard! Sixpence, is it? I am going home over the bog and round the hill, but I am going to sit on the bench outside a bit first. There's lots of swallows' nests under your eaves, Jos Hughes; that brings good luck, they say, so your shop ought to pay you well."

So saying she passed out, and sitting on the bench round the corner of the house she kissed her hand toward the swallows, who flitted in and out of their nests, twittering ecstatically.

"Hark to her," said Fani, "singing again, if you please— always light-hearted! always happy! I don't think its quite right, Jos bach, do you? You are a deacon at Penmorien and you ought to know. If it was a hymn now! but you hear it's all nonsense about the swallows. Ach y fi! she is learning them from Sara "spridion';[1] some song of the 'old fathers' in past times!"

"Yes," said Jos, sanctimoniously clasping his stubby fingers, "I'm afraid the girl is a bit of a heathen. What wonder is it? Nursed by Sara—always out with the cows or the sheep, and they say she thinks nothing of sleeping under a hedge, or out on the slopes, if any animal is sick and wants watching."

Fani went out with a toss of her head, as the sweet voice came in through the little side window with the twittering of the swallows and the cluck, cluck of a happy brood hen.

Outside, Morva had forgotten all about Jos Hughes and Fani "bakkare's" sour looks, and was singing her heart out to the sunshine.

"Sing on, little swallows," she said, "and I'll sing too. Sara taught me the 'bird song' long ago when I was a baby."

And in a clear, sweet voice she joined the birds, and woke the echoes from the brown cliffs. The tune was quaint and rapid; both it and the words had come down to her with the old folklore of generations passed away.

"Over the sea from the end of the wide world
I've come without wetting my feet, my feet, my feet,
Back to the old home, straight to the nest-home,
Under the brown thatch, oh sweet! oh sweet! oh sweet!

"When over the waters I flew in the autumn,
Then there was plenty of seed, of seed, of seed.
Women have winnow'd it, threshers have garner'd it,
Barns must be filled up indeed, indeed, indeed!

"Are you glad we have come with a flitter and twitter
Once more on the housetop to meet, to meet, to meet?
Make haste little primroses, cowslips, and daisies, we're
Longing your faces to greet, to greet, to greet!"

—Trans

"Yes, that's what you are singing. Good-bye," and waving her hand towards them again, she turned her face to the boggy moor, picking her way over the stepping-stones which led up to the dryer sheep paths.

The golden marsh marigolds glittered around her, the beautiful bog bean hung its pinky white fringe over the brown peat pools, the silky plumes of the cotton grass nodded at her as she passed, and the wind whispered in the rushes the secrets of the sea.

Allen Raine

Morva listened with a smile, a brown finger up-raised. "Yes, yes, I know what you are singing too down there in the rushes, sweet west wind," she said. "Sara has told me, but I haven't time to sing the 'wind song' to-day," and reaching the sheep path which led round the mountain, she sped against the wind, her hair streaming behind her, her blue skirt fluttering in the breeze, the ball of scarlet worsted and the shining 'bacco box held high in either hand to steady her flying footsteps, Tudor barking with joy as he bounded after her and twitched at her fluttering skirts.

It was tea-time when she reached Garthowen, and, winter or summer, that was always the pleasantest hour at the farmstead, when the air was filled with the aroma of the hot tea, and the laughter and talk of the household. On the settle in the cosy chimney corner sat Ebben Owens himself, the head of the family and the centre of interest to every member of it. He possessed that doubtful advantage, the power of attracting to himself the affection and friendship of everyone who came in contact with him; his children idolised him, and Morva was no whit behind them in her affection for him. In spite of his long grizzled locks, and a slight stoop, he was still a hale and hearty yeoman under his seventy years. His cheeks bore the ruddy hue of health, his eyes were still bright and clear, the lines of his mouth expressed a gentle and sensitive nature. It was by no means a strong face, but its very weakness perhaps accounted for the protecting tenderness shown to him by all his family. As he sat there in the shadow of the settle it was easy to understand why his children were so devotedly attached to him, and why he bore the reputation of being the kindest and most good-natured man in Pont-y-fro and its neighbourhood. Ann, his only daughter, was looking smilingly at him from the head of the table, her smooth brown hair parted over her madonna-like brows, her brown eyes full of laughter. Opposite to her, at the bottom of the table, sat Gwilym Morris, preacher at the

Calvinistic Methodist chapel, down in the valley by the shore. He had lived at Garthowen for many years as one of the family, being the son of an old friend of Ebben Owens. Having a small—very small—income of his own, he was able to devote his services to the chapel in the valley, expecting and receiving nothing in return but a pittance, for which no other minister would have been willing to work. He was a dark, pale man, of earnest and studious appearance, of quiet manners, and rather silent, but often seeking the liquid brown eyes which lighted up Ann's gentle face.

"Tis the only time father is cross when he has lost his 'bacco box," said Ann, laughing; "but then he is as cross as two sticks."

"Lol! lol!" said the old man snappishly, "give me a cup of tea; but I can't think where my 'bacco box is. I swear I left it here on the table."

Gwilym Morris hunted about in the most unlikely places, as men generally do—on the tea tray, between the leaves of some newspapers which stood on the deep window-sill. He was about to open Ann's work-bag in search of it, when Morva entered panting, and placed the shining box and ball of red wool on the table.

"Good, my daughter," said Ebben Owens, pocketing his new-found treasure, and regaining his good temper at once.

"I saw it was empty, so I took it with me to Jos Hughes's shop," she said.

Soon afterwards, seated on her milking stool, she was singing to the rhythm of the milk as it streamed into the frothing pail, for Daisy refused to yield her milk without a musical accompaniment. Very soft and low was the girl's singing, but clear and sweet as that of the thrush on the thorn bush behind her.

"Give me my little milking pail,
For under the hawthorn in the vale
The cows are gathering one by one,
They know the time by the westering sun.
Troodi, Troodi! come down from the mountain,
Troodi, Troodi! come up from the dale;
Moelen, and Corwen, and Blodwen, and Trodwen!
I'll meet you all with my milking pail."

So sang the girl, and the lilting tune caught the ears of a youth who was just entering the farmyard. He knew it at once. It was a snatch of Morva's simple milking song. He stopped to pat Daisy's broad forehead, and Morva looked up with a smile.

"Make haste," she said, "or tea will be finished. Where have you been so late?"

"Thou'll be surprised when I tell thee," said the young man; but before he had time for further conversation, Ann's voice called him from the kitchen window, and he hurried away unceremoniously.

Morva continued her song, for Daisy wanted nothing new, but was contented with the old stave which she had known from calfhood.

Will Owens, arriving in the farm kitchen, had evidently been eagerly awaited. Both Ann and Gwilym Morris came forward to meet him, and Ebben Owens rubbed his hands nervously over his corduroy knees.

"Well?" said all three together.

"Well!" echoed Will, flinging his hat across to the window-sill. "It's all right. I met Price the vicar coming down the street, so I touched my hat to him, and he saw at once that I wanted to speak to him, and there's kind he was. 'How's your father?' he said, 'and Miss Ann, is she well? I must come up and see them soon.'"

"Look you there now," said his father.

"'They will be very glad to see you sir,' I said, but I didn't know how to tell him what I wanted.

"'I am very glad to hear how well you get on with your books,' he said; 'but 'tisn't every young man has Gwilym Morris to help him and to teach him.' And then, you see, when he made a beginning, 'twas easier for me to explain."

The preacher's pale face lighted up with a smile of pleasure, and Ann flushed with gratified pride as Will continued.

"'He is a man in a hundred,' said Mr. Price, 'and 'tis a pity that his talents are wasted on a Methodist Chapel. I wish I could persuade him to enter the Church.'"

"'Well, you'll never do that,' I said. 'You might as well try to turn the course of the On. He won't come himself, but he is sending a very poor substitute to you, sir.'"

"'And who is that? You?' said Mr. Price."

"'Well, sir, that is what I wanted to see you about. You know that although we are Methodists bred and born, both my grandfather and my great-grandfather had a son in the Church,' and with that he took hold of my two hands."

"'And your father is going to follow their good example? I

am glad!' and he shook my hands so warmly."

"There for you now!" said Ebben Owens.

"'I will do all I can for you,' Mr. Price said, 'and I'm sure your uncle will help you.'"

"'Oh!' said I, 'if my father will send me to the Church, sir, it will be without pressing upon anyone else for money,' for I wasn't going to let him think we couldn't afford it."

"Right, my boy," said Ebben Owens, standing up in his excitement; "and what then?"

"Oh! then he asked me when did I think of entering college; and I said, 'Next term, sir, if I can pass.'"

"'No fear of that,' he said again, 'with Gwilym Morris at your elbow.' But I'm choking, Ann; give me a cup of tea, da chi.[2] I'll finish afterwards."

"That's all, I should think," said the preacher; "you've got on pretty far for a first interview."

"I got a little further, though," said Will. "What do you think, father, he has asked me to do?"

"What?" said the old man breathlessly.

"He asked would I read the lessons in church next Sunday week. "Twould be a good beginning,' he said; 'and tell your father and Miss Ann they must come and hear you.'

"'Well,' I said, 'my father hasn't been inside a church for years, and I don't know whether he will come.'"

"Well, of course," said the old man eagerly, "I will come to hear you, my boy, and Ann—"

"Not I, indeed," said Ann, with a toss of her head, "there will be a sermon in my own chapel."

"But it will be over before eleven, Ann, and I don't see why you shouldn't go if you wish to," said Gwilym Morris.

"I don't wish to," she answered, turning to the tea-table, and pouring out her brother's tea.

She was a typical Welsh woman, of highly-strung nervous temperament, though placid in outward appearance and manners, unselfish even to self-effacement where her kindred were concerned, but wary and suspicious beyond the pale of relationship or love; a zealous religionist, but narrow and bigoted in the extreme. In his heart of hearts Ebben Owens also hated the Church. Dissent had been the atmosphere in which his ancestors had lived and breathed, but in his case pride had struggled with prejudice, and had conquered. For three generations a son had gone forth from Garthowen to the enemy's Church, and had won there distinction and riches. True, their career had withdrawn them entirely from the old simple home circle, but this did not deter Ebben Owens from desiring strongly to emulate his ancestors. Why should not Will, the clever one of the family, his favourite son—who had "topped" all the boys at the village school, and had taken so many prizes in the grammar school at Caer-Madoc—why should not he gain distinction and preferment in the Church, and shed fresh lustre on the fading name of "Owens of Garthowen," for the name had lost its ancient prestige in the countryside? In early time theirs had been a family of importance, as witness the old deeds in the tin box on the attic rafters, but for two hundred years they had been simple farmers. They had never been a thrifty race, and the broad lands which tradition said once belonged to them had been sold from time to time, until nothing remained but the old farm with its hundred acres of mountain land. Ebben Owens never troubled his head, however, about the past glories of his race. He inherited the "happy-go-lucky," unbusiness-like temperament which had probably been the cause of his ancestors' misfortunes, but Will's evident love of learning had aroused in the old man a strong wish to remind the world that the "Owens of Garthowen" still lived, and could push themselves to the front if they wished.

As Will drank his tea and cleared plate after plate of bread and butter, his father looked at him with a tender, admiring gaze. Will had always been his favourite. Gethin, the eldest son, had never taken hold of his affections; he had been the mother's favourite, and after her death had drifted further and further out of his father's good graces. The boy's nature was a complete contrast to that of his own and second son, for Gethin was bold and daring, while they were wary and secret; he was restless and mischievous, while his brother was quiet and sedate; he was constantly getting into scrapes, while Will always managed to steer clear of censure. Gethin hated his books too, and, worse than all, he paid but scant regard to the services in the chapel, which held such an important place in the estimation of the rest of the household. More than once Ebben Owens, walking with proper decorum to chapel on Sunday morning, accompanied by Will and Ann, had been scandalised at meeting Gethin returning from a surreptitious scramble on the hillside, with a row of blue eggs strung on a stalk of grass. A hasty rush into the house to dress, a pell-mell run down the mountain side, a flurried arrival in the chapel, where Will and his father had already hung up their hats on the rail at the back of their seat, did not tend to mitigate the old man's annoyance at his son's erratic ways.

Gethin was the cause of continual disturbances in the household, culminating at last in a severer thrashing than usual, and a dismissal from the home of his childhood—a dismissal spoken in anger, which would have been repented of ere night had not the boy, exasperated at his utter inability to rule his wild and roving habits, taken his father at his word and disappeared from the old homestead.

"Let him go," Ebben Owens had said to the tearful pleading Ann. "Let him go, child; it will do him good if he can't behave himself at home. Let him go, like many another rascal, and find out whether cold and hunger and starvation will suit him. Let him feel a pinch or two, and he'll soon come home again, and then perhaps he'll have come to his senses and give us less trouble here."

Ann had cried her eyes red for days, and Will had silently grieved over the loss of his brother, but he had been prudent, and had said nothing to increase his father's anger, so the days slipped by and Gethin never returned.

His father, relenting somewhat (for he seldom remained long in the same frame of mind), made inquiries of the sea-faring men who visited the neighbouring coast villages, and learning from them that Gethin had been taken as cabin boy by an old friend of his, whom he knew to be of a kindly disposition, felt quite satisfied concerning his son's safety, and congratulated himself upon the result of his own firmness.

"There's the very thing for him," he thought; "'twill make a man of him, and 'tis time he should be brought to his senses! and he won't be so ready with his 'Amens!' again. Ach y fi!"

From time to time as the years sped on, news of Gethin came in a roundabout way to the farm, and at last a letter from some foreign port, from which it was evident that the youth, now growing up to manhood, still retained his bright sunny nature and laughter-loving ways, together with the warmth of heart which had always distinguished the troublesome Gethin. There was no allusion to the past, no begging for forgiveness, no hint of a wish to return home. His father seldom looked at the lad's letters, but flung them to Will to be read, the quarrel between him and his son, instead of dwindling into forgetfulness, seeming to grow and widen in his mind with each succeeding year, as trifling disagreements frequently do in weak but obstinate natures.

"Gethin will be an honour to us yet," Ann would say sometimes.

"Honour indeed!" the old man would answer, with a red spot on each cheek, which always denoted his rising anger. "What honour? A common sailor lounging about from one foreign port to another! 'Tis stopping at home he ought to be, and helping his old father with the farming. If Will is going to be a clergyman I will want somebody to help me with the work."

"Well, I'm sure he would come, father, and glad too, if he knew that you were wanting him."

"Oh, I don't want him. Let him come when he likes; that's fair enough."

But Gethin still roamed, and latterly nothing had been heard of him, no letters and no news. 'Tis true, a dim and hazy report had reached Garthowen from some sailor in the village "that Gethin Owens was getting on 'splendid,' that he was steady and saving." Ann had flushed with pleasure, but the old man had laughed scornfully, saying, "Well, I'll believe that when I see it—Gethin steady and saving!" And even Will had joined in the laugh, but Gwilym Morris looked vexed and serious.

"I think, indeed, you are too hard upon that poor fellow,", he said; "he may return to you some day like the prodigal son. Don't forget that, Ebben Owens—"

"Oh, I don't forget that," said the old man; "and when he comes home in the same temper as the son we read of, then we'll kill for him the fatted calf."

"Well, I'd like to know what did he do whatever?" said a girlish voice from behind the settle, where Morva Lloyd (who was shepherdess, cowherd, milkmaid, all in one), was drying her hands on a jack-towel; "what did Gethin do so very bad?"

"Look in his mother's Bible," said the old man, "and you'll see his last sin."

"I've put it away," said Ann. "Twas too wicked to leave about; but he was very young, father, and Gwilym says—"

"Oh! Gwilym," said her father, "has an excuse for everyone's faults except his own; for thine especially."

There was a general laugh, during which Morva made up her mind to hunt up the old Bible.

"I hope," said Ann, addressing Will, when he had come to an end of his tea, "you told Price the vicar that Gwilym did not spend evening after evening here helping you on with your studies, *knowing* that you were going to be a clergyman?"

"No, I didn't tell him that, but I can tell him some other time," answered Will, who would have promised anything in his desire to propitiate Ann and his father, and to gain their consent to his entering Llaniago College at the beginning of the next term.

"I'll tell him if he comes here," said Ann. "I wouldn't have him think that Gwilym Morris, the Methodist minister, spent his time in teaching a parson."

"Well," said the preacher, who was standing at the old glass bookcase looking for a book, "you certainly did spring the news very suddenly upon me, Will; you kept your secret very close; but still, Ann, it makes no difference. I would have done anything for your brother, and I'm glad, whatever his course may be, that I have been able to impart to him a little knowledge."

"Look you here now," said the old man, shuffling uneasily, for there was a secret consciousness between him and his son that they had wilfully kept Gwilym Morris in the dark as long as possible, fearing lest his dissenting principles might prevent the accomplishment of their wishes, "look you here now, Will, October is very near, and it means money, my boy, and that's not gathered so easy as blackberries about here; you must wait until Christmas, and you shall go to Llaniago in the New Year, but I can't afford it now."

Will's handsome face flushed to the roots of his hair, his blue eyes sparkled with anger, and the clear-cut mouth took a petulant curve as he answered, rising hastily from the tea-table:

"Why didn't you tell me that sooner, instead of letting me go and speak to Mr. Price? You have made a fool of me!" And he went out, banging the door after him.

There was a moment's silence.

"Will's temper is not improving," said Ann at last.

"Poor boy," said the indulgent father, "'tis disappointed he is; but it won't be long to wait till January."

"But, father," said Ann, "there is the 80 pounds you got for the two ricks? You put that into the bank safe, didn't you?"

"Yes, yes, yes, quite safe, 'merch i. Don't you bother your head about things that don't concern you," and he too went out, leaving Ann drumming with her fingers on the tea-tray.

Her father's manner awoke some uneasiness in her mind, for long experience had taught her that money had a way of slipping through his hands ere ever it reached the wants of the household.

"I went with him to the bank," said Gwilym Morris reassuringly, "and saw him put it in," and Ann was satisfied.

Under her skilful management, in spite of their dwindled means, Garthowen was always a home of plenty. The produce of the farm was exchanged at the village shops for the simple necessaries of domestic life. The sheep on their own pasture lands yielded wool in abundance for their home-spun clothing, the flitches of bacon that garnished the rafters provided ample flavouring for the cawl, and for the rest Will and Gwilym's fishing and shooting brought in sufficient variety for the simple tastes of the family. Indeed, there was only one thing that was not abundant at Garthowen, and that was—ready money!

[1] Spirit Sara.

[2] Do.

CHAPTER III

MORVA OF THE MOOR

When Will had reached the door of the farm kitchen in a fume of hot temper, the cool sea breeze coming up the valley had bathed his flushed face with so soothing an influence that he had turned towards it and wandered away to the cliffs which made the seaward boundary of the farm. A craggy hill on the opposite side of the valley cast its lengthening shadow on his path until he reached the Cribserth, a ridge of rocks which ran down the mountain side on the Garthowen land. It rose abruptly from the mountain pasturage, as though some monster of the early world were struggling to rise once more from its burial of ages, succeeding only in erecting its rugged spine and crest through the green sward. This ridge marked a curious division of the country, for on one side of it lay all the signs of cultivation of which this wind-swept parish could boast. Here were villages, fertile fields, and wooded valleys; but beyond the rugged escarpment all was different. For miles the seaward side of the hills was wild and bare, except for the soft velvet turf, interspersed with gorse and heather, which stretched up the steep slopes, covering and softening every rough outline. Even Will, as he rounded the ridge, recovered his equanimity, and his face lighted up with pleasure at the sight which met his view. Down below glistened a sea of burnished gold, with tints and shades of purple grey; above stretched a sky of still more glowing colours; and landward, rising to the blue of the zenith, the rugged moorland was covered with a mantle of heath and gorse, which shone in the evening sun in a rich mingling of gold and purple.

"What a glorious evening!" were Will's first thoughts. The birds sang around him, the sea lisped its soft whispers on the sea below, the song of a fisherman out on the bay came up on the breeze, the rabbits scudded across his path, and the seagulls floated slowly above him. All the sullenness went out of his face, giving way to a look of pleased surprise, as out of the carpet of gorgeous colouring spread before him rose suddenly the vision of a girl. It was Morva who came towards him, her hair glistening in the sunshine, her blue eyes dancing with the light of health and happiness. Behind a rising knoll stood her foster-mother's cottage, almost hidden by the surrounding gorse and heather, for, according to the old Welsh custom, it had been built in a hollow scooped out behind a natural elevation, which protected it from the strong sea wind; in fact, there was little of it visible except its red chimney-pot, from which generally curled the blue smoke of the furze and dried ferns burning on the bare earthen floor below.

Turning round the pathway to the front of the house, one came upon its whitewashed walls, the low worm-eaten door deep set in its crooked lintels, and its two tiny windows, looking out on the sunny garden, every inch of which was neatly and carefully cultivated by Morva's own hands; for she would not allow her "little mother" to tire herself with hard work in house or garden. To her foster-child it was a labour of love. In the early morning hours before milking time at the farm, or in the grey of the twilight, Morva was free to work in her own garden, while Sara only tended her herb bed. There at the further end was the potato bed in purple flower, here were rows of broad beans, in which the bees were humming, attracted by their sweet aroma that filled the evening air; there was the leek bed waving its grey green blades, and here, in the sunniest corner of all, was Sara's herb bed, which she tended with special care, whose products were gathered at stated times of the moon's age, not without serious thought and many consultations of an old herbal, brown with age, which always rested with her Bible and Williams "Pantycelyn's" hymns above the lintel of the door. For nearly seventeen years this had been Morva's home, ever since the memorable night of wind and storm which had wrecked the good ship *Penelope* on her voyage home from Australia. She had reached Milford safely a week before, after a prosperous voyage, and having landed some of her passengers, was making her further way towards Liverpool, her final destination. It was late autumn, and suddenly a storm arose which drove her out of her course, until on the Cardiganshire coast she had become a total wreck. In the darkness and storm, where the foaming waves leapt up to the black sky, the wild wind had battered her, and the cruel waves had torn her asunder, and engulphed her in their relentless depths; and when all was over, a few bubbles on the face of the water, a few planks tossed about by the waves, were all the signs left of the *Penelope*. The cottagers on the rugged coast never forgot that stormy night, when the roofs were uplifted from the houses, when gates were wrenched from their hinges, when the shrieking wind had torn the frightened sheep from their fold, and carried them over hedges and hillocks. There had never been such a storm in the memory of the oldest inhabitant, and when in the foam and the spray, Stiven "Storrom" had raked out from the debris washed on to the shore a hencoop, on which was bound a tiny baby, sodden and cold, but still alive, every one of the small crowd gathered on the beach below Garthowen slopes, considered he had added a fresh claim to his name—a name which he had gained by his frequent raids upon the fierce storms, and the harvest which he had gathered from their fury. That baby had found open arms and tender hearts ready to succour it, and when Sara "'spridion" had stretched imploring hands towards it, reminding the onlookers of her recent bereavement, it was handed over to her fostering care. "Give it to me," she said, "my heart is empty; it will not fill up the void, but it will help me to bear it. There are other reasons," she added, "good reasons." She had carried it home triumphantly, and little Morva had never after missed a mother's love and tenderness. The seventeen years that followed had glided happily over her head; in fact she was so perfect an embodiment of health and happiness, that she sometimes excited the envy of the somewhat sombre dwellers on those lonely hillsides; and when in the golden sunset, she suddenly rose from the gorse bloom to greet Will's sight, she had never appeared brighter or more brimful of joy.

"Well, indeed," said Will, casting a furtive glance behind him, to make sure that no one from Garthowen was following in his footsteps, "Morva, lass, where hast come from? I will begin to think thou art one of the spirits thy mother says she sees. I thought thee wast busy in the dairy at home!"

Morva laughed merrily.

"I had some milk to bring home, and Ann sent me early to help mother a bit. I was going now to gather dry furze and bracken to boil the porridge. Will you come and have supper with us, Will?"

"I have just had my tea," he said, "and a supper of bitter herbs into the bargain, for my father angered me by something he said. He is changeable as the wind, and I was roaming over here to seek for calmness from the sea wind,

Allen Raine

and perhaps a talk with Sara."

"Yes, come! She is in the herb garden gathering her bear's claws and rue; 'tis the proper time for them. But first we must cut the bracken."

Will took her sickle and soon cut a pile of the dry brittle fuel, binding it with a rope which she carried; and turning towards the cottage, they dragged it behind them.

"You go and seek mother," said Morva, "while I go and boil the porridge."

And in the garden Will found Sara stooping over her herb bed, and deeply intent upon her task.

The sun was setting now, and threw its ruddy beams upon the sunny corner, and upon the aged face and figure of the old woman.

"Well, 'machgen i," she said, straightening herself. "What is it?"

"Oh, nothing," said Will; "only, roaming about the moor, I came in to see you, and Morva has asked me to have supper with you—you are gathering your herbs?"

"Yes, 'tis time to dry them and hang them up under the rafters; if they will save one human being from pain 'twill be a good thing. Last night Mari Lewis came to ask me for something for her boy; I gave it to her, but she never came to tell me whether it had done him any good," and she smiled as she led the way back to the cottage carrying her bunches of herbs.

"Was it Dan?" asked Will.

"Yes."

"Then he is well, for I saw him ploughing this evening."

"That's better than thanks," said the old woman, entering the dark cottage, where Morva was stirring a crock which hung on a chain from the open chimney, the furze and bracken flaming and crackling beneath it and lighting up her beautiful face. Once in the cottage, Sara sat down on the old oak settle and waited for her supper, her herbs lying in a green heap on the floor beside her. The square of scarlet flannel, which she always wore pinned on her shoulders, made a bit of bright colour in the gloom, her wrinkled hands were clasped on her lap, and a far-away look came into her wonderful dark eyes.

Morva looked up from her work.

"Are you seeing anything, mother?"

"No, no, child, nothing. Make haste with the supper," said Sara.

And when Morva had divided the porridge in the three shining black bowls, they drew round the bare oak table, on which the red of the setting sun made a flickering pattern of the mallow bush growing on the garden hedge. They talked about the farm work, the fishing, the lime burning, the fate of the *Lapwing*, which had sailed in the autumn and had never returned, until, when supper was over, Will rose to go with a stretch and a yawn.

"Ann wants me to give the white calf his medicine to-night, mother," said Morva.

"Wilt come with me now?" said Will, "for I am going."

Allen Raine

"Yes, go," said the old woman, "go together."

But as the two young people went out under the low doorway she looked after them pensively, and remained long looking up at the evening sky, which the open door revealed. At last she tied up her herbs and began washing her bowls, and while engaged at her work she sang. Her voice had the pathetic tremble of old age, but was still true and musical, for she had once been a singer among singers, and the song that she sang—who shall describe it? from what old stores of memory did it come to light? from what old wells of ancient folklore and tradition did it spring? But Sara was full of songs and hymns—of the simplest and oldest—of the rocky path—of the golden summit—of the angelic host—of the cloud of witnesses—but of the more modern hymns of church festivals or chapel revivals, of creeds and shibboleths, she knew nothing!

Outside on the heath and gorse Will and Morva made their way along the narrow sheep paths, until, reaching the green sward where two could walk abreast, he drew nearer, and passing his arm round her shoulders, turned her gently towards the side of the cliff, where jutting crags and stunted thorns made "sheltered nooks for lovers' seats."

"Come, sit down here, Morva," he said; "all day I have wanted to talk to thee. Dost know what kept me so long at Castell On to-day? Dost know what grand thing is opening out before me? Dost know, lass, the time is coming when I will be able to put rings on thy fingers, and silken scarves on thy shoulders, and pretty shoes on thy little feet?"

Morva's lips parted, disclosing two rows of pearly teeth, as she stared in astonishment at her companion.

"Oh, Will, lad, what is the matter with thee? Hast lost thy

senses? We mustn't be long or Ann will be waiting."

"Oh, Ann!" said Will pettishly, "let her wait; listen thou. I am going to finish with them all before long; I am not going to plod on here on the farm any longer; I am going to college, lass; I am going to pass my examination and be a clergyman, like Mr. Price, or like that young curate who was stopping with him a month ago. Didst see him, Morva? Such a gentleman! dressed so grand, and went from town in the Nantmyny carriage."

Morva was still speechless.

"Oh, anwl! what art talking about, Will?" she said at last.

"Truth, Morva; I will be like that young man before long, and when I have a home ready I will send for thee; thou shalt come secretly to meet me in some large town where no one will know us. I will have a silken gown ready for thee, and we will be married, and thou shalt be a real lady."

Morva's only answer was a peal of laughter, which reached over moor and crag and down to the sandy beach below.

"Oh, Will, Will!" she gasped, with her hand on her side, "now indeed thy senses are roaming. Morva Lloyd in velvet shoes and silken gowns, and Will Owens with flapping coat tails like Mr. Price, and one of those ugly shining hats that the gentlemen wear! Oh, Will, Will! there's funny indeed!" and she laughed again until she woke the echoes from the cliffs.

"Hush-sh-sh!" said Will, a good deal nettled, "or laugh at thyself if thou wilt, but not at me, for I tell thee that's how thou'lt see me very soon."

Allen Raine

"Well, indeed, then," said the girl, "when thou tak'st that path thou must say 'good-bye' to Morva Lloyd, for such things will never suit her."

"I tell thee, girl," said Will, taking both her hands in his, "thou must come with me. I will follow that path—I feel I must, and I feel it will lead to riches and honour, but I feel, too, that I can never live without thee; thou must come with me, Morva. What is in the future for me must be for thee too! dost hear?"

"Yes, I hear," said the girl, with a gasp.

"Dost remember thy promise, Morva? When we were children together, and sat here watching the stars, didn't I hold thy little finger and point it up to the North Star and make thee promise to marry me? And if thou art going to change thy mind, 'twill break my heart," and his mouth took a sad, pathetic curve.

"But I am not going to change. I remember the star which I pointed to when I promised to marry thee. 'Twill be up there by and by when the light is gone, for it is always there, though the others move about."

"Yes, 'tis the North Star, and the English have a saying, 'As true as the North Star'—that's what thou must be to me, Morva."

"Yes, indeed. The English are very wise people. But after all, Will, I must laugh when I think of a clergyman marrying a shepherdess. Oh! Will, Will!" added the girl more seriously and in a deprecating tone, "thou art talking nonsense. Think it over for a day or two, and then we'll talk about it. I cannot stay longer—Ann will be angry."

And slipping out of his grasp, she ran with light footsteps over the soft turf, Will looking after her bewildered and troubled, until she disappeared round the edge of the ridge; then he rose slowly, picked up his book, and followed her with slow steps and an anxious look on his handsome face. He was tall and well grown, like every member of the Garthowen family; his reddish-brown hair so thick above his forehead that his small cap of country frieze was scarcely required as a covering for his head; and not even the coarse material of his homespun suit, or his thick country-made shoes, could hide a certain air of jaunty distinction, which was a subject of derision amongst the young lads of his acquaintance, but of which he himself was secretly proud. From boyhood he had despised the commonplace ways of his rustic home, and had always aimed at becoming what he called "a gentleman." No wonder, then, that with his foot, as he thought, on the first rung of the ladder, he was pensive and serious as he followed Morva homewards.

Ebben Owens, when he had risen from the tea table, had followed his son into the farmyard, but finding no trace of him there, his face had taken a troubled and anxious expression, for Will was the idol of his soul, the apple of his eye, and a ruffle upon that young man's brow meant a furrow on the old man's heart. He reproached himself for having allowed "the boy" to proceed too far with his plans for entering college before he had suggested that there might be a difficulty in finding the required funds. After a long reverie, he muttered as he went to the cowsheds:

"Well, well, I must manage it somehow. I must ask Davy my brother, to lend me the money until I have sold those yearlings."

Not having the moral courage to open his mind to his son, he allowed the subject to drift on in the dilatory fashion characteristic of his nation; and as time went on, he began to allude to the coming glories of Llaniago in a manner which soothed Will's irritation, and made him think that the old man, on reconsideration, was as usual becoming reconciled to his son's plans. As a matter of fact, Ebben Owens was endeavouring to adjust his ideas to those of his son, solving the difficulties which perplexed him by mentally referring to "Davy my brother," or "those yearlings."

Will also took refuge, as a final resource, in the thought of his rich uncle, the Rev. Dr. Owen, of Llanisderi, who, through marriage with a wealthy widow, had in a wonderfully short time gained for himself preferment, riches, and popularity.

"I will stoop to ask Uncle Davy to help me," he thought, "rather than put it off;" but he kept his thoughts to himself, hoping still that his father would relent, for he considered the want of funds was probably a mere excuse for keeping him longer at home.

It had been very easy, one day a month earlier, when, sitting in the barn together, they had talked the matter over, for Ebben Owens to make any number of plans and promises, for he had just sold two large ricks of hay, and had placed the price thereof in the bank. He was, therefore, in a calm and contented frame of mind, and in the humour to be reckless in the matter of promises. The whole country side knew how good-natured he was, how ready to help a friend, very often to his own detriment and that of his family; he was consequently very popular at fair and market. Everybody brought his troubles to him, especially money troubles; and although Ebben Owens might at first refuse assistance, he would generally end by opening his heart and his pockets, and lending the sum required, sometimes on good security, sometimes on bad, sometimes on none at all but his creditors' word of honour, whose value, alas! was apt to rise or fall with the tide of circumstances. He had many times given his own word of honour to his anxious daughter, that he would never again lend his money or "go security" for his neighbours without consulting his family; but over the first blue of beer, at the first fair or market, he had been unable to withstand the pleadings of some impecunious friend. Only a week after he and Will had talked over their plans in the barn, Jos Hughes, who was his fellow-deacon at Penmorien Chapel, had met him in the market at Castell On, and had persuaded him to lend him the exact amount which his ricks had brought him, with many promises of speedy repayment.

"Tis those hard-hearted Saeson,[1] Mr. Owens bach! They will never listen to reason, you know," he had argued, "and they are pressing upon me shocking for payment for the goods I had from them last year; and me such a good customer, too! I must pay them this week, Mr. Owens bach, and you are always so kind, and there is no one else in the parish got so much money as Garthowen. I will give you good security, and will pay you week after next, as sure as the sun is shining!"

It was a plausible tale, and Ebben Owens, as usual, was weak and yielding. He liked to be considered the "rich man" of the parish, and to be called "Mr. Owens," so Jos went home with the money in his pocket, giving in return only his "I. O. U.," and a promise that the transaction should be carefully kept from Ann's ears, for Ebben Owens was more afraid of his daughter's gentle reproofs than he had ever been of his wife's sharp tongue.

[1] English.

CHAPTER IV

THE OLD BIBLE

On the following Sunday, Morva kept house alone at Garthowen, for everyone else had gone to chapel, except Will, who had walked to Castell On, which was three miles away up the valley of the On, he having been of late a frequent attendant at Mr. Price's church. The vicar was much beloved by all his parishioners, beloved and respected by high and low, but still his congregation was sparse and uncertain, so that every new member was quickly noticed and welcomed by him—more especially any stray sheep from the dissenting fold possessed for him all the interest of the sheep in the parable, for whose sake the ninety and nine were left in the wilderness. Will had gone off with a large prayer book under his arm, determined to take special note of the Vicar's manner in reading the lessons, for on the following Sunday this important duty would devolve upon him.

No one who has not spent a Sunday afternoon in a Methodist household can really have sounded the depths of dullness; the interminable hours between the early dinner and the welcome moment when the singing kettle and the jingling of the tea-things break up the spell of dreariness, the solemn silence pervading everything, broken only by the persistent ticking of the old clock on the stairs, Morva had noted them all rather wearily. Even the fowls in the farmyard seemed to walk about with a more sober demeanour than usual, but more trying than anything else to an active girl was the fact that *there was nothing to do.*

It was a hot blazing summer afternoon; she had paid frequent visits to the sick calf, which was getting well and mischievous again, and inclined to butt at Tudor, so even that small excitement was over, and the girl came sauntering back under the shady elder tree which spread its branches over the doorway of the back kitchen. She crossed to the window, and leaning her arms on the deep sill looked out over the yard, and the fields beyond, to the sea, whose every aspect she knew so well. Not a boat or sail broke its silvery surface, even there the spell of Sabbath stillness seemed to reign. She thought of the chapel with its gallery thronged with smiling lads and lasses; she thought of Will sitting bolt upright at church. Yes; decidedly the dullness was depressing; but suddenly a brightening thought struck her. Why should she not hunt up the old Bible which Ann said was too bad to leave about? What could Gethin have written in it that was so wicked? She remembered him only as her friend and companion, and her willing slave. She was only a child when he left, but she had not forgotten the burst of bitter wailing which she sent after him as he picked up his bundle and tore himself away from her clinging arms, and how she had cried herself to sleep that night by Sara's side, who had tried to pacify her with promises of his speedy return. But he had never come, and his absence seemed only to have left in his father's memory a sense of injury, as though he himself had not been the cause of his boy's banishment. Even Ann and Will, who had at first mourned for him, and longed for his return, appeared to have forgotten him, or only to regard his memory as a kind of sorrowful dream. Why, she knew not, but the thought of him on this quiet Sunday afternoon filled her with tender recollections.

She opened every dusty book in the glass bookcase, but in vain. Here was Bunyan's "Pilgrim's Progress"; and here a worm-eaten, brown stained book of sermons; here were Williams of "Pantycelyn's" Hymns and his "Theomemphis," with Bibles old and new, but *not* the one which she sought. Mounting a chair, and from thence the table, she at last drew out from under a glass shade, covering a group of stuffed birds, a dust-begrimed book, with a brass clasp and nails at the corners. Dusting it carefully she laid it on the table before her, and proceeded to decipher its faded inscriptions. Yes— no doubt this was the book for which she had sought, and with a brown finger following the words, she read aloud:

"ANN OWENS, HER BOOK,
GARTHOWEN."

Beneath this was written in a boyish hand the well-known doggerel lines:

"This book is hers, I do declare,
Then steal it not or else beware!
For on the dreadful Judgment Day
You may depend the Lord will say,
'Where is that book you stole away?'"

It was written in English, and Morva, though she could make herself understood in that language, was not learned enough to read it easily. However, there was no difficulty in reading the signature of "William Owens" which followed. She turned over a leaf, and here indeed were signs of Gethin, for all over the title page was scrawled with many flourishes "Gethin Owens, Garthowen," "Gethin Owens," "G. O.," "Gethin," etc. It was wrong, no doubt, to deface the first page of the Bible in this way, but Ann had said "too wicked to leave about!" so Morva searched through the whole book, until on the fair leaf which fronted "The Revelations" she found evident proof of Gethin's depravity; and she quailed a little as she saw a vivid and realistic pen and ink drawing of a fire of leaping flames, standing over which was a monster in human shape, though boasting of a tail and cloven hoofs. With fiendish glee the creature was toasting on a long fork something which looked fearfully like a man, whose starting eyes and writhing limbs showed plainly that he was not as happy as his tormentor. It was very horrible, and Morva closed the book with a snap, but could not resist the temptation of another peep, as there was something written beneath in Welsh, which translated ran thus:

"Here's the ugly old Boy! I tell you beware!
If you fall in his clutches there's badly you'll fare!
Look here at his picture, his claws and his tail,
If you make his acquaintance you're sure to bewail!
Hallelujah! Amen!

—GETHIN OWENS."

At the last words Morva stood aghast; this then was Gethin's terrible crime! "Oh! there's a boy he must have been!" said the girl, clasping her fingers as she leant over the big Bible. "Oh! dear, dear! no wonder 'n'wncwl Ebben was so angry! I don't forget how cross he was one day when I let the Bible fall; didn't his face alter! 'Dost remember, girl,' he said, 'it is the Word of God!' and there's frightened I was! Poor Gethin! 'twas hard, though, to turn him away, for all they are such wicked words. 'Hallelujah! Amen!' Well, indeed! the very words that 'n'wncwl Ebben says so solemn after the sermon in Penmorien!" and she shook her head sorrowfully, "and here they are after this song about the devil. Will would never have done that," and she pondered a little seriously; "but poor Gethin! After all, he was only a boy, and boys do dreadful things—but Will never did! Mother reads her Bible plenty too, but I don't think she would have turned me out

Allen Raine

when I was a little girl if I had made this song. I'll tell her to-night, and see what she says about Gethin, poor fellow."

She closed and clasped the book, and mounting the table again, replaced it in the hollow at the top of the bookcase, with the stuffed birds and glass case over it.

When Ann and her father returned from chapel, there was a conscious look on her face which they both remarked upon at once.

"What's the matter, Morva?" asked Ann.

"Is the calf worse?" asked the old man.

"No," answered the girl, her seriousness vanishing at once. "Nothing's the matter; the calf is getting quite well."

As she spoke Will arrived from church, wearing a black coat and a white cotton tie, his prayer-book under his arm.

Ebben Owens looked at him with an air of proud satisfaction.

"Here comes the parson," he said, and Will smiled graciously even at Morva, whom he generally ignored in the presence of Ann and his father.

"Hast been stopping at home, Morva? I thought thee wast at chapel."

"I am going home now," said the girl, eyeing him rather critically. "I will tell mother I have seen the 'Rev. Verily Verily.'"

Will flushed up, though he pretended to laugh; but Ebben Owens looked annoyed.

"No more of that nonsense, Morva; thou art a bit too forward, girl; remember Will is thy master's son, and leave off thy jokes."

"Oh! she meant no harm," said Will apologetically; "'twill be hard if we can't have our jokes, parson or no parson."

"Well, indeed," said Morva, without a shade of annoyance in her voice, "'twill be hard at first; but I suppose I will get used to it some day. Will you want me again to-night, Ann?"

"No; but to-morrow early," said Ann.

And Morva went singing through the farmyard, and along the fields to the Cribserth; but to-day it was a hymn tune of mournful minor melody which woke the echoes from moor and cliff. Rounding the ridge, the same fair view greeted her eyes, as had chased away Will's ill-temper on the preceding evening, and she sat a moment under the shadow of a broom bush to ponder, for Morva was a girl of many thoughts though her mind was perfectly uneducated, her heart and soul were alive with earnest questions. Her seventeen years had been spent in close companionship with a woman of exceptional character, and although the girl did not share in the abnormal sensitiveness of her foster-mother, she had gained from her intimacy with her, an unusual receptivity to all the delicate influences of Nature. Sara claimed to be clairvoyant, though she had never heard the word. Morva was clear seeing only; her pure and simple spirit was undimmed by any mists of worldly ideas; no subterfuge or plausible excuse ever hid the truth from her, and yet in spite of this crystal innocence, she kept her engagement to Will a secret from all the world, excepting Sara.

It is the custom of the country to keep a love affair a secret as long as possible; if it is discovered and talked about by outside gossips, half its delight and charm is gone; indeed it is considered indelicate to show any signs of love-making in public. It is true that this secrecy often leads to serious mischief, but, on the other hand, there is much to be said for the sensitive modesty of the Welsh maiden, when compared with an English girl's too evident appreciation of her lover's attentions in public. So hitherto Morva had followed Will's lead, and shown no signs of more than the love and affection which was naturally to be expected from her close intercourse with the Garthowen family from babyhood. Did she feel anything more? She thought she did. From childhood she had been promised to Will; the idea of marrying him when they were both grown to manhood and maidenhood had been familiar to her ever since she could remember. It caused no excitement in her mind, no tumult in her heart. It was in the nature of things—it was Will's wish—it was her fate! She did not rebel against it, but it woke no thrill of delight within her. She had promised, and the idea of breaking that promise was one that never entered her mind; but this evening, as she sat under the broom bush, a curious feeling of unrest came over her. How was it all to end? Would it not be wiser of Will to turn his face to the world lying beyond the Cribserth ridge, where the towns—the smooth roads—the college—and the many people lay, and leave her to her lonely moor—to the sheep, and the gorse, and the heather? She looked around her, where the evening sun was flooding land and sea with golden glory.

"I would not break my heart," she thought; "here is plenty to make me happy; there's the sea and the sands and the rocks! and at night, oh, anwl! nobody knows how beautiful it is to float about in Stiven 'Storrom's' boat, in and out of the rocks, and the stars shining so bright in the sky, and the moon sometimes as light as day. Oh, no; I wouldn't be unhappy," and stretching her arms out wide, she turned her face up to the glowing sky. "I love it all," she said, "and I do not want a lover."

Catching sight of the blue smoke curling up from the heather mound behind which Sara's cottage was buried, she rose, and dropping her sober thoughts, ran homewards, singing and filling the sweet west wind which blew round her with melody. But ere she reached the cottage door, there came a whistle on the breeze, and, turning round, she saw Will standing at the corner of the Cribserth, just where the rocky rampart edged the hillside. She turned at once and slowly retraced her footsteps, Will coming to meet her with more speedy progress. He had changed his clothes, and in his work-a-day fustian looked far better than he had in the black cloth suit which he had worn to church.

"Well, indeed, Morva lass, thou runn'st like the wind; I could never catch thee. Come and sit down behind these bushes, for I want to talk to thee. Wert offended at what my father said just now?"

"Offended! no," said the girl. "Garthowen has a right to say what he likes to me, and besides, he was right, Will. I must learn to treat thee with more respect."

"Respect!" said Will, laying hold of her hands, "'tis more love I want, lass, and not respect; sometimes I fear thou dost not love me."

"But I do," said the girl calmly; "I do love thee, Will. 'Tis truth that I would lay down my life for thee and all at Garthowen. Haven't you been all in all to me—father, sister, brother? and especially you and I, Will, have been together all our lives. Ann has not been quite so much a sister to me since we've grown up, but then I am only the milkmaid, and Gwilym Morris has come between."

"Yes, true," said Will; "but between me and thee, Morva, nothing has ever come. Promise me once more, that when I have a home for thee thou wilt marry me and come and live with me. My love for thee is the only shadow on my future, because I fear sometimes that something will part us, and yet, lass, it is the brightest spot, too—dost believe me?"

"Yes," said Morva, with eyes cast down upon the wild thyme which her fingers were idly plucking, "I believe thee, Will. What need is there to say more? I have promised thee to be thy wife, and dost think I would break my word? Never! unless, Will, thou wishest it thyself. Understand, that when once I am sure that thou hast changed thy mind then I will never marry thee."

"That time will never come," said Will; and they sat and talked till the evening shadows lengthened and till the sun sank low in the west; then they parted, and Morva once more turned her footsteps homewards. She walked more soberly than before, and there was no song upon her lips.

CHAPTER V

THE SEA MAIDEN

Sara was sitting at tea when the girl arrived. Through the open doorway came the glow of the sunset, with the humming of bees and the smell of the thyme and the bean flowers.

"Thou hast something to ask me, Morva. What is it?" she said, making room for her at the little round table in the chimney corner.

"Oh, 'tis nothing, I suppose," said Morva, cutting herself a long slice of the flat barley loaf; "only 'tis the same old questions that are often troubling me. What is going to become of me? What is in the future for me? I used to think when I grew to be a woman I would marry Will, and settle down at Garthowen close to you here, mother fach, and take care of 'n'wncwl Ebben when Ann and Gwilym Morris were married; but now, somehow, it all seems altered."

The old woman looked at her long and thoughtfully.

"Wait until later, child," she said. "Clear away the tea, tidy up the hearth, and let me read my chapter while the daylight lasts," and finishing her tea Morva did as she was bid.

Later on in the evening, sitting on the low rush stool opposite to Sara, she continued her inquiries.

"Tell me, mother, about Will and Gethin when they were boys. Was Gethin so very wicked?"

"Wicked? No," said Sara, "never wicked. Wild and mischievous and full of pranks he was, but the truest, the kindest boy in the world was Gethin Owens Garthowen."

"And Will?"

"Will was a good boy always, but I never loved him as I loved the other. Gethin had a bad character because he stole the apples from the orchard, and he took Phil Graig's boat one day without asking leave, and there was huboob all over the village, and his father was mad with anger, and threatened to give him a thrashing; but in the evening Gethin brought the boat back quite safely. He had been as far as Ynysoer, and he brought back a creel full of fish for Phil, to make up. Phil made a good penny by the fish, and forgave the boy bach; but his father was thorny to Gethin for a long time. Then at last he did something—I never knew what—that offended his father bitterly, and he was sent away, and never came back again."

"Mother," said Morva solemnly, "I have found out what he did. He got his mother's Bible and he wrote some dreadful things in it, and made a fearful picture."

"Picture of what?" asked the old woman.

"A picture of flames and fire, and the devil toasting a man on it, and a song about the devil. Here it is; I remember every word," and she repeated it word for word, it having sunk deeply into her mind. "Then at the bottom he had written,

'Hallelujah, Amen! Gethin Owens Garthowen.'"

A smile overspread Sara's countenance as she observed Morva's solemnity, a smile which somewhat lessened the girl's disquietude.

"Was it so very wicked, mother?"

"Wicked? No," said the old woman. "What wonder was it that the boy drew a picture of the things that he heard every Sunday in chapel—God's never-ending anger, and the devil's gathering in the precious souls which He has created. That would be a failure, Morva, and God can't fail in anything. No, no," she added shrewdly, nodding her head, "He will punish us for our sins, but the devil is not going to triumph over the Almighty in the end."

Morva pondered seriously as she fed the fire from a heap of dried furze piled up in the corner behind the big chimney.

"I was very little when Gethin went away, but I remember it. Now tell me about the night when first I came to you. I love that story as much now as I did when I was a child."

"That night," said Sara, "oh! that night, my child. I see it as plainly as I have seen the gold of the sunset to-night. It had been blowing all day from the north-west till the bay was like a pot of boiling milk. It was about sunset (although we couldn't see the sun), there was a dark red glow over everything as if it were angry with us. Up here on the moor the wind shrieked and roared and tore the poor sheep from the fold, and the little sea-crows from their nests. I sat here alone, for it was the year when my husband and baby had died, and, oh, I was lonely, child! I moaned with the wind, and my tears fell like the rain. I heaped the furze on the fire and kept a good blaze; it was cold, for it was late in October.

It grew darker and darker, and I sat on through the night, and gradually my ears got used to the raging of the storm, I suppose, for I fell asleep, sitting here under the chimney, but suddenly I awoke. The wind was shrieking louder than ever, and there in that dark corner by the spinning-wheel I saw a faint shadow that changed into the form of a woman. She was pale, and had on a long white gown, her hair, light like thine, hung down in threads as if it were wet. She held out her hands to me, and I sat up and listened. I saw her lips move, and, though I could not hear her voice, I seemed to understand what she said, for thee know'st, Morva, I am used to these visions."

"Yes," said the girl, nodding her head.

"Well, I rose and answered her, and drew my old cloak from the peg there. 'I am coming,' I said, and she glided before me out through the door and down the path over the moor. I saw her, a faint, white figure, gliding before me till I reached the Cribserth, and there she disappeared, but I knew what she wished me to do; and I followed the path down to the shore, and there was tumult and storm indeed, the air full of spray, and even in the black night the foaming waves showing white against the darkness. Out at sea there was a ship in distress, there was a light on the mast, and we knew by its motion that the poor ship was sorely tossed and driven. Many people had gathered on the shore in the darkness. No one had thought of calling me, for here we are out of the world, Morva; but the spirits come more easily to the lonely moor than to the busy town. Ebben Owens was there, and little Ann, and all the servants and the people from the farms beyond the moor, but no one could help the poor ship in her distress. At last the light went out, and we knew the waves had swallowed her up, and all night on the incoming tide came spars and logs and shattered timber, and many of the drowned sailors. Stiven 'Storrom' was there as usual, and in the early dawn, when there was just a streak of light in the angry sky, he shouted out that he had found something, and we all ran towards him, and there, tied safely to a hencoop, lay a tiny baby, wet and sodden, but still alive. It was thee, child, so wasn't I right to call thee Morforwyn?[1] though indeed we soon shortened it to Morva. When I saw thee I knew at once 'twas thy mother who had come to me here, and had led me down to the shore, and I begged them to give me the baby. 'There is a reason,' I said, but I did not tell them what it was. What was the good, Morva? They would not understand. They would only jeer at me as they do, and call me Sara "spridion.'[2] Well, let them, I am richer than they, oh! ten thousand times, and I would not change my life here on the lonely moor, and the visions I have here, for any riches they could offer me."

"No, indeed, and it is a happy home for me, too, though I don't see your visions; but then you tell me about them, and it teaches me a great deal. Mother, I think my life is more full of happy thoughts than most of the girls about here because of your teaching. No, I don't want to leave here, except, of course, I must live at Garthowen when Will wants me."

The old woman made no answer, but continued to gaze at the crackling furze.

"You wish that too, mother?" asked the girl.

"I did, 'merch i, but now I don't know indeed, Morva. Thou must not marry without love."

"Without love, mother! I have told you many times I love Will with all my heart."

Sara shook her head with a smile of incredulity.

Allen Raine

"It is a dream, child, and thou wilt wake some day. Please God it may not be too late."

A pained look overspread the girl's face, a turmoil of busy thought was in her brain, but there was no uncertainty in the voice with which she answered:

"Mother, I love Will. I have told him so. I have promised to be his wife, and I would rather die than break my word."

"Well, well," said Sara, "there is no need to trouble, child, only try to do right, and all that will be settled for thee; but I think I see sorrow for thee, and it comes from Will."

"Well," said Morva bravely, as she flung another bunch of furze on the fire, "I suppose I must bear my share of that like other people. 'As the sparks fly upward,' mother, the Bible says, and see, there's a fine lot of them," and she raked the small fire with the lightsome laugh of youth.

"Ah!" said the old woman, "thou canst laugh at sorrows now, Morva; but when they come they will prick thee like that furze."

"And I will stamp them out as I do these furze, mother," and again she laughed merrily, but ceased suddenly, and, with her finger held up, listened intently.

"What is that sound?" she asked. "It is some one brushing through the heather and furze. Who can it be? Is it Will?"

Both women were fluttered and frightened, for such a thing as a footstep approaching their door at so late an hour was seldom heard, for at Garthowen they all retired early, and the cottagers in the village below avoided Sara as something uncanny, and looked askance even at Morva, who seemed not to have much in common with the other girls of the countryside.

"'Tis a man's step," she whispered, "and he is coming into the cwrt," and, while she was still speaking, there came a firm, though not loud, knock at the door.

Morva shrank a little under the big chimney, where she stood in the glow of the flaming furze; but Sara rose without hesitation, and going to the door, opened it wide.

"Who is here so late at night?" she asked.

"Shall I come in, Sara, and I will explain?" said a pleasant, though unknown voice. "'Twas to Garthowen I was going, but when I reached there every light was put out, so I wouldn't wake the old man from his first sleep, and I have come on here to see can you let me sleep here to-night? Dost know me, Sara?"

"Gethin Owens!" exclaimed the old woman, with delighted surprise. "My dear boy, come in!"

There was no light in the cottage except that of the fitful furze fire, so that when Gethin entered he exclaimed at the darkness,

"Sara fach, let's have a light, for I am longing to see thee!"

Morva threw a fresh furze branch on the fire. The motion attracted Gethin's attention, and as the quick flame leaped up, the girl stood revealed. While Sara fumbled about for the candle the flame burnt out, and for a moment there was gloom again.

"Hast one of thy spirits here, or was it an angel I saw

standing there by the fire?" said the newcomer; but when Sara had succeeded in lighting the candle, he saw it was no spirit, but a creature of flesh and blood who stood before him.

"No, no, 'tis only Morva," said Sara, dusting a chair and pushing it towards him. "Sit thee down, my boy, and let me have a good look at thee. Well! well! is it Gethin, indeed? this great big man, so tall and broad."

But Gethin's eyes were fixed upon the girl, who still stood astonished and bewildered under the chimney.

"Morva!" he said, "is this little Morva, who cried so bad after me when I went away, and whom I have longed to see so often? Come, shake hands, lass; dost remember thy old playmate?" and he advanced towards her with both hands outstretched.

Morva placed her own in his.

"Yes, indeed," she answered, "now in the light I can see 'tis thee, Gethin—just the same and unaltered only—only—"

"Only grown bigger and rougher and uglier, but never mind; 'tis the same old Gethin who carried thee about the slopes on his shoulders, but, dei anwl! I didn't expect to see thee so altered and so—so pretty."

Morva blushed but ignored the compliment.

"Well, indeed, there's glad they'll be to see thee at Garthowen."

"Dost think?"

"Yes, indeed; but won't I put him some supper, mother?"

"Yes, 'merch i, put on the milk porridge."

And Morva, glad to hide her embarrassment, set about preparing the evening meal, for Gethin's eyes told the admiration which he dared not speak. His gaze followed her about as she mixed the milk and the oatmeal in the quaint old iron crochon.

"'Twill soon be ready; thee must be hungry, lad," said Sara, laying the bowls and spoons in readiness on the table.

"Yes, I am hungry, indeed, for I have walked all the way from Caer-Madoc. 'Tis Sunday, thee seest, so there were no carts coming along the road. Halt, halt, lass!" he said, "let me lift that heavy crochon for thee."

"Canst sleep on the settle, Gethin?" asked the old woman, "for I have no bed for thee. I will spread quilts and pillows on it."

Gethen laughed boisterously.

"Quilts and pillows, indeed, for a man who has slept on the hard deck, on the bare ground, on a coil of ropes; and once on a floating spar, when I thought sleep was death, and welcomed it too."

"Hast seen many hardships then, dear lad?" said Sara. "Perhaps when we were sleeping sound in out beds, thou hast oftentimes been battling with death and shipwreck."

"Not often, but more than once, indeed," said Gethin.

"Thou must tell us after supper some of thy wonderful escapes."

Allen Raine

"Yes, I'll tell you plenty of yarns," said Gethin, his eyes still following Morva's movements.

A curious silence had fallen upon the girl, generally so ready to talk in utter absence of self-consciousness. She served the porridge into the black bowls, and shyly pushed Gethin's towards him, cutting him a slice of the barley bread and butter.

"I have left my canvas bag at Caer-Madoc," said Gethin, when he had somewhat appeased his appetite. "'Twill come up to Garthowen to-morrow. I have a present in it for thee, Morva."

"For me?" said the girl, and a flood of crimson rushed into her face. "I didn't think thee wouldst be remembering me."

"There thou wast wrong, then," said Gethin, cutting himself another slice.

"Well, indeed, I have never had a present before!"

"I have one for Ann, and Will, and my father, God bless him! And how is good old Will?"

"He is quite well," said Morva.

"As industrious and good as ever? Dei anwl! there's a difference there was between me and him! You wouldn't think we were children of the same mother. Well, you can't alter your nature, and I'm afraid 'tis a bad lot Gethin Owens will be to the end!" And he laughed aloud, his black eyes sparkling, and the rings in his ears shining out in the gloom of the cottage.

Morva looked at the stalwart form, the swarthy skin, the

strong, even teeth, that gleamed so white under the black moustache, the jet-black hair, the broad shoulders, and thought how proud Ann would be of such a brother.

They sat long into the night, Sara gathering from the young man the history of all his varied experiences since he had left his father's home; Morva listening intently as she cleared away the supper, Gethin's eyes following her light figure with fascinated gaze.

At last the door was bolted, the fire swept up, and Sara and Morva, retiring to the penucha, left Gethin to his musings, which, however, quickly resolved themselves into a heavy, dreamless sleep, that lasted until the larks were singing above the moor on the following morning.

[1] Sea-maiden.

[2] Spirit Sara.

CHAPTER VI

GETHIN'S PRESENTS

The corn harvest had commenced, and Ebben Owens was up and out early in the cornfields. Will, too, was there, but with scant interest in the work. It had never been a labour of love with him, and now that fresh hopes and prospects were dawning upon him, the farm duties seemed more insignificant and tedious than ever. Had it been Gethin who stretched himself and yawned as he attacked the first swathe of corn, Ebben Owens would have called him a "lazy lout," but as it was Will, he only jokingly rallied him upon his want of energy.

"Come, come," he said, "thee'st not got thy gown and bands on yet. We'll have hard work to finish this field by sunset; another hand wouldn't be amiss."

"Here it is, then," said a pleasant, jovial voice, as a sunburnt man came through the gap, holding out his brown right hand to Ebben Owens. The other he stretched towards Will, who had thrown his sickle away, and was hastily approaching.

No human heart could have steeled itself against that frank countenance and beaming smile, certainly no father's. There was no questioning "Who art thou?" for in both father's and brother's hearts leaped up the warm feeling of kinship.

"Gethin!" said Ebben Owens, clasping the hand held out to him so genially. "'Machgen i, is it thee indeed? Well, well, I am glad to see thee!"

And Will, too, greeted the long-lost one with warm welcome.

The reapers gathered round, and Gethin's reception was cordial enough to satisfy even his anticipations; for he had thought of this home-coming, had dreamt of the welcome, and had earnestly desired it, with the intense longing for home which is almost the ruling passion of a Welshman's heart.

"Here I am," he said, laughing, his eyes sparkling with happiness—"here I am, ready for anything! 'The prodigal son' has returned, father. Will you have him? Will you set him to work at once with your hired servants? For I love hard work, and if I don't get it, perhaps I'll fall into mischief again."

"No, no," said Ebben Owens, "no work for thee this morning, lad. Thee must go home with Will, and lighten Ann's heart, for she has grieved for thee many a time, and I will follow at noon. To-morrow thou shalt work if thou wilt; there is plenty to do at Garthowen, as usual. Come, boys, come, on with the work. Nothing must stop the harvest, not even the homecoming of Gethin."

The men stooped to their work again, but there were muttered comments on the master's want of feeling.

"Dei anwl! if it had been Will," said one man to his neighbour, "the reaping would have been thrown to the winds, and we would have had a grand supper on the fatted calf. But Gethin is different. There's a fine fellow he is!"

"Yes," said another; "did you notice his broad chest and his bright eyes? Will looks nothing by him."

And they looked after the two young men as they passed through the gap together, Ebben Owens taking up Will's sickle and setting to work in his place.

Meanwhile Gethin, with a sailor's light, swinging gait, hastened Will's more measured steps towards the homestead.

"Well, Will lad, there's glad I am to see thee!"

"And I," said Will. "No one knows how much I grieved after thee at first, but latterly I was beginning to get used to thy absence."

"Well, 'twas quite the contrary with me, now," said Gethin. "At first I was full of the new scenes and people around me, and I didn't think much about old Wales or any of you; but as the time went on my heart seemed to ache more and more for the old home—more and more, more and more!—till at last I made up my mind I would give up the sea and go back to Garthowen and stay, if they wanted me there, and help the old man on the farm. Dost think he will have me?"

"Yes, of course," said Will. "Thou hast come in the nick of time, and 'twill be easier for me to leave home, as I am going to do next month."

"Leave home?" said Gethin, in astonishment.

"Yes," and Will began to expatiate with pride on his new plans, and his intention of entering Llaniago College at once.

"Diwss anwl!" said Gethin; "have I got to live continually with a parson? I'm afraid I had better pack up my bundle at once; thee wilt never have patience with me and my foolish ways."

Will looked sober. "Thy foolish ways! I hope thou hast left them behind thee."

"Well, truth," said Gethin, "as we grow older our faults and follies get buried deeper under the surface; but it takes very little to dig them up with me. I am only a foolish boy in spite of my strong limbs and tall stature. But so it will always be. You can't make a silk purse out of a sow's ear, and Gethin Owens will be Gethin Owens always. There's the dear old place!" he cried suddenly; "there's the elder tree over the kitchen door! Well, indeed! I have thought of it many times in distant lands and stormy seas, and here it is now in reality! God bless the old home!" and he took off his cap and waved it round his head as he shouted, "Hoi! hoi!" to Ann, who, already apprised of his coming, was running through the farmyard to meet him.

"Oh, Gethin anwl!" she sobbed, as she clasped her arms round his neck.

Gethin gently loosed her clinging fingers, and kissed the tears from her eyes, and in her heart welled up again the tender love which had been smothered and buried for so long.

Gwilym Morris came hurrying down from his "study," a tiny room partitioned off from the hayloft. And if the fatted calf was not killed for Gethin's return, a fine goose was, and no happier family sat down to their midday meal that day in all Wales than the household of Garthowen.

In the afternoon Gethin insisted upon taking his sickle to the cornfield, and although the work was new to him his brawny arm soon made an impression on the standing corn. The field was full of laughter and talk, the sweet autumn air was laden with the scent of the blackberries and honeysuckle in the hedges, and the work went on with a will until, at four o'clock, the reapers took a rest, sitting on the sunny hedge sides.

Through the gap Ann and Morva appeared, bringing the welcome basket of tea. Gethin hurried towards them, relieving them of the heavy basket which they were carrying between them.

"Thee'll have enough to do if thee'st going to help the women folk here," said Will.

"He's been in foreign parts," said a reaper, "and learnt manners, ye see."

"Yes," said another, "that polish will soon wear off."

"Well, caton pawb!" said Gethin, "manners or no manners, man, I never could sit still and see a woman, foreign or Welsh, carry a heavy load without helping her."

The two girls spread the refreshing viands on the grass, and with merry repartee answered the jokes of the hungry reapers.

"'Twill be a jolly supper to-night, Miss Ann; we'll expect the 'fatted calf,'" said one.

"Well, you'll get it," replied Ann; "'tis veal in the cawl, whatever."

"Hast seen Gethin before?" said Will to Morva, observing there was no greeting between them.

"Well, yes," answered the girl, blushing a rosy red under her sunbonnet; "wasn't it at our cottage he slept last night? and indeed there's glad mother was to see him."

"And thee ought to be too," said one of the reapers, "for I'll never forget how thee cried the day he ran away."

"Well, I'll never make her cry again," said Gethin. "Art going at once, lass? Wilt not sit here and have tea with us?" and he drew his coat, which he had taken off for his work, toward her, and spread it on the hedge side.

Morva laughed shyly; she was not used to such attentions.

"No, indeed, I must go," she answered; "we are preparing supper."

As she followed Ann through the gap Gethin looked after her with a smile in his eyes.

"There's bonnie flowers growing on the slopes of Garthowen, and no mistake," he said.

Will examined the edge of his sickle and did not answer.

Later on, when the harvest supper was over, and the last brawny reaper had filed out of the farmyard in the soft evening twilight, the Garthowen household dropped in one by one to the best kitchen, where their own meals were generally partaken of. Ebben Owens himself, as often as not, took his with the servants, but Will, especially of late, preferred to join Ann and Gwilym Morris in the best kitchen or hall. Here they were seated to-night, a glowing fire of

Allen Raine

culm balls filling the large grate, and throwing a light which was but little helped by the home-made dip standing in a brass candlestick on the middle of the table, round which they were all gathered while Gethin displayed his presents.

"Here's a tie for you, father; green it is, with red spots; would you like it?"

"Ts-ts!" said the old man, "it has just come in time, lad, for me to wear on Sunday when I go to hear Will reading in church."

"That will be a proud day for you, father; I will go with you. And for thee, Will, here's a knife. I remember how fond thee wast of the old knife we bought in the fair together."

"Well, indeed!" said Will, clasping and unclasping the blades; "'tis a splendid one, too, and here's a fine blade to mend pens with!"

"And for Ann," continued Gethen, "I have only a hymn-book."

"What couldst thou bring me better? And look at the cover! So good. And the gold edges! And Welsh! I will be proud of it."

"Yes," said Gethin; "I bought it in Liverpool in a shop where they sell Welsh books. And for you, sir," he said, turning to Gwilym Morris.

"'Sir,'" said the preacher, laughing; "Gethin bach, this is the second time you have called me 'sir.' Drop it, man, or I will be offended."

"Well! I won't say it again. Dei anwl! I will have to be on my best behaviour here, with a parson and a preacher in the house! Well! it's a pocket-book for you, I thought very like, being a preacher, you would like to put down a word sometimes."

"Quite right, indeed," said Gwilym Morris; "and look at my old one, barely hanging together it is!"

At the bottom of the bag from which Gethin drew his treasures, lay the little painted box containing Morva's necklace.

"Where's Morva?" he asked. "I've got something for her, too."

"Oh, well," said Will, "thou art a generous man and a rich, I should think! Perhaps thou hast one for Dyc 'pigstye' and Sara "spridion' too."

"Dyc 'pigstye'; no! But Sara, indeed I'm sorry I didn't remember her, whatever."

"I hear Morva's voice in the yard. Will I call her in?" said Ann, and she tapped at the little side window.

"No, no," said Gethin, "I will take it to her," and he went out, carrying the gaudy box in his hand.

"Morva!" he called, and under the elder tree, where she was counting the chickens at roost on its branches, the girl stood facing him, the rising moon shining full upon her. "Morva, lass," he said, drawing near; "'tis the present I told thee of. Wilt have it?" and there was a diffident tremor in his voice, which was not its usual tone; for to-night he was as shy as a schoolboy as he opened the box and drew out the shining necklace. The iridescent colours gleamed in the moonlight and Morva exclaimed in admiration:

"Oh, anwl! is that for me?"

"Yes, for thee, lass; for who else?" said Gethin. "Let me fasten it on for thee. 'Tis a tiresome clasp," and as she bent her shapely neck and his fingers touched it for a moment, she gently drew further away.

"Dost like them?" said Gethin, looking from the shining shells to the glowing face above them.

"Oh, they are beautiful!" she answered, feeling them with her fingers. "I will go in and show them to Ann. I haven't said 'thank you,' but I do thank thee indeed, Gethin;" and he followed her into the "hall," where the glowing light from the fire and the candle fell on the changing glitter of the shells.

"Oh, there's beautiful!" said Ann. "Come near, Morva, and let me look at them. Well, indeed, they are fit for a lady."

"Thee must have paid a lot for that," said Ebben Owens, rather reproachfully.

"Not much indeed, father, but I wasn't going to forget my little playfellow, whatever."

"No, no, my boy, that was quite right," said the old man; and Will too tried to smile and admire, but there was a flush of vexation on his face which did not escape Morva's notice.

"I must go now," she said, a little shadow falling over her.

"Let me loosen the clasp for thee," said Gethin; but Morva, remembering the touch of the brown fingers, quickly reached the door.

"No—no, I must show them to mother."

"Hast thanked Gethin, lass?" said the old man.

"Not much, indeed," she answered, turning back at the door, "but I thank thee, Gethin, for remembering me," and, half-playfully and half-seriously, she made him a little bob curtsey.

Arrived in the cottage she drew eagerly into the gleam of the candle.

"Mother, mother, look! see what Gethin has brought me. Oh! look at them, mother; row under row of glittering shells from some far-off beach. Look at them, mother; green—blue—purple with a silver sheen over them, too. I never thought there were such shells in the world."

"They are beautiful, indeed," said Sara, "but just like a sailor. If he had given thee something useful it would have been better. They will not suit a shepherdess. Thee will have to take them off in a day or two and lay them away in their box. 'Tis a pity, too, child."

"Any way, mother, I will wear them sometimes; they are only shells after all. 'Tis hard I can't wear them because they are so lovely."

And the next day she wore them again, and, longing to see for herself how she looked, made her way up to the moor in the early morning sunshine to where a clear pool in the brown peat bog reflected the sky and the gold of the furze bushes. Here she stood on the edge and gazed at her own reflection in the clear water.

"Oh, 'tis pretty!" she said leaning over the pool, and as she gazed her own beautiful face with its halo of golden hair impressed itself on her mind as it had never done before. "And there's pretty I am, too," she whispered, and gazing at her own image she blushed, entranced with the vision. "Good-bye, Morva," she whispered again, "good-bye. I wonder does Gethin see me pretty? But I must not think that; what would be the use? Will does, and that must be enough for me;" and with a sigh she turned down the moor again.

CHAPTER VII

THE BROOM GIRL

One morning in the following week the high road leading to Castell On presented a lively appearance. It was white and dusty from the tramp of the country folk and the vehicles of all descriptions which followed each other towards the town, whose one long street would be crowded from ten o'clock in the morning till late afternoon, as it was market day. This was the weekly excitement of the neighbourhood, and there was scarcely a household within the radius of a few miles that did not send at least one of its members to swell the number of chafferers and bargainers in the market. Jolly farmers, buxom maidens, old women in witch hats and scarlet scarves, pigs, sheep, horses, all followed each other in the same direction.

Amongst the rest came a girl who rather stooped under what looked like a large bunch of blooming heather. It was Morva, who was carrying her bundle of heath brooms to the corner of the market-place, where she was eagerly waited for by the farmers' wives.

Dyc "pigstye" was accustomed to bring her a bundle of broom handles, which he had roughly fashioned in the wood in the valley, and she and Sara employed their leisure hours in tying on to them the bunches of purple heather, binding them firmly with the young withies of the willows growing here and there on the boggy moor.

There was always quite a little knot of women round her stall of brooms and wings, for she collected also from the farmhouses the wings of the geese and ducks which had been killed for the market, and after drying them carefully in the big chimney, sold them as brushes for hearth and stairs. Sometimes, too, her stock-in-trade was increased by a collection of wooden bowls, spoons, scales, and trenchers, which Stiven "Storrom," living on the shore below, turned off his lathe, and sold through Morva's agency. At such times she borrowed Stiven's donkey-cart, and stood by it in the market until her wares were sold. But to-day she had only her brooms, and tying them on her shoulders, she held the cords crossed over her bosom, stooping a little under their weight. Her head was buried in the purple blossoms, so that she did not hear the tramp of footsteps following close behind her.

Gethin and Will were going to the market together, and the latter had recognised the girl at some distance off, but had kept silence and lessened his speed a little until his brother had asked:

"Who is this lass walking before us? Let's catch her up and carry her brooms for her."

"Nonsense," said Will. "A Garthowen man may drive his sheep, his oxen, and his horses to market, but to carry a bundle of brooms would not look well. Leave them and the fowls to the women, and the pigs to the men-servants—that's my fancy."

"Well, my fancy is to help this lassie," said Gethin. "She's got a tidy pair of ankles, whatever; let's see what her face is like."

"'Tis Morva," said Will, rather sulkily.

"Then we know what her face is like. Come on, man. Who will be the first to catch her?" and Gethin hurried his steps, while Will held back a little. "Why, what's the matter? Surely thou art not ashamed to be seen with Morva?"

"Of course not," said Will irritably; "but—er—er—a broom girl!"

"Oh, jawks!" said Gethin. "Brooms or no brooms, I am going to catch her up," and coming abreast other, he laid his hand on the bunches of blooming heather.

"Morva," he said, bending round her purple burden, "where art here, lassie? Thee art buried in flowers! Come, loosen thy cords, and hoist them upon my shoulder."

And as the girl looked at him from under the brooms, his voice changed, the brusque sailor manner softened.

"'Tis not for a girl like thee to be carrying a heavy weight on thy shoulders," he said gently. "Come, loosen thy cords."

But Morva held them tightly.

"Not for the world," she said. "It is quite right I should carry my wares to market, but I would not like to see a son of Garthowen with a bundle of brooms on his shoulders."

"I will have them," he said; "come, loosen the cords," and he laid hold of one of the hands which held the rope.

A warm glow overspread Morva's face, as the large brown hand covered hers in its firm grasp.

"No, I will do this to please thee," she said, and loosening her hold of the bundle, she flung it suddenly into an empty red cart which was rattling by. "Take care of them, Shemi, thou know'st my corner in the market."

"Yes, yes," said Shemi, "they will be all right."

And Morva stood up in the sunshine freed from her burden.

Will seemed to think it the right time to join them, and suddenly appearing, greeted the girl, but rather coldly, and the three walked on together, Gethin much resenting Will's bad temper, and endeavouring to make up for his brother's somewhat silent and pre-occupied manner by keeping up the conversation himself. But a little constraint fell upon them all, Gethin chafing at the girl's apparent nervousness, and his brother's silence; Morva fearful of offending Will, and disturbed at her own pleasure at meeting Gethin. When they reached the town she bade them good-bye.

"Here's my corner," she said, "and when I have sold my brooms, I am going home in the cart from the mill at Pont-y-fro."

Will seemed relieved at this solving of his difficulties, but Gethin was not so satisfied; he roamed the market discontentedly, filling his pockets with sweets and gingerbread. Many times that day he peered through the crowd into the corner out of the sun, where Morva's purple blooms made a grand show. At last he ventured nearer, and laying his sweets and gingerbreads down beside her, said:

"Thee'll be hungry by and by, Morva; wilt have these?"

The girl's eyes drooped, and she scarcely answered, but the smile and the blush with which she took up the paper bags were quite enough for Gethin, who went home early, with that smile and blush gilding every thought and every subject of conversation with his companions of the road.

In the afternoon Morva, having sold her brooms, prepared to leave the market. Looking up the sunny street, she saw Will approaching, and the little cloud of sadness which Gethin's genial smile had banished for a time, returned, bringing with it a pucker on the brows and a droop at the corners of her mouth.

"Well, indeed," she soliloquised, "there's grand Will is looking, with his gloves and shining boots; quite like a gentleman. 'Tis not only me he will have to say good-bye to soon, I am thinking, but to all at Garthowen."

Her thoughts were interrupted by his arrival. "Art still here, Morva?" he said; "I thought thee wouldst have gone long ago."

"Only just now I have sold my brooms. There's Jacob the Mill, now I will go."

Will looked at the cart uneasily as it rumbled up the street; already he was beginning to be ashamed of his rustic surroundings.

With keen sensitiveness Morva read his thoughts.

"Nay, there's no need for you to help me, Will. I am used to the mill cart, and indeed to goodness, 'twould not suit with gloves and shining boots to be helping a girl into a red cart."

"Twt, nonsense," said Will irritably; but he nevertheless

Allen Raine

allowed her to leave him, with a wave of her hand, and an amused twinkle in her eye.

As she hurried to catch the cart, he stood a moment moodily looking after her, his better nature prompting him to follow and help her, but it was too late; already the brilliant vehicle, with Morva and the burly Jacob sitting in it side by side, was swallowed up by the crowd of market people and cattle, and Will turned on his heel with a look of vexation on his face.

The market was at its liveliest, the sunny air laden with a babel of sounds. Men and women chattered and chaffered, pigs shrieked, sheep bleated, and cattle lowed, but Will scarcely noticed the familiar sounds. A light step and a soft voice, however, attracted his attention, and he saw approaching him two girls, who evidently belonged to a different class from those whose simple ways we have hitherto followed. One was a lady of very ordinary appearance, but the other he recognised as Miss Vaughan of Nantmyny, a young lady whose beauty and pleasant manners were the frequent theme of the countryside gossip, "and no wonder," he thought, "she *is* pretty!"

"Ah! what a pity!" she was saying to her friend, who was evidently a young housekeeper intent upon her purchases, "the brooms are all gone! we're too late!"

Will walked away hastily, lest standing upon that spot he might appear to be in some way connected with the broom girl. Suddenly there was a tumult in the air, a rushing of feet, and cries of fright, and in a cloud of dust he saw rushing towards him an infuriated bull, which had evidently escaped from his attendant, for from the iron ring in his nose still hung the rope by which he had been held. With head lowered and tail curled high over his back, he dashed towards the two ladies, who fled in affright before him, one escaping through an open doorway, while the other, bewildered and terrified, catching her foot in an upturned stall-table, fell prone exactly in the path of the bull. The poor animal, as frightened as any of his shouting pursuers, increased his own mad fury by continually stepping upon the rope which dangled from the ring in his nose, thus inflicting upon himself the pain from which he endeavoured to escape.

The girl screamed with terror, as the snorting nostrils and curving horns came close upon her. In another moment she would undoubtedly have been seriously gored, had not Will, who was in no wise lacking in personal courage, rushed in upon the scene. One look at the beautiful, pale face lying helpless in the dust, and he had seized the creature's horns. The muscular power of his arms was well known at Garthowen, and now it stood him in good stead, for calling his full strength to his aid, he succeeded by a sudden wrench in turning the bull's head aside, so that the direct force of his attack came upon the ground instead of the girl's body.

In a moment the enraged animal turned upon his assailant, and probably Will would have fared badly had not a drover arrived, who, possessing himself of the rope, gave a sudden and sharp twitch at the bull's nose, a form of punishment so agonising and alas, so familiar, that the animal was instantly subdued, and brought under comparative control, not, however, before his horn had slightly torn Will's arm.

An excited crowd of market people had now reached the spot, and while the animal, frightened into submissiveness by the blows and cries that surrounded him, was led away snorting and panting, Will looked in affright at the girl who lay white and unconscious on the ground.

"Did he toss her?" asked one of the crowd, "or is she only frightened? Dear! there's white she looks, there's delicate the gentry are!"

"'Tis her foot, I think," said Will; "let be, I will hold her."

"Yes, 'tis her foot," said another, "the bull must have trampled on it, see how dusty it is—there's a pity."

It was in fact more from the pain of the crushed foot than from fright that Gwenda had fainted, for she was a brave girl. Though fully alive to her danger she had not lost consciousness until her foot had been crushed, and even then not before she had seen Will's rush to her rescue, and his energetic twist of the animal's horns.

Two or three gentlemen now came running up the street, amongst them her uncle, Colonel Vaughan, who, standing at the door of the hotel, had witnessed the escape of the bull, and the pursuit of him by the excited throng of market people. Remembering that his niece had but a few moments previously passed up the street, he too ran in the same direction, and arrived on the scene as promptly as his short legs and shorter breath permitted him. In a fever of fright and flurry he approached, the crowd making way for him as he snapped out a cannonade of irrelevant questions.

"Good heavens! Gwenda! What is it? My darling, are you hurt? Who did it? How very careless!"

"'Tis her foot, I think, sir," said Will. "She has not been gored, and if you will send for your carriage I will lift her in as I am already holding her."

"She'd have been killed for certain," said one of the crowd, "if this young man had not rushed at the bull and saved her life. I saw it all from the window of the Market Hall. He risked his life, I can tell you, sir, and you've got to thank him that the young lady is not killed."

"Yes, yes, a brave young fellow, pommy word. There comes the carriage, now raise her gently," and Will lifted the slender form as easily as he would have carried a swathe of corn.

Slipping her gently into a recumbent position in the carriage, he endeavoured to rest her foot on the opposite seat, but she moaned and opened her eyes as he did so, crying out with evident pain.

"'Tis plain the position hurts her," said her uncle.

Will lifted the foot again, and the moaning ceased.

"That's it," said the colonel; "sit down and hold it up."

Will did as he was bid in a maze of bewilderment, and while the colonel continued to wonder, to lament, and to congratulate, Will made a soft cushion of a wrap which he found beside him, and resting the foot upon it he held the two ends, so that the injured limb hung as it were in a sling, thus lessening very much the effect of the jolting of the carriage over the rough road.

"Drive slowly," said the colonel to his coachman, "and call at Dr. Jones's on your way. Can you spare time to come as far as Nantmyny?" he said, addressing Will.

"Oh! yes, sir, certainly," he answered in good English.

"Tis the right foot, I think," said the old gentleman, unbuttoning the boot.

The girl opened her eyes.

"Oh! uncle, it hurts," she said. "Keep it up," and catching sight of Will, she looked inquiringly at her uncle.

"Tis the young man who saved your life, child," he explained.

"Oh! not that, sir," said Will. "I am sorry I have not even prevented her being hurt."

At first there was a pompous stiffness in Colonel Vaughan's manner, but he added more graciously:

"I hope you were not hurt yourself. Bless me! is that blood on your hand?"

"I have cut my wrist a little, but 'tis nothing," said Will. "Please not to think about it."

"Oh! certainly, certainly, we must. Here's Dr. Jones. Come in, doctor. You must squeeze in somewhere. Gwenda has had a narrow escape, and this young fellow has hurt his wrist in saving her. A very brave young man! Mercy we were not all killed, I'm sure!"

"I'll attend to them both when we get to Nantmyny," said Dr. Jones.

"Keep her foot in that position, and be as quiet as possible, young man," said the colonel, and Will, though he resented the tone and the "young man," still felt a glow of satisfaction at the turn affairs had taken.

To have sat in the Nantmyny carriage! What a story to tell Ann and his father! and Will felt as they drove through the lodge gates that the charm of the situation outweighed the twinges of pain in his arm.

Gwenda Vaughan, recovering a little, smiled at him gratefully.

"Thank you so much for holding up my foot," she said. "It is easier so. I am sorry you have hurt your wrist. Does it pain you much?"

"Oh, 'tis nothing at all," said Will, not accustomed to think much of slight wounds or bruises.

On arriving at Nantmyny he assisted in carrying her into the house.

"Now," said the doctor, when they had laid her on a couch, "let me see, and I will look at your wrist afterwards. Young Owens of Garthowen, I think—eh?"

"Yes," said Will, quietly retreating into the background, while Colonel Vaughan and the maids pressed round the sofa. He only waited until, after a careful examination, the doctor said, "No bones broken, I'm glad to say, only rather badly bruised," and then, leaving the room unnoticed, found his way to the front door, and in a glow of excitement walked back to Castell On. His arm was getting more painful, so on his way through the town he called on Dr. Hughes, who was considered "the people's" doctor, while Dr. Jones was more patronised by "the gentry."

Allen Raine

CHAPTER VIII

GARTHOWEN SLOPES

Dr. Jones's visits to Nantmyny were very frequent during the following week, for Gwenda's foot had been rather severely crushed, and the pain was acute; but being a girl of great spirit she bore it patiently, though it entailed many long hours of wearisome confinement to the house and sofa. During these hours of enforced idleness, she indulged in frequent "brown studies," for her firm and decided character was curiously tinged with romance. She had received but a desultory education; her uncle, though providing her amply with all the means of learning, yet chafed continually against the application which was necessary for her profiting by them.

"Come out, child," he would call, standing outside the open window, his jovial face broadening into a smile of blandishment, most aggravating to Miss Howells, who, inside the window, was trying to fix her pupil's attention upon some subject of history or grammar. The rustling of the brown leaves and the whispering of the wind in the trees added their own enticements, which required all Gwenda's firmness to resist.

"No, uncle," she would say, shaking her finger at him.

"Yesterday and Monday you made me neglect my studies. You mustn't come again this week to tempt me out. I have promised Miss Howells to be industrious. It will soon be four o'clock, and then I will come."

And her uncle had perforce to be content, for at Nantmyny there was no doubt that Gwenda "ruled the roost." Somehow she emerged from the stage of girlhood with a fair amount of knowledge, although her mother's sisters, the two Miss Gwynnes of Pentre, were much dissatisfied with her want of what they called "polish."

"She'll never make a good match," they were wont to say, "never! That plain outspokenness is all very well in a man, or even in an old woman, but it's very unbecoming in a girl, and I'm sure it will ruin her prospects." And on the subject of her "prospects" they were accustomed to dilate so continually and so earnestly that Gwenda had a shrinking dislike to the word, as well as to the subject to which it referred.

"We must really speak to her again, Maria, for of course George may marry some day, and then what would become of her prospects?" And another lecture was prepared for Gwenda.

A few days after the accident which made her a prisoner, lying on the sofa in the morning-room she had fallen into a deep reverie, which had caused quite a pucker between her eyebrows. Being naturally a romantic, sentimental girl, she mentally resented the sordid necessity so continually urged by her aunts of making a "good match." It was in Gwenda to cast all their prudent manoeuvres to the winds, and to follow the bent of her own inclinations; but it was in her also to immolate herself entirely upon the altar of an imagined duty. She chafed somewhat at the want of freedom in her surroundings, her aunts declaring it was incumbent upon her to please her uncle by marrying well, and as soon as possible. And all these restrictions galled the young lady, in whom the romantic dreams of the natural woman were calling loudly for fulfilment. Perhaps these feelings would account for the little look of worry and discontent in her face on the Sunday morning while her uncle lingered round her sofa.

"Well, I'm sorry to leave you alone, Gwenda; but here are the magazines, and I'll soon be back. I don't like the Nantmyny pew to be empty, you know. Good-bye."

When the sounds of the carriage-wheels had died away, Gwenda took up one of the magazines and turned over the pages listlessly. She sighed a little wearily, and fell asleep—a sleep which lasted until her uncle returned from church, and came blustering into the room.

"Well, pommy word, child, I think you have had the best of it this morning. Price the vicar didn't preach. Some Jones of Llan something, and you never heard such a rhodomontade in your life; but I went to sleep and escaped the worst of it—all about mortar, give you my word for it, Gwenda, and about not putting enough cowhair in the mortar."

"Really!" she said, yawning. "No wonder you went to sleep. Were the Williamses there?"

"Yes, and the Griffiths of Plasdu, and the Henry Reeses, and Captain Scott is staying with them. Well, I'm going to have a smoke." But at the door he turned round with a fresh bit of news. "Oh, what d'ye think, Gwenda? A young man stood up to read the lessons, and I couldn't for the life of me remember where I'd seen him before, and I bothered my brains about it all through the sermon till I fell asleep. After service I asked Price the vicar, and who should he be but that young fellow who tackled the bull the other day? Pommy word, he's a fine-looking fellow; got his arm in a sling, though." And he went out banging the door.

Gwenda pondered with a brightening look in her face.

The young man who seized the bull! How strange! Reading the lessons! What was the meaning of that? And with his arm in a sling! It must have really required attention when he disappeared so mysteriously the other day. Handsome? Yes, he was very handsome. That broad white forehead crowned with its tawny clumps of hair! She would like to thank him once more, for he had certainly saved her life. She rang the bell, and a maid appeared.

"Lewis, can you tell me who that man was who seized the bull the other day?"

"'Twas young Owens Garthowen, miss."

"My uncle says he read the lessons in church to-day."

"Yes, I daresay indeed, miss. He's going to be a clergyman, they say. He hurt his arm shocking the other day, miss, because he went to Dr. Hughes on his way from here, and he is keeping it in a sling ever since."

"Where does he live?"

"Oh, about three miles the other side of Castell On, miss, towards the sea. 'Tis an old grey farmhouse, very old, they say; 'tis on the side of the hill towards the sea, very high up, too. 'Tis very windy up there, I should think."

Here the colonel entered again.

"Lewis tells me, uncle, that young man who read the lessons is going to enter the Church."

"Shouldn't wonder at all; every Cardiganshire farmer tries to send one son to the Church. There's Dr. Owen, now, he was a farmer's son. Bless my soul! Why, he is this young man's uncle! Never thought of that! Of course. He's own brother to Ebben Owens, Garthowen. I don't think he keeps up any acquaintance with them, though, and, of course, nobody alludes to them in his presence. I daresay he will take this young man in hand and we shall have him canon or archdeacon or bishop very soon."

This was something more for Gwenda to ponder over, and before the day was ended she had woven quite a halo of romance round Will's unconscious head.

"Shouldn't we send to ask how his arm is, uncle?"

"Yes; pommy word we ought to. I am going to the meet to-morrow at Plasdu, 'twill be very little out of my way to go up to the farm and ask how the young fellow is."

The next afternoon when he returned from the hunt, he brought a fresh item of news for his niece, for he pitied the girl lying there inactive, a state of existence which above all others would have galled him beyond measure.

"I called up at the farm, Gwenda, and saw our young friend with the lion locks. He was crossing the farmyard with a book under his arm, which was still in a sling, but when I asked him about it he only laughed (splendid teeth all those Garthowens have, old Ebben's even are perfect)! He said his arm was quite well and he didn't know why Dr. Hughes insisted upon keeping it in a sling. If he could only be sure, he said, that the young lady's foot was not giving her more pain than he felt he would be glad. I told him your foot was painful, but would soon be all right. Well-spoken young man. By the by, all the men on the field asked after you, and most of them said that was a brave fellow who sprang at the bull. I told them it was one of Ebben Owens's sons. Everybody knows him, you know. Very old family. At one time, I am told, the Garthowen estate was a large one. Griffiths Plasdu's grandfather bought a great deal of it, all that wooded land lying this side of the moor. By the by, Captain Scott is coming round this way to dine with us to-morrow and to stay the night. Pommy word, child, I think he has taken a fancy to you. He seemed quite anxious about you. Good-bye, my dear, I must go."

Gwenda turned her face to the window. The black elm branches swayed against the evening sky, a brilliant star glittered through them, a rising wind sighed mournfully and the girl sighed too.

"Yes, Captain Scott no doubt was interested in her, probably he would propose to her, and if he did, probably she would accept him, with all his money, his starting eyes, and his red nose! How dull and uninteresting life is," she said. "I wonder what we are born for?"

* * * * * *

At Garthowen the stream of life was flowing on smoothly just then. Will was happy and content. He had read the lessons on Sunday to Mr. Price's entire satisfaction, clearly and with an evident understanding of their meaning. Sometimes the roll of the "r's" and the lengthening of the "o's" showed the Welshman's difficulty in pronouncing the English tongue, but upon the whole, the accent was wonderfully good. Above all things Will had taken pains to acquire the English tone of speech, for he was sufficiently acute to know that however learned a Welshman may be, his chances of success are seriously minimised by a Welsh accent, therefore he had paid much attention to this point.

"The time is drawing near, father," he said one day. "I am determined to go to Llaniago, and if you can't pay I must get the money somewhere else, that's all," and he had risen from the table with that wilful, dogged curve on his mouth which his father knew so well, and had always been so weakly unable to resist.

"Twt, twt, my boy," he said, "that will be all right; don't you vex about that."

And thus reassured, Will gladly banished the disquieting doubt from his mind, and his good humour returned.

Gethin seemed to fall naturally into his place as eldest son of the family, taking to the farm work with zeal and energy, and making up for his want of experience by his complete devotion to his work.

Ann was calm and serene as usual, happy in her brother's prospects, and deeply interested in the grey stone house which the congregation at Penmorien were building for their minister.

Gwilym Morris devoted himself entirely to Will's preparations for his entrance examination.

And for Morva, what had the autumn brought? A rich, full tide of life and happiness. Every morning she rose with the sun, and as she opened the door and let in the scent of the furze and the dewy grass, her whole being responded to the voice of Nature around her. She was constantly running backwards and forwards between Garthowen and the cottage. Nothing went well at the farm without her, and in the cottage there were a score of things which she loved to do for Sara. There were the fowls to be fed, the eggs to be hunted for, the garden to be weeded, the cottage to be cleaned, Sara's knitting to be set straight, the herbs to be dried and sorted and tied up in bundles under the brown rafters. Oh, yes! every day brought for Morva its full harvest of lovely scenes, of beautiful sounds, and sweet scents. Certainly, Will was a little cold and irritable lately, but she was well used to his variable humours, and somehow the home-coming of Gethin had filled the only void there had been in her life, though of that she had scarcely been conscious. There was hardly an hour in the day when Morva's song might not be heard filling the autumn air with melody, for how could she help singing as she sat knitting on the moorside while she watched the cattle, and kept them from roaming too near the edge of the cliff.

On the brow of the hill Gethin was harrowing. His lively whistle reached her on the breeze, and she would look up at him as he passed along the skyline, and rejoice once more that he had returned to make their lives complete, to fill Ann's heart with happiness, and his father's with content; for the girl, generally so clear-sighted, so free from guile or pretence, was deceiving herself utterly, and imagined that the increased joy and glory of life which had permeated her whole being since Gethin's return, arose only from the deep interest she took in every member of the Garthowen family, and was due solely to the happiness which the return of the wanderer naturally evoked. Was not Gethin Will's brother? had she not every reason to be glad in his return to the old home? her playmate, the friend of her childhood? and she gave herself up unrestrainedly to the happiness which brooded over every hour of her life.

To Gethin, too, the world seemed to have changed to a

Allen Raine

paradise. Every day, every hour drew him closer to Morva; in her presence he was lost in a dream of happiness, in her absence she was ever present like a golden vision in his mind. Will's manner towards the girl being intentionally formal and distant, had completely blinded his brother to the true state of affairs, and though his daily intercourse with Morva seemed to him almost too delightful to last, he followed blindly the chain that was binding him continually more closely to her.

"Art not going to the market to-day?" he shouted out to her one morning as he drove the horses over the moor.

"No," called Morva in return.

"Will and Gwilym Morris are gone," he shouted again, beginning his way towards her between the low gorse bushes. "Art watching the sheep, lass?"

"No; 'tis the calves who will stray to the bog over yonder. Indeed, they are wilful, whatever, for the grass down here is much sweeter. There they go again—see!" and Gethin helped her with whoop and halloo, and many devious races of circumvention to recover them. "Oh, anwl, they are like naughty children," she said, sitting down, exhausted with laughter and running, Gethin flinging himself beside her, and picking idly at the gorse blossoms which filled the air with their rich perfume.

The clear, blue autumn sky was over them, the deep blue sea stretched before them, the larks sang overhead, the sheep bleated on the moor, and in the grass around them the dewdrops sparkled in the morning sun.

"'Tis a fair world," said Morva; "didst ever see more beautiful sea or land than ours in all thy voyages, Gethin?"

"Brighter, grander, warmer, but more beautiful—none, Morva. Indeed to me, since I've come home, every day seems happier and more beautiful—and thou, too, Morva. I think by that merry song thou wert singing thou art not very unhappy."

"Well, indeed, 'twas not a very happy song," said the girl, "but I suppose I was putting my own foolishness into it."

"Wilt sing it again, lass?"

"Wilt sing, too?"

"Oh, dei anwl, yes; there's no song ever reaches my ears but I must join in it. Come, sing on."

And Morva sang again, Gethin's rich tones blending with hers in full harmony. This time she was awake, and realised the sorrow of the words.

"Well, no," said Gethin, "'tis not a very merry thing, indeed, to set your heart upon winning a maiden, and to lose her as that poor fellow did. But, Morva," he said, tossing the gorse blossoms on her lap, "'tis a happy thing to love and to be loved in return."

"Yes, perhaps," said the girl, thinking of Will, and wondering why, though he loved her so much, there was always a shadow hanging over her affection for him.

Gethin longed to break the silence which fell over them, but a nervous fear deterred him, a dread of spoiling the happy freedom of their intercourse—a nameless fear of what her answer might be; so he put off the hour of certainty, and seized the joys of hope and delight which the present yielded him.

"Where's thy necklace, Morva?"

"'Tis at home in the box. Mother says a milkmaid should not wear such beautiful things every day, and on Sunday the girls and boys would stare at me if I wore them to chapel."

"What art keeping them for, then?" said Gethin. "For thy wedding-day?"

"That will be a long time; oh, no, before then very often I will wear it, now when I'm at home alone, and sometimes when the sun is gone down I love to feel it on my neck; and I go up to the moor sometimes and peep at myself in the bog pools just to see how it looks. There's a foolish girl I am!"

What a day of delight it was! The browns of autumn tingeing the moor, the very air full of its mellow richness, the plash of the waves on the rocks below the cliffs, the song of the reapers coming on the breeze, oh, yes, life was all glorious and beautiful on the Garthowen slopes just then.

"To-morrow night is the 'cynos.'[1] Wilt be there, Morva?" asked Gethin.

"Well, yes, of course," answered the girl, "and 'tis busy we'll be with only Ann and me and the men-servants, for Will never goes to the cynos; he doesn't like farm work, and now he's studying so hard and all 'twould be foolish for him to sit up all night."

"I will be there, whatever," said Gethin.

"Wilt indeed?" and a glow of pleasure suffused her face. "There's going to be fun there, they say, for Jacob the miller is going to ask Neddy 'Pandy' to dance the 'candle dance,' and Robin Davies the sailor will play the fiddle for him. Hast ever seen the candle dance?"

"No," said Gethin, his black eyes fixed on the girl's beautiful face, which filled his mind to the exclusion of what she was saying.

"'Tis gone out of fashion long ago, but Jacob the miller likes to keep up the old ways."

"The candle dance," said Gethin absently, "what is it like?"

"Well, indeed," said Morva, shyly bending her head under his ardent gaze, "thee wilt see for thyself; I have dropped a stitch."

A long silence followed while the stitch was recovered, and the furze blossoms came dropping into her lap, into her hair, and on to her neck. She laughed at last, and sprang up tossing them all to the ground.

"The calves! the calves!" she cried, and once more both ran in pursuit of the wilful creatures.

So simple a life, so void of all that is supposed to make life interesting, and yet so full of love and health and happiness that the memory of it was impressed upon the minds of both for the rest of their lives. Yes, even in old age they called it to mind with a pensive tenderness, and a lingering longing, and the words, "There's happy we were long ago on the Garthowen slopes!"

Before he went to market in the morning Will had sought out Morva as she sat on her milking-stool, leaning her head on Daisy's flank, and milking her to the old refrain:

"Troodi, Troodi! come down from the mountain!

Troodi, Troodi! come up from the dale!"

"I want to see thee, Morva; wilt meet me beyond the Cribserth to-night? 'Twill be moonlight. I will wait for thee behind the broom bushes on the edge of the cliff."

"Yes, I will come."

Will was looking his best, a new suit of clothes made by a Caer-Madoc tailor, the first of the kind he had ever had, set off his handsome figure to advantage, his hat pushed back showed the clumps of red gold hair, the blue eyes, and the mouth with its curves of Cupid's bow. Yes; certainly Will was a handsome man.

"There's smart thou art," said Morva, with a mischievous smile.

"'Tis my new suit; they are pretty well," said Will.

"And what are those? Gloves again! oh, anwl! indeed, it is time thee and me should part," and rising from her stool she curtseyed low before him with a little sarcasm in her looks and voice.

"Part, Morva—never!" said Will. "Remember tonight."

Morva nodded and bent to her work again, and the white sunbonnet leant against Daisy once more, and the sweet voice sang the old melody. When her pail was full she sighed as she watched Gwilym Morris and Will disappear through the lane to the high road.

[1] The annual corn-grinding.

CHAPTER IX

THE NORTH STAR

Ebben Owens was going to market in his rough jolting car, Dyc "pigstye" beside him, both dressed in their best frieze. In the back of the car, covered over with a netting, lay three small pigs, who grunted and squealed in concert when a rough stone gave them an extra jolt. In the crowded street at Castell On, where the bargaining was most vigorous, and the noise of the market was loudest, he stopped and unharnessed Bowler, who had "forged" into town with great swinging steps and much jingling of buckles and chains.

Having led him into the yard of the Plough Inn, he returned, and with Dyc's help proceeded to lift out the pigs and carry them to the pen prepared for them in the open street, Dyc taking them by the ears and Ebben Owens by the tail. Now, pigs have remonstrated loudly against this mode of conveyance for generations, but nobody seems to have listened to their expostulations. They are by no means light and airy creatures, indeed, for their size, they are of considerable weight, so why they of all other animals should be picked out for this summary mode of transport is difficult to understand. At any rate the Garthowen pigs resented it warmly, and the air was rent with their shrieks as Will and Gwilym Morris came upon the scene. Ebben Owens almost

Allen Raine

dropped his pig in the delight of seeing his son in his new clothes. Will nodded smilingly at him, while keeping at a respectable distance from the shrieking animals, and the old man was filled with a glow of pride and happiness which threw a *couleur de rose* over everything for the rest of the day. In truth, Morgan Jones of Bryn made an easy bargain with him for those pigs, and Ebben went home in the evening with ten shillings less in his pocket than he meant to have had when he started from home.

"Look you here," he said to Ann and Gethin, who both hovered round him on his return with loving attentions, "look you here now; wasn't a gentleman in the market looking smarter than our Will to-day! There was the young son of Mr. Vaughan the lawyer, was dressed like him exactly— same brown hat, same grey suit, and his boots not shining so well as Will's! Caton pawb! there's handsome he was! Shouldn't wonder if he didn't marry a lady some day, with plenty of money!"

"Shouldn't wonder, indeed," said Gethin, clapping him on the back; "and there's proud he'll be to drive his old father to church with him!"

"Hech! hech! hech!" laughed the old man, sitting down and rubbing his knees. "Well, indeed, he's a fine boy, whatever!"

"Wasn't Gwilym there?" asked Ann.

"Yes, yes, to be sure, and he is looking very nice always; but I didn't notice him much today."

Meanwhile, in the town, Will and Gwilym had much to do; there were books to be got—there was a horse to be looked at for the farm—and, moreover, Will was to call upon Mr. Price the vicar, so the hours passed quickly away, until late in the afternoon when the crowd was a little thinning, the Nantmyny carriage passed through the street, within it Colonel Vaughan and his niece. Will saw it at once, and turned away to avoid recognition—for although nothing would have pleased him more, he was a man of great tact and common sense, and never spoiled a good chance by indiscreet intrusion. As he turned away, Colonel Vaughan caught sight of him, and, stopping the carriage, beckoned to a bystander, who touched his hat with a knobbed stake from the hedge.

"Isn't that young Owens of Garthowen?"

"Iss, sare," said the man, knocking his hat again.

"Ask him to come here, then."

And Will came, not too hurriedly, and with assumed nonchalance.

"Well, young man," said the colonel, "I want to know how your arm is?"

"It is quite well, thank you," said Will, carefully studying his accent. "I hope," he added, taking off his hat and turning to Gwenda, who sat up interested, "I hope you are no longer suffering pain?"

"Very little, thank you. I am so glad your arm is well again, and I am glad to have this opportunity of thanking you."

And as Will prepared to withdraw again, lifting his hat and showing his tawny locks and his white teeth, Miss Vaughan placed her hand in his with a friendly good-bye.

The old colonel winced a little.

"I don't think you need have shaken hands with him, child; however, it was very nice of you, and I've no doubt it will please the young man very much. I declare he looks like a gentleman."

"And speaks like one," said Gwenda.

"Yes; pommy word I don't know what's the world coming to!"

"Very nice people those Vaughans, I should think," said Gwilym Morris, as he and Will tramped homewards in the evening.

"H'm! yes," said Will; "I daresay they thought they were honouring me very much by their notice; but, mind you, Gwilym, in a few years I'll show them I can hold up my head with any of them."

"Will," said Gwilym, after a pause, "I am afraid for you, lad; I am afraid of what the world will make of you. At Garthowen, with nothing but the simple country ways around us, we escape many temptations; but once we enter the world outside, even here in the market it reaches us, that subtle insidious glamour which incites us, not to become what we ought to be, but to appear different to what we are in reality."

"I can't follow you," said Will. "I suppose it is every man's duty to try and get on as far as he can in the path of life which he has chosen. I have chosen mine, and I don't mean to leave a stone unturned which may help me on. Yon can't blame me for that, Gwilym."

"No, no! I suppose not; and yet—and yet—"

"And yet what?" asked Will irritably.

"You may get to the very top of the ladder, and then find it has not been leaning against the right wall. That would be a poor success, Will."

"Well, well!" he said, as they entered the farmyard, "what's the matter with you to-night? You wait a few years, give me only a chance, and you'll be proud of your old pupil."

When they had separated, Gwilym looked after him thoughtfully.

"I wonder will I, indeed!" he said.

*   *   *   *   *   *

It was late in the evening when Morva made her way to the cliffs to meet her lover. The moor was bathed in a flood of silver moonlight, the sea below was lighted up by the same serene effulgence, and the silence of night was only broken by the trickle of the mill stream down in the valley, the barking of the dogs on the distant farms, and the secret scurry of a rabbit under the furze bushes.

As she neared the edge of the cliff, the peace and beauty of the scene impressed her eye but did not reach her heart, which was beating with a strange unrest.

In the dark shadow of the crags on the cliff side Will was waiting for her. He had been there some time, and was a little nettled at her delay.

"Where hast been, Morva?" he said, stretching out his hand and drawing her towards him in the shadow. "Come out of the moonlight, lass. There is Simon 'Sarndu' fishing down there with Essec Jones; they will see thee."

"Well, indeed," said the girl, "what is the good of our going on like this? It will be a weariness to thee to be always hiding thy—thy—"

"My love for thee? No, Morva, 'tis all the sweeter to me that nobody guesses it. And nobody must guess it; and that's what I wanted to speak to thee about. When a man begins his life in earnest, and takes his place in the outside world, he must be careful, Morva—careful of every step—and must act very differently to those who mean to spend their lives in this dull corner of the world."

"Dull corner!" said Morva. "To me it seems the one bright spot in the whole world, and as if no other place were of any consequence. I'm sure if I ever leave here, I will be pining for the old home, the lovely moor, and the sea and the cliffs. Oh! I can never, never be happy anywhere else!"

"Twt, twt," said Will, "thou art talking nonsense. When I send for thee to come and live with me in a beautiful home, thou wilt be happy. But listen, girl! Is thy love for me strong enough and true enough to bear what may look like neglect and forgetfulness? For a time, Morva, I want to break away from thee, lest any whispers of my love for thee should get abroad. It would blast my success in life, 'twould ruin my prospects if it were known that I courted my father's shepherdess, and so, for a time I want to drop all outward connection with thee. Canst bear that, Morva, and still be true to me?"

"I don't know," said the girl.

"Canst not believe that I shall love thee as much as ever, and more fervently perhaps than ever?"

"I will try," said Morva; "but I think thou art making a hard path for thyself and me. 'Twould be better far to drop me out of thy life, then thou couldst climb the uphill road without looking back."

"And leave thee free to marry another man? Never, Morva! I claim thy promise. Remember when thou wast a little girl how I made thee point up to the North Star and promise to marry me some day."

"Indeed the star is not there to-night, whatever."

"It is there, Morva, only the moonlight is too bright for thee to see it. It is there unchangeable, as thou hast promised to be to me."

"Yes, I have promised; what more need be?"

"Yes, more; thou must tell me again to-night, Morva, that thou wilt be true to me whatever happens—whatever thou mayst hear about me—that thou wilt still believe that in my heart I love thee and thee only. Dost hear, girl—*whatever* thou dost hear?"

"I will believe nothing I may hear against thee, Will; nothing at all. But when I see with my own eyes that thou art weary of me and art ashamed of me, *then* remember I am free."

"But thine eyes may deceive thee."

"I will swear by *them*, whatever," said Morva, with spirit.

Will sighed sentimentally.

"What a fate mine is! to be torn like this between my desire to rise in the world and my love for a girl in a—in a humbler position than that to which I aspire!"

"Oh, Will bach! thou art getting to talk so grand, and to look so grand. Take my advice and drop poor Morva of the moor!"

"I will not!" said Will. "I will rise in the world, and I will have thee too! Listen to me, lass, I am full of disquiet and anxiety, and thou must give me peace of mind and confidence to go on my path bravely."

"Poor Will!" said the girl, looking pensively out over the shimmering sea.

"Once more, Morva, dost love me?"

"Oh, Will, once more, yes! I love thee with all my heart, thee and everyone at Garthowen."

"Well," said Will, "we have been kind to thee ever since thou wast cast ashore by the storm. It would be cruel and ungrateful to return our kindness by breaking my heart."

"Oh, I will never, Will; I will never do that! Be easy, have faith in me, and I will be true to my promise."

"Wilt seal it with a kiss, then?"

Morva was very chary of her kisses, but to-night she let him draw her closer to him; while he pressed a passionate kiss upon her lips. There was no answering fervour on her part, but she went so far as to smooth back the thick hair which shaded his forehead and to press a light kiss upon his brow.

"Well done!" said Will, with a laugh, "that is the first time thou hast ever given me a kiss of thine own accord. I must say, Morva; thou art as sparing of thy kisses as if thou wert a princess. Well, lass, we must part, for to-morrow I am going to Llaniago to see about my rooms, and there's lots to do to-night, so good-bye."

And once more holding her hand in his, he kissed her, and left her standing behind the broom bushes. She passed out into the moonlight, and walked slowly back over the moor with her head drooping, an unusual thing for Morva, for from childhood she had had a habit of looking upwards. Up there on the lonely moor, the vault of heaven with its galaxy of stars, its blue ethereal depths, its flood of silver moonlight, or its breadth of sunlit blue, seemed so closely to envelop and embrace her that it was impossible to ignore it; but to-night she looked only at the gossamer spangles on her path.

"What did Will mean by 'We must part! Whatever thou mayst hear!'" and she sighed a little wearily as she lifted the latch of the cottage door.

"Morva sighing!" said Sara, who sat reading her chapter by the fireside. "Don't begin that, 'merch i, or I must do the same. I would never be happy, child, if thou wert not happy too; we are too closely knit together."

And she took the girl's strong, firm hand in her own, so frail, so slender, and so soft. Morva's eyes filled with tears.

"Mother, I am happy, I think. Why should I not be? They are all so kind to me at Garthowen, and I love them all so much. I would lay my life down for them, mother, and still be happy!"

"Yes, child, I believe thou wouldst. Come to supper, the cawl is ready."

"'Tis the cynos to-morrow night, mother, will I go?"

"Yes, of course; I wouldn't have thee go to the cynos of any other farm; there is too much foolishness going on."

"Robin Davies, the sailor, is going to bring his fiddle, and there will be fun, but Ann will not allow any foolishness."

"No, no," said Sara, "she's a sensible girl, and going to be married to Gwilym Morris too! that will be a happy thing for her I think."

Morva was silent, following her own train of thoughts while she ate her barley bread and drank her cawl, and when she broke the silence with a remark about Will, to both women it came naturally, as the sequence of their musings.

"Will is going away to-morrow, mother."

"Away to-morrow! so soon?"

"Only for a day or two, I think."

"Was that the meaning of the sigh then, Morva?"

"I don't know," said the girl, pensively chasing a fly with her finger on the table. "Oh, mother! I don't know, it is all a turmoil and unrest of thoughts here," and she drew her hand over her forehead.

"Well, never mind that, 'merch i, if it is rest and happiness *here*," and Sara laid her finger on the region of Morva's heart. "Tell me that, child; is it rest and love there?"

"Oh! I don't know, mother; I don't know indeed, indeed."

And then she did what Sara had scarcely ever seen her do since she had "gone into long frocks and turned her hair up," she crossed her arms on the table, and leaning her head upon them, she sobbed, and sobbed, and sobbed.

Allen Raine

CHAPTER X

THE CYNOS

In the old grey mill in the gorge, which ran up the moor about half a mile beyond Sara's cottage, there was a "sound of revelry by night," for the Garthowen "cynos" was in full swing. It bid fair to be the merriest, heartiest cynos of the year, and Jacob the miller was in his element.

As Morva came down the side of the moor after supper, the enlivening sounds which greeted her ear hastened her steps and quickened the blood in her veins.

Will's absence, though unconsciously, was a relief to her, and in the morning when, on rising, she had opened the cottage door, disclosing to view all the charms of the autumn day, its glow of crimson bramble, its glory of furze and heather, against the blue of the sea, her spirits had risen with a bound, and the sadness of the evening before had at once taken flight. For in the elasticity of youth, the hand of sorrow has but to be removed for a moment and the flowers of hope and happiness rise with unimpaired freshness and vigour; not so when age draws near, then the heavy hand may be lifted, and the crushed flowers of happiness may slowly revive and open once more, but there is a bruise on the stem and a stain on the petals which remain.

Ebben Owens and Ann had all day been busy with the preparations for the cynos. Gethin's whistle came loud and clear from the brow of the hill. It had been a happy day for every one, so Morva thought, knowing nothing of the anxiety which her burst of sorrow on the previous evening had awakened in her foster-mother's heart. Sara's love for her adopted child, who had come to her when her mother's heart was crying aloud in its bereavement, had in it not only tenderness deep as a mother's, but also that keen intuition and sensitiveness to every varying mood and feeling of the loved one, which is the bitter prerogative of all true love. So, while Morva had gone singing to her milking, Sara had walked in her herb garden, musing somewhat sadly. There was neither sorrow nor anxiety in the girl's heart as she hastened her steps down the side of the gorge. She saw the twinkling light in the window of the old mill kitchen, she heard the trickling of the stream, and the sound of laughter and merry voices which issued from the wide open mill door.

When she arrived there was Gethin busy with the sacks of corn, there was the hot kiln upon which the grain would be roasted, while ranged round it stood the benches which Jacob had prepared for the company.

Already some of the young men and girls from the surrounding farms were dropping in to share in the evening's amusement and work. Shan, the miller's wife, was busy in the old kitchen with preparations for the midnight meal. Ebben Owens had caused a small cask of beer to be tapped, and Jacob was unremitting in his attentions to it during the night.

"Garthowen's is worth calling a cynos," he said. "He doesn't forget how the flour gets into one's throat and makes one thirsty. I'm no Blue Ribbonite, no, not I, nor intend to be, and that's why I try always to make the Garthowen cynos a jolly one."

"Yes, yes," said Shan, "you needn't trouble to tell me the reason; I know it well now these many years."

When Morva entered she was warmly greeted by all. The farm lads particularly were loud in their welcome.

"Come in, lass, where'st been lately? We haven't seen thee a long time."

"Well, indeed, I've been on the moor every day with the calves or the sheep; they are grazing there now."

Everyone said something except Gethin, who only glanced at her with a smile and a sparkle of black eyes, for he had seen her many times during the day, and he was already, according to the fashion of his country, beginning to hide his love under an outward appearance of stolid indifference; but this did not offend Morva, for it saved her from the ordeal of curious eyes and broad comments, and Gethin felt that the tender flower of love was well shielded from rude contact with the outside world, by the secrecy behind which a Welshman hides his love, for, in a hundred ways unnoticed and unseen by those around him, there were opportunities of apprising the girl of his constant and watchful interest. How sweet was the chance touch of her brown fingers in the course of the mill work. If her eyes met his, which they did not often, how easy it was to send a meaning glance from his own! how delightful to sit beside her in the circle round the glowing kiln!

Robin Davies and Neddy "Pandy" were late, so to beguile the time Jacob struck up a merry tune, the whole company joining in the chorus. Song after song followed each other, interspersed with stories, some of old times and traditions, others of modern adventures at market or fair, until at midnight they all adjourned to the mill kitchen, where Shan had prepared the usual meal of steaming coffee with bread and butter. There was bread of all sorts, from the brown barley loaf to the creamy, curled oatcake, flanked by piles of the delicious tea-cakes for which Pont-y-fro was noted. The men washed down their cakes with foaming "blues" from the beer barrel.

Robin Davies and Neddy "Pandy" arrived just in time for the coffee, and when the meal was over they all returned to the kiln room, where the air was filled with the aroma of the roasting corn.

It was only at such gatherings as these that Neddy ever experienced the full enjoyments of life, for he was a homeless wanderer from place to place.

Nature had been bountiful to him in the matter of bodily size and strength, but she had not been correspondingly generous in her allotment of mental capacities. No one knew anything of his parentage or birthplace. Nobody cared sufficiently to inquire, and no one knew of his weary hours of tramping over moor and mountain, led only by some stray rumour of a fair or festive gathering, at which he might at least for a few hours enjoy the pleasures of a "blue" of beer, a cheerful greeting, and a seat in the chimney-corner, in return for a song, or a turn at the "candle-dance," for which he was famous. He had called at the old mill the week before, and Jacob had engaged his services for the coming cynos. He had spent the day on board the *Speedwell*, where Robin Davies was mate, and had had a good rest and a feast of music, for Robin was a genius, and played his fiddle with wonderful taste and skill, and Neddy, though wanting in many things, was behind no one in his love for and appreciation of music. He was therefore unusually bright and fresh when he arrived at the mill. He and Robin had walked up all the way from Abersethin through the surf, carrying their shoes under their arms.

"'Twill freshen thy feet, and make them hard for the candles," said Robin.

Neddy's thin haggard face, surmounted by a thick crop of grizzled curly hair, lighted up with pleasure as he felt the warm air of the roasting room.

"Here, sit down by the kiln, man," said Gethin, "and rest a bit before thou begin'st."

"Yes, and sing us 'Aderin pur'," said Jacob, "'twill prepare the air for the dancing."

And Neddy struck up at once. He never required pressing, for his songs seemed always on his lips. He sang his ballads as he passed through the country towns and villages, and the people came out and pressed pennies into his hand, or invited him into their houses for a rest, a hunch of bread and cheese, or a bowl of cawl; and he sang as he tramped over the lonely hillsides, sometimes weary and faint enough, but still singing; and when at night he retired to rest in some hay-loft or barn, or perhaps alone under the starry night sky, he was wont to sing himself to sleep, as he had done when a child in the old homestead of which nobody knew.

When he began the words of the song so sweet to every Welshman's ear:

"Oh! lovely bird with azure wing
Wilt bear my message to her?"

every ear was intent upon the melody, and as the rich sonorous voice carried it on through its first fervid strains of love, to the imploring cadences of the ending, heads and hands beat time, eyes glistened, humid with feeling, and when the song had come to an end, there was a breathless silence and a sigh of satisfaction.

"There's lovely it is! Sing us again, Neddy bach."

And Neddy sang again the song of the red-cheeked little prince, who slept in his golden cradle, a red-cheeked apple in his hand. It was but a simple nursery rhyme, but Neddy put his soul into it, for he was but a child himself in spite of his tall stature and grizzled locks.

Morva was sitting on the steps which led up to the rickety, windy loft, Gethin beside her on an upturned barrow.

"I might go on with my knitting," said the girl, "if somebody would hold my skein for me to wind."

Gethin held it, of course; and while the ball increased in size there was plenty of time and opportunity for talk, which was interrupted by Robin's fiddle striking up a merry jig time. Wool and ball were laid aside, while Ann placed six lighted candles on the floor—four in the centre and one at each end, with space enough between them for the figures of the dance.

Neddy listened a few moments, seemingly to get the rhythm well into his mind; then starting up, and flinging his heavy shoes aside, he took his place at the end of the space cleared for him, his ragged corduroy trousers hanging in tatters round his bare ankles. With his thumbs in the armholes of his waistcoat, he began the dance, singing all the time an old refrain descriptive of its measure; keeping at a little distance from the group of candles, but gradually approaching nearer and nearer, and at length flinging his bare feet around the flaring lights. Round them and over them, in between them and outside them, until it was a mystery how the bare feet were not burnt and the ragged trousers did not catch fire. Over and over again he stopped for breath, until the loud stamping of feet and cries of applause, in which Tudor joined vociferously, encouraged him to begin again. The music waxed faster and faster, and Neddy danced with more marvellous rapidity, until he seemed to lose himself in the intricate mazes of the dance. He was pale, and beads of perspiration stood on his forehead, when at last, with a trick of his bare foot, he extinguished every light, and staggered to his seat in the corner by the kiln.

"Hooray, Neddy! as good as ever he was! Well done, bachgen! fetch him a 'blue.'"

And Neddy, triumphant and thoroughly enjoying the cheering and *eclat* of his exploit, leant back panting to recover himself.

"The corn! The corn!" said Ann, turning to the roasting-pan over the kiln. "We mustn't forget that with our dancing and our singing, and thee mustn't have another 'blue' yet, Neddy."

"Oh, indeed 'tis wonderful!" said Morva.

"Yes, 'tis a pretty dance indeed," said Gethin, "and something like the sailor's hornpipe we used to dance on board ship sometimes."

"Canst dance?" said the girl, with wide-open eyes of intense interest.

"Well, yes—I was considered to have a pretty good foot for a fling."

"Oh, dance!" said Morva, clasping her hands, "Ann, Ann, Gethin can dance!"

"But not in these boots," he said.

"Oh, Gethin, try!" said his sister.

"Well, if I had my shoes. Run, Grif, to Garthowen and fetch them."

And in a short time the boy returned, bringing Gethin's best Sunday shoes under his arm.

The floor was cleared again, and everybody watched eagerly while the sailor took his stand, with arms folded across his chest and head well thrown back.

"Now, Robin, a jig tune for me."

"Yes, yes, the sailor's hornpipe proper," said Robin; and he struck up the time with spirit, and Gethin began the dance with equal vigour.

The company looked on with breathless admiration, Neddy with critical nods of approval; but Morva's delight was indescribable. With eagerness like a child's she followed every dash, every scrape, and every fling of the dance, and when it was ended, and Gethin returned, laughing and panting, to his seat on the barrow, alas! alas! he had danced into her very heart.

"Oh! there's handsome he is!" said Magw, the dairymaid, with a sigh; and Morva echoed the sentiment, though she did not give it utterance.

"Yes, 'twas very well," said Neddy; "but thee couldn't do it if thou hadst the candles."

"That I couldn't, Neddy; nobody but thee could," and the old man was quite satisfied.

In the early grey of the morning the stray visitors dropped off one by one, and Neddy, having slept for an hour in his cosy corner, shook himself awake and betook himself, crooning an old song, once more to his solitary rambles over the hills. It was not until the sun had well risen, and the whole remaining party had breakfasted together in the mill kitchen, that the Garthowen household returned home, leading with them the lumbering blue and scarlet carts, laden with the sacks of meal sufficient for the coming year, Tudor following the procession with the air of a dog who congratulates himself upon having brought affairs to a satisfactory conclusion. Ebben Owens was already up to receive them, the big oak coffers in the grain room were swept out, the dry meal poured into them, and Twm the carter, with white cotton stockings kept for the occasion drawn over his feet and legs, stood in the coffers treading the meal into as hard a mass as possible. When they were full to the brim the heavy lids were closed with a snap, and the Garthowen cynos was over for the year. Afterwards the work of the farm went on as usual, but there were many surreptitious naps taken during the day, in hay loft or barn, or behind some sunny hedgerow or stack.

Gwilym Morris and Will did not return that day, as had been expected.

"Wilt stay a little later, Morva?" said Ann; "they may come by the carrier at seven o'clock, and I will want to prepare supper for them."

Morva's heart sank, but she made no outward sign; she had been full of restless excitement all day, and had looked forward to the quiet of the cottage under the furze bank, and to Sara's soothing company.

All day she had been haunted by the memory of the sailor's

hornpipe, Gethin's flashing eyes, his handsome person, his supple limbs! She tried to banish the vision and to turn her thoughts to Will, but found it impossible! and she went about her work in a dream of happiness, unwillingly recalling every word that Gethin had spoken, every hidden compliment, and every look of tenderness. She avoided him when he returned from the fields at midday, she trembled and blushed at the sound of his name, and when he came home in the evening to his supper she feigned some excuse and was absent from the evening meal; but when at last Will's return was despaired of, and Morva took her way round the Cribserth towards home, Gethin, no longer to be baulked, followed her with rapid steps, and caught her up just as she turned the rugged edge of the ridge.

"Morva!" he called, and she turned at once and stood facing him in the light of the full moon.

She bent her head a little and let her arms fall at her sides, standing like a culprit before his accuser. The attitude pained Gethin, whose whole being was overflowing with tenderness.

"Morva, lass! what is the matter? Where art going? Art running away from *me*?"

The girl raised her eyes to his, and in a low but firm voice answered, "Yes."

"Why? Why?" he asked, and taking her hands hastily he drew her away from the path, and down to the shadow of a broom bush on the cliff side.

She remembered it was the very bush behind which she had met Will two evenings before. For a moment they were silent, both feeling too agitated to speak. Beyond the shadow of the bushes the world lay silent in the mellow moonlight, a soft breathing stole up to them from the heaving sea below, a whispering breeze played on their faces, and through it all the insidious glamour of the dance, which had enchanted the simple rustic girl, wove like a silver thread.

"Morva," he said at last, pressing the hand which he held in his, "thou knowest well what I want to say. If I had learning like Will's now, I would not be hunting for words like this, but indeed, lass, I am fair doited with love of thee. Answer me, dost love me too? I think, Morva," and he drew her closer, "I think thou dost not hate me?"

"Oh, no," she whispered, "but—but—" and she slowly endeavoured to withdraw from his detaining grasp, "but, Gethin, I am promised to Will."

"What? What didst say, girl?" said Gethin, in an agitated voice. "Thou hast promised to marry Will?"

There was a long pause of silence, during which the lapping of the waves on the beach, the rustle of the leaves in the bushes, together with their own fluttering breaths, were distinctly audible.

"Didst say that, Morva?"

"Yes, indeed, 'tis true," said the girl, in a low voice.

"But—but does Will love thee?"

"Yes, he loves me," answered Morva sadly, but steadily, "and I love him, and I must listen to no other man, for I have promised him."

"Promised him! when?" said Gethin, trying to steady his voice.

"Oh, many times, many times; two nights ago, here, under this very broom bush, I promised to be true and unchangeable."

"Is this true indeed, then? Hast promised thyself away from me?" said Gethin, looking round as if dazed and stunned.

"Yes," she answered again, in a low voice. "Will asked me if I loved him, and I said 'Yes, I love thee with all my heart, and I love everyone at Garthowen the same, and would willingly give my life for them.'"

"And what did he say to that?" asked Gethin in a scornful tone.

"He said, 'twas right I should feel like that, for they had all been kind to me, ever since the sea cast me up here, a little helpless baby; and he said 'twould ill repay their kindness to break his heart."

Gethin snatched at her hand hungrily.

"Will I tell thee, lass, what I would have answered if I had been Will? I would have said, 'Love me, Morva, *more* than all the others at Garthowen; love me more than all the world beside; love me as I love thee, girl! Nothing less will satisfy me; no riches, no worldly goods, no joy, no happiness will be of any account to me if I have not all thy love.'"

"Stop, Gethin, stop," said Morva, turning away.

But Gethin continued, still detaining her hands in his, "That is what I would have said, Morva, if I were Will. Canst say nothing to me, lass?"

Morva had turned her face to the broom bush, and was sobbing with her apron to her eyes.

Allen Raine

"Why didst thou promise him?" Gethin said again, in a fierce tone.

"I promised him when I was a little girl, and ever since, whenever he has asked me, I have said, 'Oh, Will, there is no need to say more, for I have promised,'" and she turned slowly to move away; but Gethin drew her back.

"Thou shalt not go," he said; "I cannot live without thee; all through the long years I too have loved thee, Morva, ever since that day when I tore myself from thy clinging arms and heard thee crying after me; but because I was away, and could not tell thee of my love, I have lost thee."

"I have promised," was all her answer.

"Well, then, I suppose there is nothing else to be said, and I must live without thee; but 'twill be hard, very hard, lass. I thought—I thought—but there; what's the use of thinking? I suppose I must say 'Good-bye.' Wilt give me one kiss before we part? No? Well, indeed, an unwilling kiss from Morva would kill me, so fforwel, lass! At least shake hands."

Morva turned towards him, placing her hand in his, and by the bright moonlight he saw her face was very pale.

"Fforwel!" he said once more, and dropping her hand, he left her suddenly, standing alone under the night sky. She looked after him until he had passed round the Cribserth, and then turned homewards with a heavier heart than she had ever borne before.

"'As the sparks fly upward!'" she whispered, as she reached the cottage door, "Yes, mother was right, 'as the sparks fly upward!'"

CHAPTER XI

UNREST

"Ach y fi!" said Ann one day as the autumn slipped by, "only a week before Will goes; there's dull it will be without him!"

"Twt, twt!" said Will, tossing his tawny mane, "'twill only be for three months. Christmas will be here directly, and I will be home then for the holidays—vacation, I mean."

"Vacation; is that what they call it? Dear! dear! we must mind our words now with a college man among us."

Gethin seldom came into the house; from morning to night he worked hard on the farm, and his father was obliged to confess that, after all his roving, he showed more aptitude for steady work than Will did. When he did enter the house, it was only to take his meals hurriedly and silently, and if by chance he encountered Morva, as was unavoidable some-times in the day's work, he was careful not to look at her. The girl, though conscious of his change of manner, showed no outward sign of the acute suffering she was undergoing. Her whole life seemed upturned, full of discordant elements and strained relations. To bear Will's apparent indifference was not difficult, for she had been accustomed to that all her life; but to know that she was bound to him—that he still

Allen Raine

loved her, and would carry with him his faith and trust in her, was a heavy burden. The change in Gethin's manner, the averted look, the avoidance of her, the formal question or request, were positively so many sharp thorns that pierced her like some tangible weapon, and added to this was a deep regret that she was so unworthy of Will's love. He did not ask her to meet him again behind the broom bushes, and only one night in the old beudy,[1] where she had carried a pail of grain to a sick cow, had he tried to speak to her alone. Gethin, who watched his brother with eager interest, was astonished at the indifference he showed towards her.

Surely they must meet somewhere secretly! Well, what was it to him? What was anything to him? For Morva's love he would willingly have laid down his life; but now that that was denied him, nothing else was of any consequence; and in troubled thought he sauntered out to cross the farmyard on his way to Pont-y-fro. The moor beyond the Cribserth he avoided carefully, and when his work led him along the brow of the hill, he tried to avert his eyes as well as his thoughts from its undulating knolls, a background, against which memory would picture a winsome girl, red-cloaked and blue-kilted.

Will had preceded him about a quarter of an hour, and had found Morva pensively holding the empty pail before the cow, who had eaten up the grain, and was licking round in search of more; she did not see him until he was close upon her, and then she started from her dreams.

"Oh, Will!" she said, and nothing more.

"I wanted to see thee once more, lass, to say good-bye, and to remind thee of thy promise."

"You will be back before Christmas, Will, and we will be

together again."

"Yes," he answered, "and then we must manage to meet sometimes, for I find I cannot live without thee. I cannot break away from thee entirely; but we must be careful, very, very careful. I would not have anyone suspect our courtship for all the world. Thou wilt keep my secret, Morva?"

"Yes," she said wearily.

"Come, cheer up, lass, 'twill soon be over. A year or two and I will have a home for thee—I know I will. And now good-bye, I hear footsteps. Good-bye, Morva."

He clasped her once to his heart, and whispered a word of endearment in her ear; but she stood like a statue, and only answered "Good-bye," and even that he did not hear, for he had already slipped away, and by a circuitous path reached the house.

Crossing the farmyard, Gethin's approaching footsteps made but little sound on the soft stubble; and Morva, thinking herself quite alone, stood leaning just within the doorway, crying softly in the darkness, for the flaring candle had gone out.

"Who is there?" said Gethin.

There was no answer, Morva checking her sobs, and standing perfectly still.

"Morva, is it thee crying here by thyself? What is it? Tell me, child."

"Oh! nothing," said the girl. "Only Will has been here."

"Oh! I see," said Gethin bitterly, "to bid thee fforwel, I suppose. Well, it won't be for long; he will be back soon, and then thou wilt be happy, Morva."

"Gethin, thee must promise me one thing."

"And what is that?" he said.

"Never to tell anyone what I told thee over yonder beyond the Cribserth. Will wants it to be a secret."

"Fear nothing," said Gethin, "I will never tell tales. Gethin Owens has not many good qualities, but he has one, and that is, he would never betray a trust, so be easy, Morva. I am going to Pont-y-fro. Good-night!"

"Good-night," echoed the girl, and, taking up her pail, she closed the beudy door, and as she crossed the yard under the bright starlight she recalled Gethin's parting words, "Be easy, Morva," and repeated them to herself with a sorrowful smile.

* * * * * *

"'Tis Martinmas Fair to-morrow," said Ann, as Morva entered the best kitchen. "Are you going, father?"

"Yes," he said. "I have those yearlings to sell."

"I will come with you," said Gwilym Morris, for they seldom let the old man go alone. "I can see about Will's coat, and I want some books. Come on, Ann, come with us; 'twill be a lively fair, I think."

"Very well, I'll come and look after you both."

"That's right," said the old man, rubbing his knees. "Twm

will drive the yearlings. Art coming, Will?"

"No," he answered, "I have promised to go to Caer-Madoc to-morrow."

And so Garthowen was empty next day, for Gethin did not return to the midday meal. Morva, as usual in Ann's absence, took charge of the house, and very sad and lonely she felt as she roamed from one room to another, dusting a chair or table occasionally, and looking out through the windows at the dull, leaden sea, for outside, too, the clouds were gathering, and the wind whispered threatenings of change.

Three nights ago! Was it possible? So lately as that was she bright and happy, and was the world around her so full of light and warmth?

She leant her elbows on the deep window-sill and mused. How long ago, too, it seemed since she had taken down the old Bible and hunted up Gethin's delinquencies. She saw it now in her mind's eye, and, getting upon the table, she reached it down again, and turned to the disfigured page.

Now she knew how little harm there had been in those foolish, boyish rhymes; now she knew the bright black eyes which had guided the pen in those brown fingers were full of nothing but mischief. "Oh, no! no harm," she said, "only fun and mischief." She read the lines again, and a sad little smile came over her mouth, then she looked at the signatures below. "Gethin Owens, Garthowen." "G. O." "Gethin." She half-closed the old book, and then, with a furtive glance round the room and through the window, opened it again, and, stooping down, pressed her lips on the name, then, blushing a vivid red, she mounted the table once more and replaced the Bible.

It was a long, weary day, but it came at last to a close. She made up the fire, prepared the tea, with piles of buttered toast and new-laid eggs in plenty, and soon the jingling car drove into the farmyard, Gwilym Morris lifting Ann bodily out, and both assisting the old man with tender care, Morva hovering round. She was to sleep at the farm that night in order to be ready for the early churning next day, so when they were all seated at the tea-table she left the house with the intention of seeing if Sara required any help.

"I will be back before supper," she said, and hurried homewards over the moor, where the wind was rising and sighing in the broom bushes. The clouds were hurrying up from the north-west, and threatening to overcast the pale evening sky, quivering flocks of fieldfares whirred over her, and the gold and purple were fast losing their brilliant tints. As she neared the cottage in the darkening twilight, a patch of scarlet caught her eye, and a warm glow of comfort rushed into her heart. It was Sara's red mantle and she knew the faithful heart was waiting for her.

"The dear old mother," she said, and hastening her footsteps soon reached Sara, who stood leaning on her stick and peering over the moor.

"Here I am, mother!" she said, as cheerfully as she could.

"'Merch fach i!" said Sara tenderly, and they turned into the cottage together.

The tea was laid on the little round table in the chimney corner.

"Did you expect me, then, mother?"

"Yes; I thought thou wouldst come, child, to see how I fared as thou art sleeping there to-night," and sitting down together they chatted over their tea.

At Garthowen there was much chat going on, too. Ebben Owens had not sold his yearlings.

"I wasn't going to give them away for half price, not I!" he said. "I'd rather keep them till next fair." So Twm had driven them home again, and was even now turning them into the old cowhouse.

"Well! I have a wonderful piece of news to give you all," said Gwilym Morris, leaning back in his chair and diving deep into his pocket. Having pulled out a canvas bag he laid it triumphantly on the table with a bang.

"What is it?" said all, in a breath.

Gwilym did not answer, but undoing the pink tape which tied it, he poured out on the table forty glittering sovereigns.

"There!" he said, "what do you think; old Tim 'Penlau' paid me the 40 pounds he has owed me so long!"

"Well, wonders will never cease!" said Ebben Owens.

"How long has he had them?" asked Will.

"Oh! these years and years. I had quite given them up, but he was always promising that when he sold his farm he would repay me. Now they have come just in time to furnish the new house, Ann."

"But why didn't you put them into the bank?" asked Will.

"'Twas too late, the bank was closed; but I will take them in to-morrow."

"I saw you talking to Gryny Lewis in the market," said Ebben Owens. "What were you saying to him? You weren't such a fool as to tell him you had received the 40 pounds?"

"Well, yes, indeed I did," replied Gwilym.

"Well, I wouldn't tell him. Don't forget how he stole from Jos Hughes's till."

"Well, indeed, I never remembered that. Oh, I'll take care of them," he said, tying them once more in his bag, and returning them to his pocket. "I'll put them in my drawer to-night, and to-morrow I'll take them to the bank."

When Morva returned they were still discussing the preacher's good fortune in the recovery of the loan which he had almost despaired of.

"Oh, there's glad I am!" said the girl; and Gethin put in a word of congratulation as he sauntered out to take a last look at the horses.

Long before ten the whole household had retired for the night. Ann and Morva slept in a small room on the first landing, just beyond which, up two steps, ran a long passage, into which the other bedrooms opened.

Morva, who generally found the handmaid of sleep waiting beside her pillow, missed her to-night. Hour after hour she lay silent and open-eyed, vainly endeavouring to follow Ann into the realms of dreamland.

Tudor, too, who usually slept quietly in his kennel, seemed

disturbed and restless, and filled the air with mournful howling.

The girl was in that cruellest of all stages of sorrow, when the mind has but half grasped the meaning of its trouble. She had no name for the deep longing which rebelled in her heart against the fate that was closing her in; for she had as yet scarcely confessed to herself that her whole being turned towards Gethin as the flower to the sun, and that in her breast, so long calm and unruffled as the pools in the boggy moor, was growing as strong a repulsion for one brother as love for the other. And as she lay quietly on her pillow, endeavouring not to disturb her companion's rest, a tide of sorrowful regrets swept over her, even as outside, under the shifting moonlight, the bay, yesterday so calm, was torn and tossed by the rising north-west wind. Through all, and interwoven even with her bitter grief, was the memory of that happy night—surely long ago?—when she had sat in the warm air of the cynos, and Gethin had danced into her heart. Oh, the pity of it! such love to be offered her, and to be thrust aside! "That is what I would say if I were Will!" And all night every sorrowful longing, every endeavour after resignation, every prayer for strength, ended with the same refrain, "If he were Will! if he were Will!"

Tick, tack, tick, tack! the old clock filled the night air with its measured beat. "Surely it does not tick so loudly in the day?" she thought.

Ten, eleven, and twelve had struck, and still Morva lay wakeful, with wide-open eyes, watching the hurrying clouds. At last she slept for an hour or two, and her uninterrupted breathing showed that the invigorating sleep of youth had at length fallen upon her weary eyelids. For an hour or two she slept, but at last she suddenly stirred, and in a moment was wide awake, with every sense strained to the utmost.

What had awakened her she could not tell. She was conscious only of an eager and thrilling expectancy.

She was about to relapse into slumber when a gliding sound caught her ear, and in a moment she was listening again, with all her senses alert. Was it fancy? or was there a soft footfall, and a sound as of a hand drawn over the white-washed wall of the passage? A board creaked, and Morva sat up, and strained her ears to listen. After a stillness of some moments, again there was the soft footfall and the gliding hand on the wall. She rose and quietly crept into the passage just in time to see a dark figure entering the preacher's room.

Who could it be?

Intense curiosity was the feeling uppermost in her mind, and this alone prevented her calling Ann. Standing a few moments in breathless silence, she heard the slow opening of a drawer; another pause of eager listening, while the stealthy footsteps seemed to be returning towards the doorway.

At this moment the moon emerged from behind a cloud, and in her light Morva saw a sight which astonished her, for coming from the preacher's room a well-known form stood plainly revealed. It was Gethin! and the girl shrank a little into the shadow of a doorway. But her precaution was needless, for he walked as if dazed or asleep, and with unsteady footstep seemed to stagger as he hurriedly gained his own room.

Morva, frightened and wondering, returned to bed, and if the early hours of the night had been disturbed and restless, those which followed were still more so.

What could it mean? What could Gethin want in Gwilym's room? She had thought it was a thief, and if not a thief what was the meaning of those stealthy footsteps and the opening of the drawer? and full of unrest she lay awake listening to the ticking of the clock, and to Tudor's continued howling. Should she wake Ann? No! for Gethin had evidently desired secrecy, and she would not be the one to frustrate his intentions, for whatever might be the object of his secret visit to the preacher's room, she never doubted but that it was right and honourable.

All night she lay in troubled thought, rising many times to look through the ivy-framed window towards the eastern brow of the slopes. At length the pale dawn drew near, and Morva slept a heavy dreamless sleep, which lasted till Ann called her for the churning.

[1] Cowhouse.

CHAPTER XII

SARA'S VISION

"Morva, lass," said Ann, "what's the matter to-day? No breakfast; after thy work at the churn, too?"

"Well, indeed," said Morva, "I drank so much butter milk that I don't want much breakfast."

"Come, lass," said Ebben Owens, "hard work wants good feeding."

"Well," said Ann, "you are not eating much yourself. Did you sleep well, father?"

"Yes, of course," said the old man; "I always sleep like a top. Here's Will; he'll satisfy thee in the eating line, whatever."

"Yes; especially when there's fresh butter and new bread," said Will, sitting down and cutting a thick slice for himself. "What was the matter with Tudor last night? He was howling all night. Did you hear him, father?"

"Not I. 'Twas the moonlight, I suppose. Dogs often howl on a moonlight night."

"Tudor doesn't," said Ann. "I'm glad I didn't hear him, ach y fi! I don't like it at all. But where's Gwilym and Gethin? There's late they are."

At this moment the former entered and took his seat silently at the table, looking pale and flurried.

"Where can Gethin be?" said Ann again; "not back from the mountain?" and Magw was sent to the top of the garden to call him, which she did with such stentorian tones that his name flew backwards and forwards across the valley, but no Gethin came.

Breakfast over, the big Bible was placed before Ebben Owens as usual, and all the farm servants assembled for prayers. When they rose from their knees and the wooden shoes had clattered out of the kitchen, Gwilym said, as he drew his chair to the table:

"Ann, we must wait a little longer for our furniture. My bag of sovereigns is gone!"

"Gone?" echoed everyone, and Morva, who was putting away the Bible, turned white with a deadly fear, which seemed to freeze the blood in her veins. In the excitement of the moment her change of countenance escaped the notice of the other members of the family.

"Gone," said Will, "gone where? What do you mean, man? Stolen?"

"Yes, no doubt, for the window and the drawer were open."

"The window?" said Ebben Owens. "Then the thief must have come in that way."

"And gone out, too, I suppose," said Gwilym.

"Tis that devil, Gryffy Lewis," said Will. "He could easily creep up from his cottage. You ought not to have told him."

"No, I ought not," said the preacher; "but, indeed, I was so glad of the money and to find that Tim 'Penlau' was honest after all our doubts, and Gryffy Lewis seemed as glad as I was."

"The deceitful blackguard!" said Ebben Owens.

"Well, we don't know it was he after all," suggested Gwilym. "Poor man, we must not blame him till we are certain. I hoped and believed that he had taken a turn for the better, and this would be a dreadful blow to me."

"Blow to you!" said Will excitedly. "I'll go to Castell On for a policeman, and it'll be a blow to Gryffy when he feels the handcuffs on his wrists."

"No—no," said Gwilym Morris, "that I will never allow." For in his daily life the preacher carried out his Master's teaching in its spirit, and forgave unto seventy times seven, and with curious inconsistency abhorred the relentless anger which on Sundays in the pulpit he unconsciously ascribed to the God whom he worshipped. "No, let him have the money, it will bring its own punishment, poor fellow! I have lived long enough without it, and can do without it still, only poor Ann won't have mahogany chairs and a shining black sofa in her parlour—deal must do instead."

"Deal will do very well," said Ann soothingly,

"Well," said Ebben Owens, "you take your trouble like a Christian, Gwilym."

"Like a Christian!" said Will. "Like a madman I call it! I think you owe it to everyone in the house, Gwilym, to send for a policeman and have the matter cleared up."

"It wouldn't do," said Ebben, "to charge Gryffy without any proofs, so we had better hush it up and say nothing about it before the servants."

"Yes, that is the best plan," said the preacher, "and perhaps in time and by kindness I can turn Gryffy's mind to repentance and to returning the money."

"But where's Gethin this morning?" inquired Will. "I hope nothing has happened to Bowler."

The morning hours slipped by, and yet Gethin did not appear. At dinner in the farm kitchen there were inquiries and comments, but nobody knew anything of the absent one.

In the best kitchen the meal was partaken of in silence, a heavy cloud hung over the household, and terrible doubts clutched at their hearts, but no one spoke his fears. When, however, the shades of evening were closing in, and neither on moor nor meadow, in stable nor yard, was Gethin to be seen, a dreadful certainty fell upon them. It was too evident that he had disappeared from the haunts of Garthowen. Will swore under his breath, Gwilym Morris was even more tender than usual to every member of the family, and Ebben Owens went about the farm with a hard look on his face, and a red spot on each cheek, but nobody said anything more about sending for a policeman. Ann cried herself to sleep that night. Morva went home to her mother, white and dry-eyed, her mind full of anxious questioning, her heart sinking with sorrow.

Sara held out her wrinkled hand towards her.

"Come, 'merch fach i, 'tis trouble, I know; but what is it, lass?"

"Oh, mother, 'tis too dreadful to think of! How can such things be? You say the spirits come and talk to you, they never come to me; ask them to be kind to me, too, and to take me to themselves, for this world is too full of cruel thorns!"

Sara's kind eyes filled with tears.

"Oh! that I could bear thy sorrow for thee, my little girl; but it is one of the thorns of life that we cannot raise the burden of sorrows from our dear ones and bind it on our own shoulders. God alone can help thee, my child."

"Mother, do you know what has happened?"

"Yes," said the old woman. "I was quite failing to sleep last night, so I got up and lighted the fire, and I read a chapter sitting here on the settle. After I had read, looking I was at the flames and the sparks that flew upwards, and a vision came before me. I was at Garthowen in the dark, I saw a figure creeping quietly into a room; it was a man, but I could not recognise him. He opened a drawer, and took something out of it, and I did not see anything more. When I awoke the fire had gone out, and I was very cold, so I went back to bed, and slept heavily all night, and when I awoke this morning I knew thou wouldst come to me in sorrow and fright."

"Well, mother, can you gather some comfort from your vision? Oh! tell me the meaning of it all. What did Gethin want in Gwilym's room?"

"Gethin?" said Sara, in astonishment, "in Gwilym Morris's room!"

"Yes, I saw him; and from there a bag of sovereigns has been stolen. He has gone away without a word to anyone, and I know they all think that he has done this dreadful thing? but I will *not* believe it, never! never! never!"

"No, it is all dark, but one thing is plain to me and thee, Gethin did not do this shameful thing. Let me be, child, and perhaps it will all come before me again, or perhaps Gethin will come back. I know, whatever, that my message to thee is Gethin is not guilty of this wickedness."

"Mother, I believe you," said the girl; "and though all the world should swear it was Gethin, I should know better, for you know, mother. We only see with our bodily eyes, but your spirit sees. Mother, I know it—but he is gone! What is the meaning of that; he is gone like the mist of the morning—like a dream of the night, and he will never return, and if he did return it could never be anything to me!"

And leaning on the table as she had done once before, her face buried on her arms, she sobbed unrestrainedly, Sara sitting by her and crying in sympathy.

All day they discussed the unhappy event.

"Who did it, mother? and why did Gethin go away?"

"I don't know," said the old woman. "I shall never know perhaps who did it, but I know it was not Gethin."

"Why did I see him, mother? I awoke suddenly and went into the passage, and there he was. I wish I had slept sounder, for that sight will always be on my mind. When we came down to breakfast he was gone, and every one will think he stole the money. Forty sovereigns, mother! Will he ever come back and clear it up?"

Allen Raine

"Some day it will be plain, but now we must be satisfied to know it was not Gethin."

"No one else will believe us, mother."

"Oh! I am used to that," said the old woman, with a patient smile; "that makes no difference in God's plans. Thou must pluck up thy heart, and have courage, child, for there is a long life before thee. A dark cloud is shading thy path now, but 'twill pass away, and thou wilt be happy again."

"Never! unless Gethin comes back to clear his name. Oh! 'tis a cold grey world. Only here with you, mother, is the comfort of love. When I draw near the cottage I look out for your red mantle, and if I see it, it sends a warm glow through me."

And so they talked until, as the twilight gathered round them, Morva said:

"I must go; the cows must be milked. Poor Garthowen is a sad house to-day! I wish I could comfort them a little, but 'tis all dark."

And as she crossed the moor to the Cribserth, she looked round her, but found no shred of comfort. The sea, all rough and torn by the high wind, looked cold and cruel; the brow of the hill, which Gethin's whistle had so often enlivened, looked bare and uninteresting; the moor had lost its gorgeous tints; a rock pigeon, endeavouring to reach its nest, was driven by the wind against a thorn bush.

"Tis pricked and beaten like me," thought the girl, and struggling with the high wind, she helped the bird with tender fingers to extricate himself.

When she entered the farmyard Daisy stood waiting, and Morva, knowing that without her song there would be no milk, began the old refrain, but her voice broke, and while she sang with trembling lips the tears ran down her cheeks.

The news of Gethin's absence was soon bruited abroad, and many were the conjectures as to its cause.

"He seemed so jolly at the cynos," said the farm servants; "who'd have thought his heart was away with the shipping and the foreign ports?"

"Well, well," said the farmers, "Garthowen will have to do without Gethin Owens, that's plain; the roving spirit is in him still, and Ebben Owens will have to look alive, with only Ann and Gwilym Morris to help him."

"Well, he needn't be so proud, then! Will a clergyman indeed! 'tis at home at the plough I'd keep him!"

But nobody knew anything of the robbery, which added so much poignancy to the sorrow at Garthowen. Ebben Owens seemed to take his son's disappearance much to heart, and to feel his absence more in sorrow than in anger.

Will grew more and more irritable, so that it was almost a relief when one day in the following week he took his departure for Llaniago, his father accompanying him in the car, and returning next day with glowing accounts of his son's introduction to the world of learning and collegiate life.

"If you were to see him in his cap and gown!" he said, "oh, there's a gentleman he looks; in my deed there wasn't one in the whole college so handsome as our Will! so straight and so tall, and everybody noticing him."

And so Will was launched on the voyage of clerical life with full sails and colours flying, while Gethin was allowed to sink into oblivion; his name was never mentioned, his place knew him no more, and the tide of life flowed on at Garthowen with the outward monotonous peace and regularity common to all farm life. Ebben Owens leant more on Gwilym and Ann, and Twm took his own way more, but further than this there was no difference in the daily routine of work.

The grey house at Brynseion was nearing completion, but Ann put off her marriage again and again, and even hinted at the desirability of breaking off her engagement entirely, unless it could be arranged for her and her husband to live on at Garthowen, and let the grey house to somebody else.

"Well!" said Gwilym, "'tis for you and your father to settle that. I will be happy with you anywhere, Ann, and I see it is impossible for you to leave the old man while both his sons are away; so do as you wish, 'merch i, only don't keep me waiting any longer."

And so it was settled, and Ann sat down to indite a letter to Will in the fine pointed handwriting which she had learnt during her year of boarding-school at Caer-Madoc, fine and pointed and square, like a row of gates, with many capitals and no stops. The letter informed her brother with much formality, "that having known Gwilym Morris for many years, he and she had now decided to enter upon the matrimonal state. Our father and mother," she continued, "having been married in Capel Mair at Castell On, I have a strong wish to be married in the same place, and Gwilym consents to my wish. We will fix our wedding for some day after your return from Llaniago at Christmas, as we would like you to be present as well as my father. Elinor Jones of Betheyron will be my bridesmaid, and Morva and Gryffy

Jones will be the only others at the wedding."

By return of post Will's answer came, requesting them not to count upon him, as he might accept the invitation of a friend to spend part of his vacation with him. "In any case," he added, "it would scarcely look well for a candidate for Holy Orders in the Church of England to attend a service in a dissenting chapel."

Gwilym Morris folded the letter slowly, and returned it to Ann without a word.

"Well, well!" said Ebben Owens, "'tis disappointing, but Will knows best; no doubt he's right, and thee must find someone else, Ann. I wish Gethin was here," the old man said, with a sigh.

It was strange, Ann thought, how tenderly and wistfully he longed for Gethin, once so little cared for; and as the memory of the sinister event which she believed caused his absence crossed her mind she coloured with shame.

"Oh, father," she said, clasping her hands. "Poor Gethin! how could I have him at my wedding? I never thought one of our family could be dishonest."

"Nor I—nor I, indeed!" said Ebben Owens, shaking his head sorrowfully.

"It is too plain, isn't it?" said Ann, "going away like that— oh! to think our Gethin was a thief!" and throwing her apron over her face she burst into a fit of sobbing, a thing so unusual with the placid Ann that her father and Gwilym both watched her in surprise.

Gwilym took her hand in silence, and the old man, leaning

his elbow on the table and shading his eyes with his hand dropped some bitter tears. He had looked forward to Will's return with intense longing, had counted the days that must elapse before that happy hour should arrive when, great-coated and gloved, he should drive his son over the frosty roads, and usher him like a conquering hero into the old home. Through her own tears Ann observed the old man's sorrowful attitude, and instantly she dried her eyes and ran towards him.

"Father, anwl," she said, in an abandon of love, kneeling down beside him, and throwing her strong white arm around him, "is it tears I see dropping down on the table? Well, indeed, there's a foolish daughter you've got, to cry and mourn, and make her old father cry. Stop those tears at once, then, naughty boy," she said cheerily, patting the old man's back; "or I'll cry again, and Gwilym will be afraid to enter such a showery family."

Her father tried to laugh through his tears, and Ann, casting her sorrow to the winds, laid herself out with "merry quips and cranks" to restore him to cheerfulness.

"Now see," she cried, with assumed childish glee, "what a dinner I have for you! what you've often called 'a dinner for a king' and so it is, and that king is Ebben Owens of Garthowen!" and she placed before him a plate of boiled rabbit, adding a slice of the pink, home-cured bacon, which Gwilym was cutting with a smile of amusement at her playful ruse.

"Now, potatoes and onion sauce, salt, cabbages, knife and fork, and now the dear old king is going to eat a good dinner."

Ebben Owens laughingly took his knife and fork, and in spite of the previous tears, the meal was a cheerful one, even Tudor stood up with his paws on the table with a joyous bark.

Will's letters were the grand excitement of the farm, coming at first pretty regularly once a week—read aloud by Ann in the best kitchen, examined carefully by her father lest a word should have escaped the reader, carried out to farm kitchen or stable or field, and read to the servants, who listened with gaping admiration.

"There's a scholar he is! Caton pawb! Indeed, Mishteer, there's proud you must be of him!" And all this was incense to Ebben Owens's heart.

CHAPTER XIII

THE BIRD FLUTTERS

In the first term of his college life Will fully realised his pleasantest anticipations, and now, if never before, he acknowledged to himself his deep indebtedness to Gwilym Morris; his own abilities he had never doubted. The ease, too, with which he had matriculated much elated him, and he began his studies with a light heart and a happy conscious-ness of talent, which, coupled with a dogged perseverance and a determination to overcome every obstacle in his path, ensured success in the long run. He had one fixed and constant aim, namely, advancement in the career upon which he had entered, and in furtherance of this object, he was determined to let no hankering after the past stand in his way. In his own opinion there were but two hindrances to his progress, two shadows from the past to darken his path, and these were his obscure birth and his love for Morva, for this he had not yet succeeded in crushing. Before he left home his constant intercourse with her and the ease with which they met had prevented the usual anxieties which are said to beset the path of love. With innate selfishness, he had taken to himself all the pleasure derivable from their close companionship, without troubling himself much as to the state of the girl's feelings. That she was true to him, he had never had reason to doubt. Since he left home things had taken a different aspect; true, the thought of Morva was interwoven with all he did or read or studied, but there was an accompanying feeling of disquietude, a shrinking from the memory of her simple rustic ways, which he began to realise were incompatible with his new hopes and aspirations. It was becoming very evident to him, therefore, that his love for her must be banished, with all the old foolish ties and habits which bound him to the past. A vision of the clear blue eyes, the winsome smile, the lissom figure *would* rise persistently before him, and alas! the threadbare woollen gown, the wooden shoes, the pink cotton neckerchief, were also photographed upon his brain.

He heard from Ann of her approaching marriage, no longer deferred in expectation of his presence, and he was much relieved by this arrangement; but still, when the morning dawned clear and frosty, he was cross and irritable, for he could not banish from his mind the thought of the old ivy-covered homestead, with the few gnarled trees over-shadowing its gables, its bare sea front turned bravely to the north-west, the elder tree over the back door, the farm servants, all with white favours pinned on their breasts; the gentle bride, the handsome thoughtful bridegroom, the dear old father excited and merry, and above all, Morva decked out in wedding finery! How lovely she would look! Why was it that this sweet picture of home filled Will's heart only with discontent and an abiding unrest? The answer is plain, because he had determined, come what would, to sever himself from that homely, simple life, to cast the thought of it into the background, to live only for the future, and that future one of success and self-aggrandisement. Morva alone held him back; how could he hope to rise in his career, while his heart was fettered by the memory of a milkmaid, a cowherd, a shepherdess? No, it was very evident that from her he must break away. "But not now," he said to himself, as he paced round the quadrangle, "not yet." She was so sweet—he loved her so much; not yet must the severance come. "It will be time enough," so his reverie ended, "when my future is more defined and certain, then it will be easy to break away from poor Morva."

The invitation of which he had spoken had not been renewed, and though he was far too proud to show his annoyance, the omission galled and fretted his haughty nature, for the lowliness of his birth and circumstances chafed him continually, and engendered a sensitiveness to small annoyances which would not have troubled a nobler nature. In spite of all this, he found himself, as the term drew near its close, looking forward with pleasure to the old home ways, and the old home friends, and when he climbed into the jingling car beside his father, in the yard of the hotel, not even the rough country shabbiness of the equipage could altogether spoil the pleasant anticipations of a first vacation at home, although, it must be confessed, that as he drove out of the town, he earnestly hoped he would escape the observation of his fellow collegians.

Ebben Owens's happiness should now have been complete, for he had his much-loved son at home at his own hearth; but a shadow seemed to have fallen on the old man's life, a haunting sadness which nothing seemed to dispel. Ann rallied him upon it playfully, and he would laughingly promise to reform.

"Will at home and all," she said, "and everything going on so well—except, of course, 'tis dreadful about Gethin; but we have been used to his absence, father; and you never seemed to grieve about him."

"No, no," said her father, "I have never grieved about him much, but lately I had got so fond of him; he was so kind to me, so merry he was, and so handsome, and always ready to help!" and again he would relapse into silence.

On market day he was very anxious to drive Will into Castell On.

"Come on, 'machgen i; I will give you a new waistcoat. Come and show yourself to Mr. Price and to all the young ladies. Be bound, if they were to see you in your cap and gown, not the highest among them but would be proud to shake hands with you!"

But Will declined the offer. Later in the day, however, he walked in alone, and only that sad angel, who surely records the bitter wounds inflicted by children upon the tender parent hearts, knew how sharp a stab entered the old man's soul; but next day he had "got over it," as the phrase is.

With a slow, dragging step Morva walked home on the evening of Will's arrival. He had nodded at her in a nonchalant manner, with a kindly, "Well, Morva!" in passing, just as he had done to Magw and Shan, but further than that had not spoken to her again, though his eyes followed her everywhere as she moved about her household duties.

"Prettier than ever!" he thought. "My word! there is not one of the Llaniago young ladies fit to tie her shoe!"

As soon as the cows were milked and the short frosty day had ended, the moon rose clear and bright over the Cribserth.

"I am going to see Sara," said Will, taking his hat off the peg in the blue painted passage.

No one was surprised at that, for both Will and Gethin, ever since their mother's death, had been accustomed to run to Sara for sympathy with every pleasure or misfortune, and after being two months away it was quite natural that he should want to see her; so Morva had scarcely rounded the bend of the Cribserth before Will had caught her up. A little shiver ran through her as she recognised the step and the whistle which called her attention. It was Will, whom she once thought she had loved so truly, and the coldness which she had felt towards him of late was strangely mingled with remorse and tender memories as she turned and walked a few steps back to meet him.

"Stop, Morva; let me speak to thee. Give me thy hand, lass. After so long a parting thou canst not deny me a kiss too."

Ah, how sweet it was to return to the dear old Welsh, and the homely "thee" and "thou"!

"Art well, Will? But I need not ask. Indeed, there is life and health in thy very face."

"Yes, I am well," said Will, drawing her towards him. "I am coming with thee to see Sara."

"Yes, come," said Morva.

"Art glad to see me, lass?"

"Yes, indeed, I am very glad, whatever. Garthowen will be full again; it has been very empty lately."

She was thinking of Gethin, unconsciously, perhaps, and hung her head a little guiltily when Will said:

"Thou didst miss me, then?"

"Of course we all missed thee—thy father especially."

"More than thee, Morva?"

She sighed. "'Tis this way, Will. I am tired of this secrecy. We grew up like brother and sister. Can't we remain like that? Don't ask me for more, and then thou canst rise as high as thou pleasest, and I will be always glad to see thee, and so proud to hear of thy getting on. Will, it will never do for a clergyman to marry his father's milkmaid!"

"Twt, twt," said Will, "let us not think of the future, lass— the present is enough for me; and I promise thee not to allude to our marriage if thou wilt only meet me like this whenever I come home, and let me feel thee close to my heart as thou hast to-night."

"But I will not," said the girl suddenly, withdrawing herself from the arm which he had passed round her waist.

"Why not?" he asked.

"Because," said Morva, "'tis only my promise to marry thee that makes me meet thee as I do, and deceive them all at Garthowen. Let me tell them how it is between us, Will."

"What! Morva talk about her sweetheart as the English girls do! No, thou art too modest, lass."

"That is quite different," said Morva. "I do not want to talk about my—my—"

"Lover," said Will.

"Yes, but I don't want any longer to deceive my best friends. Let me go, Will, or let us be married soon. I am willing for either."

"Indeed, lass," said Will, beginning to hedge, "I would almost think thou hadst found another sweetheart, only I know how seldom any other man comes across thy path, unless indeed Gethin the thief has stolen thy love from me. Morva, dost love any other man?"

"Gethin is no thief," she answered hotly, "and thou knowest it as well as I do. Thou knowest his nature; 'twould be impossible for him to do a mean thing."

"Thou hast a high opinion of him," said Will scornfully. "Is it he, then, who hast stolen thine heart?"

Morva walked with bent head, pulling at her apron-strings.

"I am not saying that," she answered, in a very low tone, "but I wish to be free, or marry thee soon."

It was now Will's turn to be anxious. The possibility of Morva's loving any other man had never before disturbed him, but now her words, her attitude, all impressed him with a strong suspicion, and a flame of anger and jealousy rushed through his veins.

"Free!" he said, "after all thy promises to me—free to marry another man! Is it that, Morva?" and as he spoke his hot temper gathered strength. "Never!" he said, "I will never free thee from thy promise. Thou canst break it an thou wishest, and break my heart at the same time; 'twill be a fine return for all our kindness to thee, 'twill be a grand ending to all thy faithful vows!"

"I am willing to marry thee, Will," she said, "if thou wilt let it be soon."

"Marry thee soon! How can that be, Morva?—a student

without home or money, and a girl without a penny in the world! What madness thou art talking. I only ask thee to have patience for a year or two, and I will have a home for thee. And who is thy new sweetheart?"

"I have no sweetheart; but, Will, I want to be free."

"And I will never give thee back thy freedom. Take it if thou lik'st. The absent are always forgotten. How could I expect thee to be true?"

Morva began to cry silently.

"I see I have set my heart upon a fickle, cruel woman, one who, after years of faithful promises, forgets me, and wishes to take back her vows. I have but to leave her for two months, and she at once breaks her promises and forgets the past, while I," said Will, with growing indignation and self-pity, "have found all my studies blurred by thine image, and the memory of thee woven with all my thoughts. Oh, Morva! had I known when we were boy and girl together that thou couldst be so false, I would never have treasured thee in my heart, but would have turned and fled as Gethin did, instead of clinging to thee, and for thy sake stopping in the dull old home when the world was all before me. And now to come home and find that thou art tired of me—art cold to me, and hast forgotten me! 'Tis a hard fate, indeed!"

"Oh, Will, no, no!" sobbed the girl, "'tis not so; indeed. God knows I love thee still as much as ever I did. 'Tis only that I have grown older, and wiser, and sadder perhaps, because it seems that knowing much brings sorrow with it. I was so young when I made all those promises."

"Two months younger than thou art now!" scoffed Will.

"Two months is a long time," she said, "when you begin to think, and I have thought and thought out here at night when the stars are glittering overhead, when the sea is sighing so sad down below, and after all my thinking only one thing is plain to me, Will; let there be no promises between us."

"Never!" said Will, a vindictive feeling rising within him, "never will I set thee free to marry another man, whoever he is!"

"He is no one," interpolated Morva, in a low voice.

"Whoever he is," repeated Will, as though he had not heard her, "I will never set thee free, never—never, never!"

All the dogged obstinacy of his nature was roused, and the feeling that he was a wronged and injured man gave his voice a tone of indignant passion which told upon the girl's sensitive nature.

"Oh, Will," she said, stretching out her hand towards him, "I did not think thou loved me like that! I cannot be cruel to thee; thou art a Garthowen, and for them I have often said I would lay down my life. I will lay down my life for thee, Will. Once more I promise."

"Nay," he said, laughing, "I will never ask thee to do that for me, lass; only be true to me and wait patiently for me, Morva;" and he drew her towards him once more.

"I will," she answered.

They had reached the cottage, and Will passed round into the court, leaving her standing with eyes fixed steadfastly on the bright north star.

"I will," she repeated, "for I have promised, and there are many ways of laying down one's life."

For a moment she stood alone in the moonlight, and what vows of self-sacrifice she made were known only to herself.

"Anwl, anwl!" said Sara, as Will entered, "will I make my door bigger? Will I find a stool strong enough for this big man?"

Will laughed and tossed back his hair.

"Will I ever be more than a boy to thee, Sara?"

"Well, indeed," said the old woman, "I am forgetting how the children grow up. Sit down, my boy, and tell us all about the grand streets and the college at Llaniago, and the ladies and gentlemen whom thou art hand and glove with there—and so thou ought to be, too. Caton pawb! I'd like to see the family whose achau[1] go back further than Garthowen's!"

Here Morva entered.

"I thought thou hadst run away, lass!" said Will, with a double meaning as he looked at her.

She only smiled and shook her head.

"Oh! 'twouldn't do for me," said Sara, "whenever Morva stops out under the night sky to think she has run away; she often strays out when the stars are shining."

Gethin had always been Sara's favourite, and Will's visit therefore did not give her so much pleasure as his brother's had done; but she would have belied her hospitable nature had she allowed this preference to influence the warmth of her welcome.

Morva seemed to have regained her cheerfulness, and spread the simple supper, sometimes joining in the conversation, while Will and Sara chatted over the blaze of the crackling furze. It was quite late when he rose to go.

"Well," he said, "they will be shutting me out at Garthowen, and thinking I have learnt bad ways at Llaniago. Good-night, Sara fach, I am glad to see thee looking so well. Good-night, Morva. Wilt come with me a little way? 'Twill be an excuse for another ten minutes under the stars, Sara."

And they went out together, their shadows blending into one in the bright moonlight.

Once more Will extracted the oft-repeated promise, and Morva returned to the cottage, her chains only riveted more firmly, and her heart filled with a false strength, arising from an entire surrender of self and all selfish desires to an imaginary duty.

[1] Pedigree.

CHAPTER XIV

DR. OWEN

It was New Year's Day, the merriest and most festive day of the year, and Ebben Owens, sitting under the big chimney, seemed for a time at least to have shaken off the cloud that had hung over him of late.

Christmas Day in Wales is by no means the day of festivity that it is in England, the whole day being taken up with religious services of some kind; but the first day of the year is given up entirely to pleasure and happy re-unions. For the children it is the day of days. Before the sun has risen they congregate in the village streets, and set out in the dark and cold of the frosty morning in noisy groups, on expeditions into the surrounding country, with bags on their shoulders, in which they collect the kindly "calenigs," or New Year's gifts, prepared for them in every farm and homestead. 'Tis a merry gathering, indeed, the tramp through the frost and snow under the bright stars in the early morning, adding the charm of novelty and mystery to the usual delight of an expedition.

Ann and Morva had cut the generous hunches of barley bread and cheese overnight, and well it was that they were thus prepared, for before the hens and turkeys had flown down from their roosting-place, and before the cows had

Allen Raine

risen from their warm beds of straw in the beudy, or the sheep had begun to shake off the snow which had fallen on their fleeces in the night, fresh young voices were heard in the farmyard singing the old refrain familiar to generations of Welsh children:

"Calenig i fi, calenig i'r ffon,
Calenig i fytta ar hyd y ffordd.
Un waith, dwywaith, tair!"

Translation.

"A gift for me and a gift for my staff,
And a gift to eat as I trudge along.
Once, twice, thrice!"

It is a peremptory demand, sung in a chanting kind of monotone, and very seldom refused. A boy is chosen to knock at the farm door and rouse the inmates, it being considered unlucky for the household if a girl first crosses the threshold.

The family at Garthowen had risen hurriedly, and with smiling faces had opened the door to the children. Bags were filled, greetings were interchanged, and the happy troop were sent on their way rejoicing, shouting as they went, "A happy New Year to you all!"

When the bread and cheese had come to an end, Ebben Owens had distributed pennies from a large canvas bag which he had filled for the occasion; and in the afternoon, when the calls were becoming less frequent, he sat under the open chimney with an almost empty bag.

Suddenly the doorway was darkened by a portly figure in black. A genial face glowing from the frosty air, a voice of peculiar mellowness, which always added a musical charm of its own both to singing and conversation; a chimney-pot hat not of the newest, his black clerical coat uncovered by greatcoat or cloak, a strong knobbed walking-stick in the right hand, while the finger and thumb of the left hand were generally tightly closed on a pinch of snuff, well-shined creaking shoes, completed the costume of the visitor, who was no other than Mr. Price, the vicar of Castell On.

"I saw the children coming to the back door, and I am come with them," said the vicar as he entered, pointing with his stick to a queue of children in the yard. "How do you do, Owens?" and he shook hands warmly with the old man, who rose hurriedly to greet his visitor.

"Caton pawb, Mr. Price!" he said, flinging his remaining pence into the yard, where the children scrambled for them. "Come in, sir, come in," and he opened the door of the best kitchen, where the rest of the family were sitting in the glow of the culm fire.

Will started to his feet, exclaiming, "Mr. Price!" and for a moment he hesitated whether to speak in English or in Welsh, but the visitor settled the matter by adhering to his mother-tongue.

Ann rose, calm and dignified, and held out her hand without much empressement. Mr. Price was a clergyman, and a little antagonism awoke at once in her faithful bigoted heart.

"My husband," she said, pointing to Gwilym, who flung away his book and came forward laughing.

"My dear girl," he said, "although Mr. Price and I work apart on Sundays, we meet continually in the week, and need no introduction, I think."

Mr. Price joined in the laugh, and shook hands warmly with the preacher and Will, and the conversation soon flowed easily. Will's career was the chief topic, the vicar appearing to take a personal interest in it, which delighted the old man's heart.

"I am very glad, indeed," said the former, with his pinch of snuff held in readiness, "to hear such a good account of you from my friend, the dean," and he disposed of his snuff. "He wrote to me, knowing I was particularly interested, and also that we are neighbours. He says, 'There is every reason to think your young friend will be an honour to his father, and to his college, if he goes on as he has begun. I have seldom had the privilege of imparting knowledge to one whose early teaching presents such well prepared ground for cultivation. Who was his tutor?' I have told him," added the vicar, "how much you owe to your brother-in-law."

"It has been a pleasure to instruct Will," said the preacher. "For one thing he has a wonderfully retentive memory. Of course it is useless to pretend that I should not have been better pleased if he had remained a member of 'the old body'; but, wherever he is, I shall be very grateful if the small seeds I have sown are allowed to bear the blossom and fruit of a useful Christian life."

"Yes, yes! just so, exactly so!" said the vicar; "but having chosen the Church of his own free will, I am very anxious he should get on well and be an honour to her."

He held out his silver snuff-box towards the preacher, who declined the luxury, but Ebben Owens accepted it with evident appreciation.

"There is one thing," said the vicar, turning to Will, "which I think very necessary for your advancement. You must make your uncle's acquaintance. Dr. Owen is a personal friend of the bishop's, and they say no one to whom he is unfriendly gets on in the Church."

"I hope he is not unfriendly to me," said Will, tossing his hair off his forehead. "I have never troubled him in any way, or claimed his acquaintance."

"Have you never spoken to him?"

"Only as a child," said Will haughtily. "He has not been here for a long time, and when he came I did not see him for I was not at home."

As a matter of fact Will had been ploughing on the mountain-side when the Dr. had honoured his brother with a call. He was beginning to be ashamed of the farm work and kept it out of sight as much as possible.

"Well, well!" said his father apologetically, "we are three miles from Castell On, you see, and it is uphill all the way, and Davy my brother, never comes to the town except to some service in the church, and so I can't expect him to spend his time coming out here."

"No, no, perhaps not! He is a very busy man," said the vicar, who was never known willingly to hurt anyone's feelings or to speak a disparaging word of an absent person. "Well, now, he is coming to lunch with me on Friday on his way to the archidiaconal meetings at Caer-Madoc, and I want you to come too."

"He won't like it, perhaps," said Will, "and I should be sorry to force my company upon him."

"Oh! you have no reason to think that," said the vicar. "I

think when he has seen you he will like you; anyway, I hope you will come."

"Of course, Will, of course," said Ebben Owens. "He'll come, sir, right enough."

"You are very kind, sir," said Will, slowly and reluctantly. "I would give the world if it could be avoided, but if you think it is the right thing for me to do I will do it."

"I am sure it is! I'm sure it is!" said the vicar, taking snuff vigorously; "so I shall expect you. Well, Miss Ann, I beg pardon—Mrs. Morris, I mean, I have not congratulated you yet. 'Pon me word, I am very neglectful; but I do so now heartily, both of you. May you live long and be very happy. In fact, my call was intended for the bride and bridegroom as well as for my young friend here. And where is Morva Lloyd? She works with you, does she not?"

"She's at home to-day. 'Tis a holiday for her.

"She is a great favourite of mine; what a sweet girl she is! I never have a great beauty pointed out to me but I say 'Very lovely; but not so lovely as Morva of the Moor.'"

"Yes; she is a wonderful girl," said Ann, "for a shepherdess."

"Well, yes!" said Gwilym Morris; "I think she owes her charm in a great measure to her foster-mother. Do you know old Sara?"

"Oh, yes!" said the vicar; "we have all heard of old Sara "spridion.' Something uncanny about the old woman, they say. But, 'pon me word, there is something very interesting about her, too."

"Yes," said Gwilym Morris, "she has a wonderful spiritual insight, if I may call it so. She often shocks me by her remarks, but if I lay a subject before her upon which I have been pondering deeply but have not succeeded in elucidating, she grasps its meaning at once and explains it to me in simple words, and I come away wondering where the difficulty lay."

After the vicar was gone, Will accompanying him half a mile down the road, the whole family were loud in his praise.

"There's a man now!" said Ebben Owens; "if every clergyman was like him 'twould be a good thing for the Church. No difference to him whether a man is a Methodist, a Baptist, or a Churchman, always the same pleasant smile and warm greeting for them all, and as much at home in a Dissenter's house as a Churchman's."

"Yes, a true Christian," said Gwilym Morris, "and so genial and pleasant. At 'Bethel' on Wednesday night, when Jones 'Bethesda' was preaching, he was there, and seemed much impressed by the sermon; and well he might be! I have never heard such an eloquent preacher. Wasn't he, Ann?"

"Oh, beautiful!" she replied. "I wish Mr. Price could have stopped to tea, but, of course, that meeting prevented him."

Next day when Will, having rung the bell, stood waiting on the vicar's doorstep, he was certainly not in as equable a frame of mind as his outward demeanour would lead one to suppose. He was in a few moments to meet face to face the man who of all others had interested him most deeply, though his feeling towards him was almost akin to hatred. It was a sore point at Garthowen that Ebben Owens' own brother had so completely ignored his relationship with him; and Will's hopes of success were greatly sweetened by the thought that in time he might hold his head as high as his uncle's, and bring that proud man to his senses; but to-day as he stood waiting at Mr. Price's door he called to mind the necessity of hiding his feelings, and conciliating the great man, who perhaps might have the power of helping him in the future.

When shown into the hall he heard voices within; the vicar's jovial laugh, and a pleasant voice so like his own, that he was startled.

"Hallo! Owen, how do you do? so glad to see you," said the vicar in English.

And the tall man who was standing by the window received him with an equally pleasant greeting.

"My nephew, I am told. Well, to be sure, this makes me realise how old I am getting."

"Nay, sir," said Will, "you are many years younger than my father."

The Rev. Dr. Owen looked over Will with secret surprise and satisfaction. He had expected a raw country youth, his angles still unrubbed off, his accent rough and Welshy, but Will was on his guard; it was his strong point, and though the care with which he chose his words was sometimes a little laboured and pedantic, yet they were always well chosen and free from any trace of Welsh accent. Dr. Owen was delighted; he had dreaded a meeting with his brother's uncouth progeny, and had been rather inclined to resent the vicar's interference in the matter, but when Will entered, well dressed, simple and unaffected in manner, and yet perfectly free from gaucherie, a long-felt uneasiness was set at rest, and the unexpected relief made Dr. Owen affable and pleasant.

Will was relieved too. He had feared a haughty look, a contemptuous manner, and dreaded lest his own hot temper might have refused to be controlled.

The vicar was delighted; he felt his little plan had succeeded, and his kind heart rejoiced in the prospective advantages which might accrue to Will from his acquaintance with his uncle.

"And how is my brother Ebben?" said Dr. Owen. "Well, I hope. I am ashamed to think how long it is since I have called to see him; but, indeed, I never come to Castell On except on important Church matters, and I never have much time on my hands. You will find that to be your own case, young man, when you have fully entered upon your clerical duties. The Church in Wales is no longer asleep, and she no longer lets her clergy sleep. I hope it is not with the idea that you will gain repose and rest that you have entered her service, for if it is you will be disappointed."

"Certainly not, sir," answered Will; "my greatest desire is a sphere in which I can use my energies in the services of the Church. I don't want rest, I want work."

"That being so," said the Dr., "we must see that you get it. I have no doubt with those feelings and intentions you will get on. You will take your degree, I suppose, before leaving college?"

"I hope so," said Will, modestly; "that is my wish."

"Your sister Ann," inquired his uncle at last, "how is she? And your eldest brother? Turned out badly, didn't he?"

"Well," said Will, "he is of a roving disposition, certainly; but that is all. My sister is quite well."

He intentionally left unmentioned the fact of her marriage, but the vicar, whose blunt, honest nature never thought of concealment, imparted the information at once.

"She was married about a month ago, and I should think has every prospect of happiness."

"Married! Ah, indeed! To whom? A farmer, I suppose?"

"No; to the minister of the Methodist Chapel at Penmorien. A very fine fellow, and one of the best scholars in the county. You know his 'Meini Gobaith,' published about a year ago?"

"Oh, is that the man?" said the doctor. "Ts! ts! you have left a nest of Dissenters, William. I am glad you have escaped."

"Yes," said Will, laughing; "a nest of Dissenters, certainly."

"Well," said the vicar, "you owe a great deal to Gwilym Morris. You would never have begun your college career on such good standing had it not been for him. In fact, you have had exceptional advantages."

"Yes," said Will; "he is a splendid teacher, and a good man."

"Well, well," said his uncle, "let the superstructure be good, and the foundation will soon be forgotten."

"A good man's silent influence is a very solid foundation to build upon, whatever denomination he may belong to," said the vicar.

"Oh, certainly, certainly," agreed Dr. Owen. "My carriage is at The Bear; perhaps you will walk down with me, both of you?"

"Of course, of course," said Mr. Price; "if you must go."

"Yes, I must go; I must not be late for the meeting at Caer-Madoc."

The vicar hunted for his walking-stick, and Will helped his uncle to get into his greatcoat.

"Thank you, my boy," said the old man, almost warmly, for he was beginning to feel the ties of blood awakening in his heart.

In truth, he was so pleasantly impressed by his new-found nephew's appearance and manners that already visions of a lonely hearth passed before him, lightened by the presence of a young and ardent spirit, who should look up to him for help and sympathy, giving in return the warm love of relationship, which no heart, however cold and isolated, is entirely capable of doing without.

Will was elated, and conscious of having stepped easily into his uncle's good graces, he walked up the street with the two clergymen, full of gratified pride.

On their way, to his great annoyance, they met Gryff Jones of Pont-y-fro, a farmer's son holding the same position as his own. He would have passed him with a nod, but the genial vicar, to whom every man was of equal importance, whether lord or farmer, stopped to shake hands and make kindly inquiries.

Will and the doctor moved on, and John Thomas the draper, standing at his shop-door, turned round with a wink at his assistant and a knowing smile.

"Well, well," he said, "Will Owens Garthowen *is* a gentleman at last. That's what he's been trying to be all his life."

At the door of the Bear Hotel they came upon a knot of ladies, who at once surrounded Dr. Owen. He was a great favourite amongst them, his popularity being partly due to his good looks and pleasant manners, partly to his good position in the Church, and in some measure certainly to his reputed riches.

Soon after entering the Church he had married a lady of wealth and good position, who was considerably older than himself, and who, having no children, at her death had bequeathed to him all her property. Many a net had been spread for the rich widower, but he had hitherto escaped their toils, and appeared perfectly content with his lonely life.

Will was almost overwhelmed with nervousness and shyness as they reached the group of ladies; but, true to his purpose, he put on a look of unconcern which he was far from feeling.

"How do you do, Mr. Owen?" said one of the girls, holding out her hand with a shy friendliness, "I am Miss Vaughan, you know, whom you saved from that furious bull."

"Yes, of course," said Will, shaking hands.

"I thought perhaps you had forgotten me," she said.

Will had flushed to the roots of his hair from nervousness, but he quickly regained his self-possession. He looked down the side of his leg and pondered his boot.

"Would that be possible, I wonder?" he said, half aloud.

"I don't see much difficulty," said the girl laughingly.

Will laughed too, and his laugh was always charming, the ice was broken, and the chat was only disturbed by the Dr.'s hurried good-bye.

"Good-bye, ladies," he said, as he stepped briskly into his gig. "I am grieved to have to leave you, but that meeting calls. Good-bye, Will, I shall see you at Llaniago, and you, Miss Vaughan, I hear I am to have the pleasure of meeting you at Llwynelen." And the Dr. drove off amongst a flutter of hands and handkerchiefs.

And now Will would have been in a dilemma had not the vicar arrived on the scene. Again there were many "How do you do's?" and much shaking of hands, while Will was debating within himself what he should do.

The vicar at once introduced him to each and all of the young ladies, some of whom would have drawn back in horror had they known that the young man who addressed them with such sang-froid was the son of a farmer, and a brother-in-law of a dissenting preacher.

Will knew this obstacle in his path, and was determined to overcome it. Gwenda Vaughan, he thought, was delightfully easy to get on with, and their conversation followed on uninterruptedly until they reached the vicarage door, where they parted, the ladies separating, and Will staying to bid the vicar good-bye.

"Who on earth was that handsome man, Gwenda?" asked Adela Griffiths before parting. "I don't know how it is, but you always manage to get hold of handsome men.

"And nothing ever comes of it," whispered Edith Williams.

"Why, he's Dr. Owen's nephew," said Gwenda; "didn't you

Allen Raine

hear Dr. Owen introduce him?"

And she said no more, but carried away with her a distinct impression of Will's handsome person and charming smile.

* * * * * *

About this time a strange thing happened at Garthowen. It was midday. Ann had just laid the dinner on the table, and Ebben Owens had lounged in.

"Well, the threshing will be done soon," said the old man; "Twm is a capital fellow. Don't know in the world what I should do without him."

"What is that noise?" asked Morva, pushing back her hair to listen, as a curious sound as of shaking and thumping was heard by all.

"'Tis upstairs, and in your room, Gwilym," said Ann.

Suddenly there was a jingling sound and rolling as if of money, followed by a satisfied bark.

"Run up Morva and see," said Ann; "what is that dog doing?"

The girl ran up, passing Tudor on the stairs, who entered the kitchen with waving tail and glistening eyes carrying in his mouth a canvas bag from which hung a draggled pink tape, and at the same moment Morva's voice was heard calling, "Oh, anwl! come up and see!"

Ann and Gwilym hurried up, followed by Ebben Owens and Will, to find Morva pointing to the floor which was strewn with pieces of gold.

"My sovereigns!" said Gwilym, "no doubt! and Tudor has emptied the bag. Where could they have come from?" and everyone looked through the open window down the lane to where in the clear frosty air the blue smoke curled from a little brown thatched chimney.

Ebben Owens jerked his thumb towards the cottage.

"There's no need to ask that," he said. "'Twould be easy to stand on the garden wall and throw it in through the window."

Ann was busily counting the sovereigns which had rolled into all sorts of difficult corners.

"Thirty-eight, thirty-nine, forty!"

"Every one right," said Gwilym; "how fortunate! but how I should like to tell Gryffy Lewis I forgive him, and that he has done right in returning the money."

"I expect fear as well as a guilty conscience made him return them, the blackguard!" suggested Will.

"No doubt; no doubt," said the old man.

As for Morva, she was so overcome with joy at this proof of Gethin's innocence that she was scarcely able to hide her agitation from those around her.

When all the money had been gathered into Ann's apron they returned to their dinner to find Tudor occupying the mishteer's chair, with a decided expression of satisfaction on his face, the canvas bag lying beside him.

"Well," said Ebben Owens, ousting Tudor unceremoniously

from his seat, and speaking in an agitated and tremulous voice, "one thing has been made plain, whatever, and that is that poor Gethin had nothing to do with the money. You all see that, don't you?"

"Well I suppose he hadn't," said Will; "but why then did he go away so suddenly? That, I suppose, must remain a mystery until he chooses to turn up again."

"Yes, it is strange," said his father, with a deep sigh.

"Well, thank God!" said Gwilym; "'tis plain he never took the money, Ann. There is no more need for tears."

"No, indeed," she said, "but will he ever come back? Oh! father, anwl! no more sighs. Will is a collegian and getting on well. Gethin is an honest man wherever he is. He will come back suddenly to us one day as he did before, and there is no need for heavy hearts any longer at Garthowen. Morva, lass, art not glad?"

"Yes, indeed," said the girl, "but I never thought it was Gethin."

Ebben Owens looked up at her quickly.

"Who then?" he said.

"Oh, I didn't know," said the girl, "but I thought God would make it plain some day."

"I don't think there is much doubt about it," said Gwilym. "Poor Gryffy; we know he must have suffered much remorse before he threw that bag in at the window again."

"'Twas not Gethin, and that's all we need trouble our heads

about now," said the old man rising from the table.

The frosty wind was scarcely more fleet than Morva's flying footsteps as she crossed the moor that evening.

"Mother, mother!" she called, even before she had reached the doorway. "Mother, mother! the money is found and everyone knows now that Gethin is innocent!" and the whole story was poured into Sara's ears.

Tudor, who sat beside the girl on the settle, her arm thrown round his neck, looked from one face to another as the story proceeded, interpolating a bark whenever there was a pause.

"So the clouds roll by," said Sara. "Patience 'merch i! and the sun will shine out some day!"

"How can that be, mother, when I am bound to Will? A milkmaid to a clergyman; and he already ashamed of her!"

CHAPTER XV

GWENDA'S PROSPECTS

"I am going to walk into town," said Dr. Owen one morning as he turned over the sheets of his newspaper; "is anyone inclined for a walk?"

He was sitting in the sunny bay-window of the breakfast-room at Llwynelen, a large country house about a mile out of Llaniago.

"I am," answered Gwenda Vaughan, who sat at work near him. "Such a lovely day! I was longing for a walk."

"And I too," said Mrs. Trevor, their hostess. "I have some shopping to do, and will come with you."

"Do. Will you be ready in half an hour, ladies? I am going to call upon my nephew; I can go to his rooms while you are doing your shopping."

"Yes," said Mrs. Trevor, "and bring him back to lunch with us. I shall be glad to make his acquaintance. I hear he is a very promising young man."

"Thank you. I am sure he will be delighted to come. I think

you will like him; but I forgot that you, Miss Vaughan, have already seen him."

"Oh, yes!" said Gwenda. "He once saved my life; so of course I am very grateful."

"Saved your life, child; how," asked Mrs. Trevor.

And Gwenda related the story of the runaway bull, and the manner in which Will had gone to her rescue.

"Dear me," said Dr. Owen, "he never mentioned it to me! Well! I'll go and look him up today."

Noontide found Will seated at lunch at Llwynelen, Mr. Trevor plying him with questions concerning his studies and college life; Dr. Owen not a little pleased with his nephew's self-possessed, though unobtrusive, manner. He was pleased, too, to see that he made a favourable impression upon the genial host and hostess.

Gwenda was as delightfully agreeable as she knew how to be, and that is saying a good deal. Her naive remarks and honest straightforward manner had made her a favourite with Dr. Owen, and it gratified him to see an easy acquaintance springing up between her and his nephew.

"It is Will's twenty-fourth birthday to-day, he tells me," he said.

"How odd!" said Gwenda; "it is my twenty-second."

"That is strange," said Mrs Trevor; "and you never let me know! But you need not tell everyone your age."

"Why not?"

"Oh! well, young ladies don't usually tell their ages; but you are not quite like other girls."

Gwenda laughed; and Will thought how charming were the dimple in her chin, the perfect teeth, the sparkling black eyes! Yes, she was very pretty, no doubt!

"Is that remark meant to be disparaging or complimentary?" asked the girl.

"Oh! a little of both," said Mrs. Trevor; "girls are odd nowadays."

"Yes; I think the days are gone by when they were all run into the same mould," remarked Dr. Owen.

"And I'm afraid the mould got cracked before I was run into it," replied Gwenda.

"Well, you are not very misshapen," said the Dr. warmly, "and if you do run into little irregularities, they are all in the right direction."

"Let us hope so," said the girl.

Will said nothing; but Gwenda, catching the look of ardent admiration, blushed vividly, and looked down at her plate.

"In the meantime," she remarked, "no one has wished me or Mr. Owen many happy returns of the day."

"Bless me, no!" said Mr. Trevor; "but I do so now, my dear, with all my heart."

"And I—and I," echoed the others.

"Let us drink the health of the two young people," said the host.

"Thank you very much for your kind wishes," said Will.

"Yes, thank you very much," echoed Gwenda. Will was in danger of losing his head as well as his heart. To have his name (from which, by the by, he had dropped the plebeian "s") bracketed with Miss Gwenda Vaughan's was a state of things which, though occasioned only by a simple coincidence, elated him beyond measure. He had indeed, he thought, stepped out of the old order of things and made his way into a higher grade of life by an easy bound. He was careful, however, to hide his gratified pride entirely from those around him.

After lunch, Mrs. Trevor proposed a stroll through the conservatories, and while the elders stopped to admire a fern or a rare exotic, Will and Gwenda roamed on under the palms and greenery to where a sparkling fountain rose, and flung its feathery spray into the air.

"Will you sit down?" said Will, pointing to a seat which stood invitingly near. "You must be tired after your long walk."

"Tired? Oh no, I love walking, and am very strong, but we can rest till the others come up."

And sitting down together they watched the gold fish in the fountain's rustic basin. Through the glass they could see the sparkling frosty branches outside against the pale blue sky of a winter's day, the sun shining round and red through the afternoon haze.

"What a glorious day," said Gwenda at last.

"Yes," answered Will, adding a little under his breath, "one I shall never forget."

There was something in the tone of his voice which caused a little flutter of consciousness under Gwenda's fur necklet. She made no answer, and, after a moment, changed the subject, though with no displeasure in her voice.

"Do you see those prismatic colours in the spray?"

"Yes, beautiful!" answered Will, rather absently.

He was wondering whether all this was a dream—that he, Will Owen of Garthowen Farm, was sitting here under the palms and exotics with Miss Gwenda Vaughan of Nantmyny. At last Gwenda rallied him.

"You are dreaming," she said playfully.

"I am afraid I am."

At this moment the rest of the party appeared, and they all returned to the house together.

Will looked at his watch.

"I think I must go," he said. "I have a lecture to attend."

"Well," said his uncle, "we won't detain you from that. Quite right, my boy, never neglect your lectures. I shall see you again to-morrow."

"Now, don't wait for an invitation," said Mrs. Trevor hospitably, "but come and see us as often as you can. Your uncle is quite at home here, and we shall be delighted if you will make yourself so too!"

"I shall only be too glad to avail myself of your kindness."

"I will come with you to the gate," said his uncle, and Will went out in a maze of happiness.

"My dear boy," said Dr. Owen, taking his arm as they passed together up the broad avenue, "I have done a good thing for you to-day. I have introduced you to the nicest family in the neighbourhood. Keep up their acquaintance, it will give you a good standing."

"You are very good to me, sir," said Will. "I don't know how to thank you."

"By going on as you have begun, William. I am very pleased to find you such a congenial companion. I mean to be good to you, better than you can imagine. I am a lonely old man, and you must come and brighten up my home for me."

"Anything I can do," said Will warmly.

"Well, well, no promises, my dear boy. I shall see how you go on. I believe we shall get on very well together. Good-bye, I shall see you tomorrow."

"You evidently take a great interest in your nephew," said Mrs. Trevor, on the Dr.'s return to the house, "and I am not surprised. He seems a very nice fellow, so natural and unaffected, and so like you in appearance; he might be a son of yours."

"Yes," said Dr. Owen thoughtfully, "I am greatly pleased with him. You see I am a lonely man. I have no one else to care for, so I shall watch the young man's career with great interest. He will be everything to me, and with God's help I will do everything for him."

"He is a lucky fellow indeed," said Mrs. Trevor.

"Well, yes, I think he will be."

Gwenda was sitting quietly at work in the bay window, where not a word of this conversation was lost upon her. Was it possible that bright hopes were dawning even for her, who had been tossed about from early girlhood upon the sea of matrimonial schemes? Schemes from which her honest nature had revolted; for Gwenda Vaughan had within her a fund of right feeling and common sense, a warmth of heart which none of the frivolous, shallow-minded men with whom she had come in contact had ever moved. Attracted only by her beauty, they sought for nothing else, while she, conscious of a depth of tenderness waiting for the hand which should unseal its fountain, turned with unsatisfied yearnings from all her admirers and so-called "lovers." She had felt differently towards Will from the day when he had, as she thought, saved her life, and when he had ridden home with her foot in his hand. A strange feeling of attraction had inclined her towards him, all the romance in her nature, which had been stunted and checked by the manoeuvres and manners of country "society," turned towards this stalwart "son of the soil" who had so unexpectedly crossed her path. She had not thought it possible that her romantic dreams could be realised; such things were not for her! In her case everything was to be sacrificed to the duty of "making a good match," of settling herself advantageously in the world, but now what did she hear? "I will do everything for him," surely that meant "I will make him my heir!" For wealth and position for their own sakes she cared not a straw, but Will's "prospects," the sickening word that had been dinned into her ears for years, began to arouse a deep interest in her mind. Her heart told her that he was not entirely indifferent to her, and experience had taught her that when she laid herself out to please she never failed to do so. All day she was very silent until at last Mrs. Trevor said:

"You are very quiet to-day, love; I really shall begin to think you have fallen in love with Dr. Owen's nephew. A charming young man, certainly, and I should think his prospects—"

"Oh, stop, dear Mrs. Trevor! *Prospects*! I am sick of the word. Shall I play you something?" And in the twilight she sat down to the piano.

"Do, dear; I love to see you on that music stool," said the good lady; and well she might, for Gwenda was a musician from the soul to the finger tips, and this evening she seemed possessed by the spirit of music, for long after the twilight had faded into darkness, she sat there pouring her very heart out in melody, and when she retired to rest her pillow was surrounded by thoughts and visions of happiness, more romantic and tender than had ever visited her before.

As the year sped on its course, Will's college life became more and more absorbing. The greater part of his vacations were always spent at Isderi, his uncle's house, situated some twenty miles up the valley of the On. Invited with his uncle to all the gaieties of the neighbourhood, he frequently met Gwenda Vaughan. Their attraction for each other soon ripened into a deeper feeling, and in the opinion of her friends and acquaintances Gwenda was a fortunate girl, Will being regarded only as the nephew and probable heir of the wealthy Dr. Owen, very few knowing of or remembering his connection with the old grey-gabled farm by the sea.

A hurried scrap-end of the time at his disposal was spent at Garthowen, where his father was consumed alternately by a feverish longing to see him, and a bitter disappointment at the shortness of his visit. He was beginning to find out that the love—almost idolatry—which he had lavished upon his son did not bring him the comfort and happiness for which he had hoped.

Will was affable and sometimes affectionate in his demeanour while he was present with his father; but he showed no desire to prolong his visits beyond the time allotted him by his uncle, who seemed more and more to appropriate to himself the nephew whose acquaintance he had so lately made. This in itself chafed and irritated Ebben Owens, and he felt a bitter anger against the brother who had ignored him for so long, and was now stealing from him what was more precious to him than life itself. He tried to rejoice in his son's golden prospects, and perhaps would have succeeded had Will shown himself less ready to drop the old associations of home and the past, and a more tender clinging to the friends of his youth; but this was far from being Will's state of feeling. More and more he felt how incongruous were the simple ways of Garthowen with the formal and polished manners of his uncle's household, and that of the society to which his uncle's prestige had given him the entree. He was not so callous as to feel no pain at the necessity of withdrawing himself entirely from his old relations with Garthowen, but he considered it his bounden duty to do so. He had chosen his path; he had put his hand to the plough, and he must not look back, and the dogged persistence which was a part of his nature came to his assistance.

"*I* could pay all your expenses, my boy," said his father, with a touching humility unnoticed by Will. "I have been saving up all my money since you went to college, and now there it is lying idle in the bank."

"Well, father, it would only offend my uncle if I did not let him supply all my wants; and as my future depends so much upon him, would it be wise of me to do that?"

"No, no, my boy, b'tshwr, it wouldn't. I am a foolish old man, and must not keep my boy back when he is getting on so grand. Och fi! Och fi!" and he sighed deeply.

"Och fi!" laughed Ann and Will together.

"One would think 'twas the downward path Will was going," said the former.

"No, no!" replied the old man, "'tis the path of life I was thinking of, my children. You don't know it yet, but when you come to my age perhaps you will understand it," and he sighed again wearily.

He had altered much of late, a continual sadness seemed to have fallen on his spirit, the old pucker on his forehead was seldom absent now, he was irritable and ready to take offence, and if not spoken to, would remain silently brooding in the chimney corner.

On the contrary, Ann's whole nature seemed to have expanded. Her happy married life drew out the brightness and cheerfulness which perhaps had been a little lacking in her early girlhood.

Gwilym Morris was an ideal husband; tender and affectionate as a woman, but withal firm and steady as steel; a strong support in worldly as well as spiritual affairs. Latterly the extreme narrowness of the Calvinistic doctrines, which had made his sermons so unlike his daily practice, had given place to broader views, and a more elevating realisation of the Creator's love. Many hours he spent with Sara in her herb garden, on the moor, or sitting by the crackling fire, conversing on things of spiritual import; and the well-read scholar confessed that he had learnt much from the simple woman, the keen perception of whose sensitive soul, had in a great measure separated her from her kind, and had made her to be avoided as something uncanny or "hyspis."

And what of Morva? To her, too, time had brought its changes. She was now two years older, and certainly more than two years wiser, for upon her clear mind had dawned in unmistakeable characters of light, the truth, that her relations with Will were wrong. She knew now that she did not love him—she knew now it would be sinful to marry him, and she sought only for a way in which she could with the least pain to him, sever the connection between them. She saw plainly, that Will had ceased to love her, and she rejoiced at the idea that it would not be difficult therefore to persuade him to release her from her promise. When one day she met him on the path to the moor, and he tried as of old to draw her nearer and imprint a kiss on her lips she started from him.

"No, Will," she said, "that must not be. You must let me go now. Do you think I do not see you have changed, that you have ceased to love me?"

Will noticed at once the dropping of the familiar "thee" and "thou"; and in his strange nature, where good and bad were for ever struggling with each other, a fierce anger awoke. That she—Morva! a shepherdess! a milkmaid! should dare to oppose the wishes of the man who had once ruled her heart, and at whose beck and call she would have come as obediently as Tudor—that she should now set her will in opposition to his, and dare to ruffle the existence which had met with nothing but favour and success, was unbearable.

"What dost mean by these words, lodes?[1] how have I ever shown that I have forgotten thee? Dost expect me, who have my studies to employ me, and my future to consider—dost expect me to come philandering here on the cliffs after a shepherdess?"

"No," said Morva, trying to curb her hot Welsh temper, which rushed through her veins, "no! I only ask you to free me from my promise. I have sworn that I would keep it, but if you do not wish it, He will not expect me to keep my vow. I see that plainly. It would be a sin—so let me go, Will," and her voice changed to plaintive entreaty; "I will be the same loving sister to you as ever—set me free!"

"Never," said Will, the old cruel obstinacy taking possession of him, a vindictive anger rising within him against the man whom he suspected had taken his place in the girl's heart. Gethin—the wild and roving sailor! No! he should never have her.

"Thou canst break thy promises," he said, turning on his heel, "and marry another man if thou wilt, but remember *I* have never set thee free. I have never agreed to give thee up;" and without another word he passed round the broom bushes, leaving Morva alone gazing out over the blue bay.

As he returned to the farm he was filled with indignation and anger. The obstinacy which was so strong a trait in his character was the real cause of his refusal to give Morva her freedom, for the old love for her was fast giving place to his new-born passion for Gwenda Vaughan, which had grown steadily ever since he had first met her.

[1] Girl.

CHAPTER XVI

ISDERI

Three miles above Llaniago, the river On, which had flowed peaceably and calmly for some miles through fair meadows and under the spanning arches of many a bridge, seemed to grow weary of its staid behaviour and suddenly to return to the playful manners of its youth. In its wild exuberance it was scarcely recognisable as the placid river which, further in its course, flowed through Llaniago and Castell On. With fret and fume and babbling murmurs it made its way through its rocky channel, filling the air with the sound of its turmoil. Both sides of its precipitous banks down to the water's edge were hidden in woods of stunted oak, through whose branches the sound of its flow made continual music, music which this evening reached the ears of a solitary man, who sat at the open window of a large house standing near the top of the ravine, its well-kept grounds and velvet lawn reaching down to the very edge of the oak wood, and even stretching into its depths in many a green glade and avenue. There was no division or boundary between the wood and the lawn, so that the timid hares and pheasants would often leave their leafy haunts to disport themselves upon its soft turf. It was Dr. Owen who, contrary to his usual careful habits, sat at that open window in the gathering twilight, dreaming dreams which were borne to him on the sound of the rushing waters, which lulled his senses, and brought before him the scenes of his past life. The twilight darkened into gloom, and still he sat on in brooding thought, letting the voice of the river bear to him on its wings sweet memories or sad retrospect as it chose. The early days of his childhood came back to him, when with a light heart he had roamed over moor and sandy beach, or over the grassy slopes of Garthowen. The river still sang on, and before him rose the vision of a man of homely and rustic appearance, who urged and encouraged his youthful ardour in the pursuit of knowledge, who rejoiced at his successes, and supplied his wants, who laid his hand upon his young head with a dying blessing. How vividly the scene returned to him! The dismay of the household when that rugged figure disappeared from the scene, the difficulties which had crowded his path in the further pursuance of his education, the arduous steps up the ladder of learning, the perseverance crowned with success! Still the rushing river filled his ears and brought before him its phantom memories—his successful career in the Church—his prosperous marriage, the calm domestic life which followed—the wealth—the honour—the prestige—what had they led to?—an empty home, a solitary hearth, no heir to inherit his riches, no young voices to fill the house with music and laughter—no—it had all turned to dust and ashes—there was no one to whom he could confide his joys or his sorrows—he was alone in the world, but need it always be so? and again he listened, deep in thought, to the spirit voices which the roar of the river seemed to carry into his soul. What a change would Will's presence bring into his life. How much ruddier would be the glow of the fire! how much more cosy the lonely hearth! How pleasant it would be to see him always seated at the well-appointed table! how the silver and glass would sparkle! how they would wake the echoes of the old house with happy talk and merry laughter! and the old man became quite enamoured of the picture which his imagination had conjured up.

"Yes," he said aloud, for there was no one to hear him, "I will no longer live alone; I will adopt Will as my son and heir. I think he is all I could wish him to be, and I believe he will reflect credit on my choice."

And when he closed the window and turned to his book and reading-lamp it was with a pleased smile of content, and a determination to carry out his plans without delay. Will should be fully informed of his intentions.

"It will give him confidence," thought the old man, and the feeling of kinship which had so long slept within him began to awake and to fill his heart with a warm glow which he had missed so long, though perhaps unconsciously.

In the following week Will came for a two days' visit, and Dr. Owen looked forward to their evening smoke with eager impatience. When at last they were seated in the smoking-room and Will had, with thoughtful care, pushed the footstool towards him and placed the lamp in his favourite position on the table at his back, he no longer delayed the hour of communication.

"Thank you, my boy, I quite miss you when you are away; you seem to fall into your place here so naturally I almost wish your college life was over so that I might see more of you."

"It would be strange if I did not feel at home here, you are so indulgent to me, uncle. If I were your own son I don't think you could be kinder."

"Well, Will, that is what I want you to become—my own son, the comfort of my declining years, and the heir to my property when I die. Does that agree with your own plans for the future, or does it clash with your inclination?"

"Sir! Uncle!" exclaimed Will, in delighted astonishment, "how can I answer such a question? Such a change in my prospects takes my breath away. What can I say to you? I had never thought of such a thing," and he rose, with a heightened colour and an air of excited surprise, which left Dr. Owen no doubt as to the reality of his feelings. They were not, however, altogether real, for Will had latterly begun to suspect the true meaning of his uncle's kindness to him.

"There is only one thing to be said, sir. Did it clash with my own plans there would be no sacrifice too great for me to make in return for your kindness. But you must know, uncle, that not only the ties of gratitude compel me, but the bonds of relationship and affection (may I say love) are strong upon me, and I can only answer once more that I accept your generosity with the deepest gratitude. I little thought a year ago that I should ever feel towards you as I do now. I felt a foolish, boyish resentment at the enstrangement between you and my father, but now I am wiser, I see the reason of it. I know how impossible it would be to combine the social duties of a man in your position with continued intimate relations with your old home. The impossibility of it even now hampers me, uncle, and I feel that it will be well for me to break away from the old surroundings if I am ever to make my way up the ladder of life. Your generous intentions towards me smooth this difficulty, and I can only thank you again, uncle, from my heart. I hope my conduct through life may be such that you will never regret the step you have taken, certainly I shall endeavour to make it so."

"Agreed, my boy!" said the Dr., holding out his hand, which Will grasped warmly, "we understand each other, from this time forward you are my adopted son; the matter is settled, let us say no more about it," and for a few moments the two men followed the train of their own thoughts in silence.

"How plainly we hear the On to-night," said Will, "it seems to fill the air. Shall I close the window?"

"Yes," said Dr. Owen, "if you like, Will; I have never heard it so plainly before. There is something solemn at all times in the sound; but to you it can bring no sad memories from the days gone bye, you have so lately left that wonderful past, which, as we grow older, becomes ever more and more bathed in the golden tints of imagination, 'that light which never was on sea or land.' You owe something to those rushing waters, Will, for while I sat here alone one evening, they flooded my soul with old and tender memories, and bore in upon me the advisability of the offer which I have just made you, and to which you have agreed."

Not a word was said as to the possibility of Ebben Owens objecting to the arrangement, in fact, neither of them thought of the old man, who even now was sitting in the chimney corner at Garthowen, building castles in the air, and dreaming dreams in which Will ever played the part of hero.

Later on, when the latter lay wakeful in the silent hours of night, the distant roar of the river carried home to his heart too, the memory of the old homestead, of many a scene of his careless and happy boyhood, and of the old man, the warmth of whose affection for him he was beginning to find rather irksome and embarrassing.

On the following day Dr. Owen called all his servants together, and in a few words but with a very decided manner, made them acquainted with the important step which he had taken with regard to Will, and bade them bear in mind, that for the future, his nephew would hold, next to himself, the highest place in the household. Will had been careful to ingratiate himself as much as possible with the old servants, whose opinions he thought might weigh somewhat in their master's decisions, the younger ones he treated with a somewhat haughty bearing.

"You will be coming again next week," said the Dr., as they both sat at dinner together; "the Trevors are coming, you know, to spend a few days with me, a long promised visit. We shall have a day with the otter hounds. Colonel Vaughan and Miss Gwenda are coming too, did I tell you?"

"No," said Will, "I did not know that. Do they often stay with you?"

"No, they have never been here before. They were dining at the Trevors. I included them in the invitation, and they promised to come. Miss Gwenda is a great favourite of mine, and of yours, Will, eh? Am I right?"

Will's handsome face flushed as he answered with some embarrassment, for he was not at all sure that his uncle would approve of the entanglement of a love affair.

"I—I. Well, sir, no one can be acquainted with Miss Vaughan without being impressed by her charms both of mind and person, but further than that, it would—I have no right to—in fact, uncle, it would be madness for a young man in my station, I mean—of my obscure birth, to think of a young lady like Miss Vaughan."

"Oh, that you can leave out of your calculations henceforth, I imagine. I know the world better than you do, Will, and I shall be much surprised if the advantages of being my adopted son and my heir will not far outweigh the fact of your rustic birth. Money is the lever which moves the world now-a-days. That has been my experience, and, if you act up to the position which I offer you, your old home will not stand in your way much. Of course I need not tell a young

Allen Raine

man of your sense and shrewdness that it will not be necessary for you to allude to it. Let the past die a natural death."

This was exactly what Will meant to do, but, expressed in his uncle's cold, business-like tones, its callousness jarred upon him, and he felt some twinges of conscience, and a regretful sympathy with his old father rose in his heart, which brought a lump in his throat and an unwonted moisture in his eyes. But he mastered the feeling, and assumed an air of pleased compliance which for the moment he did not feel.

"As for Gwenda Vaughan," continued his uncle, "you could never make a choice that would please me better; and, if she is at all inclined towards you, I fancy you will find your stay together here will mark a new era in your acquaintance."

"I do not think she dislikes me," said Will; "but more than that it would be presumption on my part to expect."

"H'm. Faint heart never won fair lady," laughed the Dr.

Will left Isderi much elated by his good fortune. Fortunately for him, he was possessed of a full share of common sense which came to his aid at this dangerous crisis of his life and prevented his head being completely turned by the bright hopes and golden prospects which his uncle's conversation suggested to him. It had been settled between them that it would be advisable not to make Ebben Owens at once acquainted with their plans, but to let the fact dawn upon him gradually.

"He will like it, my dear boy," said his uncle, when Will a little demurred to the necessity of keeping his father in the dark; "he will be proud of it when he sees the real and tangible advantages which you will gain by the arrangement.

You will go and see him sometimes as before, and it need make no difference in your manner towards him, which, I have no doubt, has always been that of a dutiful son."

One day in the following week, Will returned to Isderi; and it was with a delightful feeling of prospective proprietorship that he slipped into the high dog-cart which his uncle sent for him. He took the reins, naturally, into his own hands, and the servant seemed to sink naturally into his place beside him; and if, as he drove with a firm hand the high-stepping, well-groomed horse along the high-road, he felt his heart swell with pride and self congratulation, can it be wondered at?

On reaching the drive, which wound through the park-like grounds, he overtook his uncle and Colonel Vaughan. Alighting, he joined them; and Dr. Owen introduced him to his visitor.

"Ah! yes, yes, your nephew of course—we have met before," said the old man awkwardly, and he shook hands with Will in a bewildered manner. "Of course, of course; I remember your pluck when you tackled that bull. Pommy word I think Gwenda owes her life to you. I shall never forget that, you know."

"Well, you must give me a fuller account of that affair some day," said Dr. Owen. "You are come just in time, Will. Colonel Vaughan suggests that a break in those woods, so as to show the river, would be an improvement, and I think I agree with him. What do you say to the idea?"

"I think Colonel Vaughan is quite right, uncle; the same thing had already struck me."

"That's right; then that settles the matter," said Dr. Owen, who had determined to leave no doubt in his guest's mind of his nephew's importance in his estimation, and of his generous intentions towards him.

Gwenda was sitting alone in the drawing-room when Will entered, and it was a great relief to him that this was the case, for he was not yet so completely accustomed to the small convenances of society as to feel no awkwardness or nervousness upon some occasions. Free from the restraint of Mrs. Trevor's presence, however, he made no attempt to hide the pleasure which his meeting with Gwenda aroused in him. She was looking very beautiful in a dress of some soft white material, and as she held out her hand to Will a strange feeling came over him, a feeling that that sweet face would for ever be his lodestar, and that firm little white hand would help him on the path of life. He scarcely dared to believe that the blush and the drooping eyes were caused by his arrival, but it was not long before he had conquered his diffidence, and remembering his golden prospects had recovered his self-confidence sufficiently to talk naturally and unrestrainedly.

"Never saw such a thing," said the old colonel, later on in the day, to his niece, sitting down beside her for a moment's talk, under cover of a song which Mrs. Trevor was singing. "Dr. Owen seems wrapped up in his nephew, and the fellow seems to take it all as naturally as a duck takes to the water. Pommy word, he's a lucky young dog."

And naturally and quietly Will did take his place in the household, never pleasing his uncle more than when he sometimes unconsciously gave an order to the servants, and so took upon himself the duties which would have devolved upon him had he been his son instead of his nephew.

Gradually, too, Colonel Vaughan became accustomed to the change in the "young fellow's" circumstances, and accepted the situation with equanimity. Will left no stone unturned to ingratiate himself with the old man, and was very successful in his attempts. So much so, that when he and Gwenda would sometimes step out of the French window together, and roam through the garden and under the oak trees side by side, her uncle noticed it no more than he would have had Will been one of the average young men of On-side society.

Meanwhile, for the two young people, the summer roses had a deeper glow, the river a sweeter murmur, and the sky a brighter tint than they had ever had before; and while Gwenda sat under the shade of the gnarled oaks, with head bent over some bit of work, Will lying on the green sward beside her in a dream of happiness, Mrs. Trevor watched them from her seat in the drawing-room with a smile full of meaning, and Dr. Owen with a look of pleased content.

"You must find it a very pleasant change from hard study to come out here sometimes," said Gwenda, drawing her needle out slowly.

"Yes, very," said Will; "I never bring a book with me, and I try to banish my studies from my mind while I am here."

"Do you find that possible? I am afraid I have a very ill-regulated mind, as an interesting subject will occupy my thoughts whether I like it or not."

"Well, of course," said Will, plucking at the grass, "there are some subjects which never can be banished. There is one, at all events, which permeates my whole life; which gilds every scene with beauty, and which tinges even my dreams. Need I tell you what that is, Miss Vaughan?"

Gwenda's head bent lower, and there was a vivid glow on her cheek as she answered:

Allen Raine

"Your life here must be so full of brightness, the scenes around you are so lovely, it is no wonder if they follow you into your dreams. But—but, Mr. Owen, I will not pretend to misunderstand you."

"You understand me, and yet you are not angry with me? Only tell me that, Miss Vaughan, and I shall be satisfied; and yet not quite satisfied, for I crave your love, and can never be happy without it."

There was no answer on Gwenda's lips, but the eyes, which were bent on her work, grew humid with feeling.

"I love you, but dare I have the presumption to hope that you return my love? You know me here as my uncle's nephew, but it is not in that character that I would wish you to think of me now."

What was it in the girl's pure and honest face which seemed to bring out Will's better nature?

"I am only William Owens" (he even added the plebeian "s" to his name) "the son of the old farmer Ebben Owens of Garthowen; 'tis true my uncle calls me his son, and promises that I shall inherit his wealth, but there is no legal certainty of that. He might die to-morrow, and I should only be William Owens, the poor student of Llaniago College, and yet I venture to tell you of my love. I think I must be mad! I seek in vain for any possible reason why you should accept my love, and I can find none."

"Only the best of all reasons," said Gwenda, almost in a whisper.

"Gwenda! what is that?" said Will, rising to his feet, an action which the girl followed before she answered.

"Only because I love you too."

"Gwenda!" said Will again.

They had been resting on the velvet lawn that reached down to the oak wood, and now they turned towards its shady glades, and Mrs. Trevor, who had been watching them with deep interest, was obliged to control her curiosity until, when an hour later, they entered the house together, Will looking flushed and triumphant, and Gwenda with a glow of happiness which told its own tale to her observant friend.

"It's all right, my love, I see it is! I needn't ask any questions, he who runs may read! You have accepted him?"

"I don't know what my uncle will say, it all depends upon that."

"Never mind what he says, my dear. You and I together will manage him, we'll make him say just what we please, so *that's* settled!"

In fact, Will's wooing seemed to belie the usual course of true love. Upon it as upon everything else connected with him, the fates seemed to smile, and Colonel Vaughan was soon won over by Gwenda's persuasions.

"Well! pommy word, you know, Gwenda, I like the young fellow myself. Somehow or other he has taken us by storm. Of course, I should have been better pleased if he were Dr. Owen's son instead of his nephew."

"Well, he is next thing to it, uncle," said the girl coaxingly. "He is his adopted son, and will inherit all his wealth, and you know how necessary it is for me to marry a rich man, as I haven't a penny myself. Of course I will never marry him without your consent, uncle dear, but then I am going to get it," and she sat on his knee and drew her soft hands over his bald head, turning his face up like a cherub's, and pressing her full red lips on his wiry moustache.

"Not a penny yourself! Well! well! we'll see about that. Be good, girl, and love your old uncle, and I daresay he won't leave you penniless. But, pommy word! look here, child, we must ask him here to stay a few days. He won't be bringing old Owens Garthowen here, I hope; couldn't bear that, you know."

"I am afraid he doesn't see much of his old father and sister," she said pensively.

"Afraid! I should think you would be delighted."

"No, I should prefer his being manly enough to stick to his own people, and brave the opinion of the world. *I* should not be ashamed of the old man; but, of course, I would never thrust him upon my relations."

"Well! well! you are an odd little puss, and know how to get over your old uncle, whatever!"

And so all went smoothly for Will. At the end of two years he took his degree, and another year saw him well through his college course; complimented by his fellow students, praised and flattered by his uncle, and loved by as sweet a girl as ever sprang from a Welsh stock.

Before entering upon the curacy which his uncle procured for him with as little delay as possible, he spent a few days at Garthowen, during which time he was made the idol of his family. Full of new hopes and ambitions, he scarcely thought of Morva, who kept out of his way as much as possible, dreading only the usual request that she would meet him by the broom bushes; but no such request came, and, if the truth be told, he never remembered to seek an interview with her, so filled was his mind with thoughts of Gwenda.

He had been studiously reticent with regard to his engagement to her, at her special request. She knew how much gossip the news would occasion, and felt that the less it was talked about beforehand the less likelihood there would be of her relations being irritated and annoyed by ill-natured remarks. She was happier than she had ever hoped to be, and if she sometimes saw in her lover a trait of character which did not entirely meet the approbation of her honest nature, she laid the flattering unction to her soul, "When we are married I will try to make him perfect."

CHAPTER XVII

GWENDA AT GARTHOWEN

On the slope of the moor, where the autumn sun was burnishing the furze and purpling the heather, Morva sat knitting, her nimble fingers outrun by her busy thoughts.

She was sitting half way up the moor, an old cloak wrapped round her and its hood drawn over her head, for the wind was keen, blowing fresh from the bright blue bay, which stretched before her to the hazy horizon. Her eyes gazed absently over its azure surface, flecked with white, as though with scattered snowflakes, and dotted here and there with the grey sails of the boats which the herring fishery called out from their moorings under the cliffs. She sat at the edge of a rush-bordered pool in the peaty bog, occasionally bending over it to look at her own image reflected on its glassy surface. Between the folds of the old cloak glistened the necklace of shells which Gethin had given her. It was her twentieth birthday, so she seized the excuse for wearing the precious ornament which generally lay locked in its painted casket on the shelf at her bed head. It was not at herself she gazed, but the ever-changing gleam of the shells was irresistible. How well she remembered that evening when in the moonlight under the elder tree at Garthowen, Gethin had held them out to her, with a dawning love in his eyes, and her heart had bounded towards him with that strong impulse, which alas! she now knew was love!—love that permeated her whole being, that drew her thoughts away on the wings of the wind, over the restless sea, away, away, to distant lands and foreign ports. Where did he roam? What foreign shores did his footsteps tread? In what strange lands was he wandering? far from his home, far from the hearts that loved him and longed for his return! The swallows flew in fluttering companies over the moor, beginning to congregate for their departure across the seas. Oh! that she could borrow their wings, and fly with them across that sad dividing ocean, and, finding Gethin, could flutter down to him and shelter on his breast, and twitter to him such a song of love and home that he should understand and turn his steps once more towards the old country!

Will never troubled her now, never asked her to meet him behind the broom bushes. He had ceased to love her, she knew, and although he had never freed her from her promise, Morva had too much common sense to feel bound for ever to a man who had so evidently forgotten her. If sometimes the meanness and selfishness of his conduct dawned upon her mind, the feeling was instantly repressed, and as far as possible banished, in obedience to the instinct of loyalty to Garthowen, which was so strong a trait in her character.

She turned again to look at her necklace in the pool, and caught sight of a speck of vivid scarlet on the brow of the hill—another and another. They were the huntsmen returning from their unsuccessful run, for she had seen the breathless panting fox an hour before when he crossed the moor and made for his covert on the rocky sides of the cliffs. Once there, the hunters knew the chase was over. And there were the tired hounds for a moment appearing at the bare hill-top. In a few moments they had passed from sight, leaving the moor to its usual solitude and silence. But surely no! Here was one stray figure who turned towards the cliffs, and, alighting, led her horse down the devious paths between the furze and heather. Such an uncommon sight roused Morva from her dreams.

"Can I come down this way?" said a clear, girlish voice, as Gwenda Vaughan drew near. She spoke in very broken Welsh, but Morva understood her. "Does it lead anywhere?"

"It leads nowhere," said Morva, "but to the cliffs; but round there beyond the Cribserth," and she pointed to the rugged ridge of rocks, "is Garthowen; up there to the right is nothing but moorland for two miles."

"Oh, then I will turn this way," said Gwenda. "Will they let me rest at the farm a while, do you think? I am very tired and hungry."

"Oh, of course," said Morva, her hospitable instincts awaking at once. "Come into mother's cottage," and she pointed to the thatched roof and chimney, which alone were visible above the heathery knoll.

"Is that a cottage?"

"Yes—will you come?"

"Yes, just for a moment, and then perhaps you will show me the way to the farm. That Cribserth looks a formidable rampart. Are you sure there is a way round it?"

"Oh, yes; I will come and show you," said Morva. "Here is mother," and Sara approached from her herb garden with round, astonished eyes.

"Well, indeed!" she said; "this is a pleasant sight—a lady

coming to see us, and on Morva's birthday, too! Come in, 'merch i, and sit down and rest. The horse will be safe tied there to the gate."

And Gwenda passed into the cottage with a strange feeling of happiness.

"Now, what shall I give you?" said Sara. "A cup of milk, or a cup of tea? or, I have some meth here in the corner. My bees are busy on the wild thyme and furze, you see, so we have plenty of honey for our meth."

"I would like a cup of meth," said Gwenda; and as she drank the delicious sparkling beverage, Sara gazed at her with such evident interest that she was constrained to ask:

"Why do you look at me so?"

"Because I think I have seen you before," said the old woman.

"Not likely," replied Gwenda, "unless in the streets at Castell On."

"I have not been there for twenty years," said Sara. "It must be in my dreams, then."

"Perhaps! What delicious meth! Who would think there was room for house and garden scooped out on the moor here; and such a dear sheltered hollow."

Sara smiled.

"Yes; we are safe and peaceful here."

Morva had taken the opportunity of doffing her necklace and

Allen Raine

placing it in the box.

"I am going to show the young lady the way to Garthowen, mother."

"Yes; it is easy from there to Castell On," said Sara; "the farm lane will lead you into the high road. But 'tis many, many years since I have been that way."

The chat fell into quite a friendly and familiar groove, for Sara and Morva knew nothing of the restraints of class and conventionality.

"I am so glad I came; but I must go now," said Gwenda, rising at last. "My name is Gwenda Vaughan," she added, turning to Morva. "What is yours?"

"Mine is Morva Lloyd; but I am generally called Morva of the Moor, I think. Mother's is Sara."

"Good-bye, and thank you very much," said Gwenda, and Sara held her hand a moment between her own soft palms, while she looked into the girl's face.

"You have a sweet, good face," she said. "Thank you for coming, 'merch i; in some way you will bring us good."

And again that strangely happy feeling came over Gwenda. Rounding the Cribserth, the two girls soon reached Garthowen. It was afternoon, and drawing near tea-time. Ebben Owens was already sitting on the settle in the best kitchen, waiting for it, when the sound of voices without attracted his attention.

"Caton pawb!" he said, "a lady, and Morva is bringing her."

Ann hastened to the front door, and Morva led the horse away, knowing well that she was leaving the visitor in hospitable hands.

"I am Miss Vaughan of Nantmyny! I have been out hunting today, and on the top of the hill I felt so tired that I made up my mind to call here and ask if you would let me rest awhile."

"Oh, certainly! Come in," said Ann, holding out her hand, which Gwenda took warmly.

"Miss Owen, I suppose?"

"I was Ann Owens," she said, blushing. "I am Mrs. Gwilym Morris now these three years. This is my little boy," she added, as a chubby, curly-headed child toddled towards her. She had already opened the door of the best kitchen. "There is no fire in the parlour," she apologised, "or I would take you there."

"Oh, no; please let me come to your usual sitting-room. Is this your father?"

And she held out her hand again. There was something in her face that always ensured its own welcome.

"Yes, I am Ebben Owens," said the old man, "and very glad to see you, though I not know who you are."

"I am Gwenda Vaughan of Nantmyny, come to ask if you will let me rest awhile. I have been out with the fox-hounds; we have had a long run, and I am so tired."

She had no other excuse to give for her inroad upon their hearth; but in Wales no excuse is required for a call.

"Well, indeed," said the old man, rubbing his knees with pleasure, "there's a good thing now, you come just in time for tea. I think I have heard your name, but I not know where. Oh, yes. I remember now; 'twas you the bull was running after in the market, and my boy Will stop it; 'twas good thing, indeed, you may be kill very well!"

Gwenda stopped to pat Tudor to hide the blush that rose to her cheek as she answered:

"Yes, indeed, and of course we were very grateful to him!"

"Oh, yes; he's very good fellow. Will you take off your hat? 'Tis not often we're having visitors here, so we are very glad when anybody is come."

"I was afraid, perhaps, I was taking rather a liberty," said Gwenda, laying her hat and gloves aside, "but you are all so kind, you make me feel quite at home."

"That's right," said the old man; "there's a pity now, my son-in-law, Gwilym Morris, is not at home. He was go to Castell On to-day to some meeting there. What was it? Let me see— some hard English word."

"I can speak Welsh," said Gwenda, turning to that language.

"Oh! wel din!" said the old man, relieved, and continuing in Welsh, "'tisn't every lady can speak her native language nowadays."

"No. I am ashamed of my countrywomen, though I speak it very badly myself," said Gwenda.

"There's my son Will now, indeed I'm afraid he will soon forget his Welsh, he is speaking English so easy and smooth.

Come here, Ann," the old man called, as his daughter passed busily backwards and forwards spreading the snowy cloth and laying the tea-table. "The lady can speak Welsh!"

"Oh! well indeed, I am glad," said Ann; "Will is the only one of us who speaks English quite easily."

"Oh! there's Gwilym," said her father.

"Yes, Gwilym speaks it quite correctly," said Ann, with pride, "but he has a Welsh accent, which Will has not—from a little boy he studied the English, and to speak it like the English."

"Will is evidently their centre of interest," thought Gwenda, "and how little he seems to think of them!"

Here the little curly pate came nestling against her knee.

"Hello! rascal!" said the old man, "don't pull the lady's skirts like that."

But Gwenda took the child on her lap.

"He is a lovely boy," she said, thus securing Ann's good opinion at once.

The little arms wound round her neck, and before tea was over she had won her way into all their hearts.

"I am sorry my sons are not here," said the old man; "they are good boys, both of them, and would like to speak to such a beautiful young lady."

"Have you two sons, then?" asked Gwenda.

"Yes, yes. Will, my second son, is a clergyman. He is curate of Llansidan, 'tis about forty miles from here; but Gethin, my eldest son, is a sailor; indeed, I don't know where he is now, but I am longing for him to come home, whatever; and Will does not come often to see me. He is too busy, I suppose, and 'tis very far."

And Gwenda, sensitive and tender, heard a tremble in the old man's voice, and detected the pain and bitterness of his speech.

"Young men," she said, "are so often taken up with their work at first, that they forget their old home, but they generally come back to it, and draw towards it as they grow older; for after all, there is nothing like the old home, and I should think this must have been a nest of comfort indeed."

"Well, I don't know. My two sons are gone over the nest, whatever; but Ann is stopping with me, She is the home-bird."

Gwenda thought she had never enjoyed such a tea. The tea cakes so light, the brown bread so delicious; and Ann, with her quiet manners, made a perfect hostess; so that, when she rose to go, she was as reluctant to leave the old farmhouse as her entertainers were to lose her.

"Indeed, there's sorry I am you must go," said Ebben Owens. "Will you come again some day?"

"I will," said Gwenda, waving them a last good-bye; and as she rode down the dark lane beyond the farmyard she said to herself, "And I *will* some day, please God!"

Reaching the high road, she hurried down the hill to the valley below, where Castell On lay nestled in the bend of the river. It was scarcely visible in the darkening twilight, except here and there where a light glimmered faintly. The course of the river was marked by a soft white mist, and above it all, in the clear evening sky, hung the crescent moon. The beauty of the scene before her reached Gwenda's heart, and helped to fill her cup of happiness. Her visit to the farm had strengthened her determination to turn her lover's heart back to his old home. It was all plain before her now; she had a work to do, an aim in life, not only to make her future husband happy, but to lead him back into the path of duty, from which she clearly saw he had been tempted to stray. There was no danger that she would take too harsh a view of his fault, for her love for Will was strong and abiding. There was little doubt that in that wonderful weaving of life's pattern, which some people call "Fate" and some "Providence," Gwenda and Will had been meant for each other.

When she reached home she found a letter awaiting her—a letter in the square clear writing which she had learned to look for with happy longing. She hastened to her room to read it. It bore good tidings—first, that Will had acceded to Mr. Price's request to preach at Castell On the following Sunday; secondly and chiefly, that the living of Llanisderi had been offered him, and had been accepted.

"The church is close to my uncle's property, and as he has always wished me to make my home at Isderi, he now proposes that we should be married at once, and take his house off his hands, only letting him live on with us, which I think neither you nor I will object to. There is no regular vicarage, so this arrangement seems all that could be desired. Does my darling agree?" etc., etc.

Of course "his darling" agreed, stipulating only that their marriage should take place in London, for she thought this plan would obviate the necessity for inviting her husband's relations to her wedding, and still cause them no pain.

Will was delighted with the suggestion, for he had not been without some secret twinges of compunction at the idea of being married at Castell On, and still having none of his people at the wedding. That, of course, in his own and his uncle's opinion was quite out of the question; and so the matter was settled.

* * * * * *

One day there was great excitement at Garthowen.

"Well, Bendigedig!"[1] said Magw under her breath, as crossing the farmyard she met Mr. Price the vicar making his way through the stubble to the house-door, "well, Bendigedig! there's grand we are getting. Day before yesterday a lady on horseback, to-day Price the vicare coming to see the mishteer! Well, well! Oh, yes, sare," she said aloud, in answer to the vicar's inquiry, "he's there somewhere, or he was there when I was there just now, but if he is not there he must be somewhere else. Ann will find him."

And she jerked her thumb towards the house as Mr. Price continued his way laughing.

"I am come again," said the genial vicar, shaking hands with Ebben Owens, whom he found deeply studying the almanac, "I am come to congratulate you on your son's good fortune. I hear he has been given the living of Llanisderi, and I think he will fill it very well. You are a fortunate man to have so promising a son and such an influential brother, and I expect you will be still better pleased with the rest of my news. He is going to preach at Castell On next Sunday."

Ebben Owens gasped for breath.

"Will!" he said, "my son Will? Oh! yes, he is a good boy, indeed, and is he going to preach here on Sunday? Well, well, 'twill be a grand day for me!"

"Yes," said Mr. Price, "I hear he is a splendid preacher, and I thought 'twas a pity his old friends in this neighbourhood should not hear him, so I asked him, and he has agreed to come. You must all come in and hear him—you too, Mrs. Morris, and your husband."

"My husband," said Ann, drawing herself up a little, "will have his own services to attend to; but on such an occasion I will be there certainly."

"Well, you must all dine with me," said the hospitable vicar.

"No, no, sir," said Ebben Owens, "I'll take the car, and we'll bring Will back here to dinner. We'll have a goose, Ann, and a leg of mutton and tongue."

"Yes," said Ann, smiling, "Magw will see to them while we are at church."

Mr. Price stayed to tea this time, and satisfied the old man's heart by his praises of his son. On his departure Ebben Owens sat down at once to indite a letter to Will, informing him of the great happiness it had given him to hear of his intention to preach at Castell On.

"Of course, my boy," he went on to say in his homely, rugged Welsh, "we will be there to hear you, and I will drive you home in the car, and we will have the fattest goose for dinner, and the best bedroom will be ready for you. These few lines from

"Your delighted and loving father,

"EBBEN OWENS,
"Garthowen."

Will crushed the letter with a sigh when he had read it, and
threw it into the fire, and the old Garthowen pucker on his
forehead was only chased away by the perusal of a letter
from Gwenda, whose contents we will not dare to pry into.

Never were there such preparations for attending a service,
as were made at Garthowen before the next Sunday morning.
Never had Bowler's harness received such a polish, every
buckle shone like burnished gold. Ebben Owens had brushed
his greatcoat a dozen times, and laid it on the parlour table in
readiness, and had drawn his sleeve every day over the
chimney-pot hat which he had bought for the occasion.

When the auspicious morning arrived Ann arrayed herself in
her black silk, with a bonnet and cape of town fashion; and
in the sunny frosty morning they set off to Castell On, full of
gratified pride and pleasant anticipations.

Leaving the car at a small inn near the church, they entered
and took their places modestly in the background. No one
but he who reads the secrets of all hearts knew what a tumult
of feelings surged through the breast of that rugged, bent
figure as Will passed up the aisle, looking handsomer than
ever in his clerical garb. Thankfulness, pride, love, a longing
for closer communion with his son, were all in that throbbing
heart, but underneath and permeating all was the mysterious
gnawing pain that had lately cast its shadow over the old
man's life.

During the service both he and Ann were much perplexed by
the difficulty of finding their places in the prayer-book, and

they were greatly relieved when at last it was over and the sermon commenced.

Mr. Price had not been misinformed. Will was certainly an eloquent preacher, if not a born orator, and possessed that peculiar gift known in Wales as "hwyl"—a sudden ecstatic inspiration, which carries the speaker away on its wings, supplying him with burning words of eloquence, which in his calmer and normal state he could never have chosen for himself. Will controlled this feeling, not allowing it to carry him to that degree of excitement to which some Welsh preachers abandon themselves; on the contrary, when he felt most, he lowered his voice, and kept a firm rein upon his eloquence. His command of English, too, surprised his hearers, and Dr. Owen, himself a popular preacher, confessed he had never possessed such an easy flow of that language. As for Ebben Owens himself, as the sermon proceeded, although he understood but little English, not a word, nor a phrase, nor an inflection of the beloved voice escaped his attention; and as he bent his head at the benediction tears of thankfulness, pride, and joy filled his eyes. But he dried them hastily with his bran new silk handkerchief, and followed Ann out of the church with the first of the congregation.

"We'll wait with the car," he said, "at the top of the lane. We won't push ourselves on to him at the church door when all the gentry are speaking to him."

And Ann sat in the car with the reins in her hand, while the congregation filed past, many of them turning aside to congratulate warmly the father and sister of such a preacher. One by one the people passed on, two or three carriages rolled by, and still Will had not appeared.

"Here he is, I think," said Ebben Owens, as two gentlemen walked slowly up the lane, and watching them, he scarcely caught sight of a carriage that drove quickly by. But a glance was enough as it turned round the corner into the street. In it sat Will, accompanied by Dr. Owen, Colonel Vaughan, and his niece.

"Was that Will?" said Ann, looking round.

"Yes," said her father faintly, looking about him in a dazed, confused manner. He put his hand to his head and turned very pale.

Ann was out of the car in a moment, flinging the reins to the stable boy who stood at Bowler's head.

"Come, father anwl!" she said, supporting the old man's tottering steps, for he would have fallen had she not passed her strong arm round him. "Come, we'll go home. You will be better once we are out of the town," and with great difficulty she got him into the car. "Cheer up, father bach," she said, trying to speak cheerfully, though her own voice trembled, and her eyes were full of tears. "No doubt he meant to come, or he would have written, but I'm thinking they pressed him so much that he couldn't refuse."

"Yes, yes," said the old man in a weak voice; "no doubt, no doubt! *'tis all right*, Ann; 'tis the hand of God."

Ann thought he was wandering a little, and tried to turn his thoughts by speaking of the sermon.

"'Twas a beautiful sermon, father, I have never heard a better, not even from Jones Bryn y groes."

"Yes, I should think 'twas a good sermon, though I couldn't understand the English well; only the text 'twas coming in very often 'Lord, try me and see if there be any wicked way

in me,'" and he repeated several times as he drove home
"'any wicked way in me.' Yes, yes, 'tis all right!"

When they reached home without Will, Gwilym Morris
seemed to understand at once what had happened, and he
helped the old man out of the car with a pat on his back and a
cheery greeting.

"Well, there now! didn't I tell you how it would be? Will had
so many invitations he could not come back with you. There
was Captain Lewis Bryneiron said, 'You must come and dine
with me!' and Colonel Vaughan Nantmyny said, 'He must
come with me!' and be bound Sir John Hughes wanted him
to go to Plasdu; so, poor fellow, he *had* to go, and we've got
to eat our splendid dinner ourselves! Come along; such a
goose you never saw!"

Ebben Owens said nothing, as he walked into the house,
stooping more than usual, and looking ten years older.

There was dire disappointment in the kitchen, too, when the
dinner came out scarcely tasted.

It is not to be supposed that by such observant eyes as
Gwenda's, the Garthowen car, with the waiting Ann and the
old man hovering about, had escaped unnoticed. Nay! To her
quick perception the whole event revealed itself in a flash of
intuition. They were waiting there for Will. He had
disappointed and wounded his old father, but at the same
moment she saw that the slight had been unintentional; for as
the carriage dashed by the waiting car, she saw in Will's face
a look of surprise and distress, a hurried search in his pocket,
and an unwelcome discovery of a letter addressed and
stamped—but, alas! unposted. The pathetic incident troubled
her not a little. An English girl would probably have spoken
out at once with the splendid honesty characteristic of her

nation, but Gwenda, being a thorough Welshwoman, acted differently. With what detractors of the Celtic character would probably call "craftiness," but what we prefer to call "tact and tenderness," she determined not to ruffle the existing happy state of affairs by risking a misunderstanding with her lover, but would rather wait until, as a wife, she could bring the whole influence of her own honest nature to bear upon this weak trait in his character.

A few days later the announcement of his approaching marriage reached Garthowen, in a letter from Will himself, enclosing the unposted missive, which he had discovered in his pocket as he drove to Nantmyny on the previous Sunday.

It pacified the old man somewhat, but nothing availed to lift the cloud which had fallen upon his life; and the intimation of the near approach of his son's marriage with "a lady" coming upon him as it did unexpectedly, was the climax of his depression of spirits. He sat in the chimney-corner and brooded, repeating to himself occasionally in a low voice:

"Gone! gone! Both my boys gone from me for ever!"

Ann and Gwilym's arguments were quite unheeded. Morva's sympathy alone seemed to have any consoling effect upon him. She would kneel beside him with her elbows on his knees, looking up into his face, and with make-believe cheerfulness would reason with a woman's inconsequence, fearlessly deducing results from causes which had no existence.

"'Tis as plain as the sun in the sky, 'n'wncwl Ebben bach! Gethin is only gone on another voyage, and so will certainly be back here before long. Well, you see he *must* come, because he wouldn't like to see his old father breaking his heart—not he! We know him too well. And then there's his best clothes in the box upstairs! And there's the corn growing so fast, he will surely be here for the harvest."

She knew herself it was all nonsense, realising it sometimes with a sudden sad wistfulness; but she quickly returned to her argument again.

"Look at me now, 'n'wncwl Ebben!—Morva Lloyd, whom you saved from the waves! Would I tell you anything that was not true? Of course, I wouldn't indeed! indeed! and I'm sure he'll come soon. You may take my word for it they will both come back very soon. I feel it in my heart, and mother says so too."

"Does she?" said the old man, with a little show of interest. "Does Sara say so?"

"Yes," said Morva; "she says she is sure of it."

"Perhaps indeed! I hope she is right, whatever!" And he would lay his hands on Morva's and Tudor's heads, both of whom leant upon his knees and looked lovingly into his face.

[1] "Blessed be!"

CHAPTER XVIII

SARA

For Gwenda and Will, from this time forward, all went "merry as a marriage bell." Early in the spring their wedding took place in London, and when one morning Morva brought from Pont-y-fro post office a packet for Ebben Owens containing a wedge of wedding cake and cards, he evinced some show of interest. On the box was written in Gwenda's pretty firm writing,

"With love to Garthowen, from William and Gwenda Owen."

Ebben rubbed his knees with satisfaction.

"There now," he said, "in her own handwriting, too! Well, indeed! I thought she was a nice young lady that day she came here, but, caton pawb! I never thought she would marry our Will."

A second piece of cake was enclosed and addressed. "To my friends Sara and Morva of the Moor," and Morva carried it home with mingled feelings of pride and pleasure, but paramount was the joy of knowing that she was completely released from the promise which had become so galling to her.

"I knew," said Sara, "that that face would bring us a blessing," and she looked with loving inquiry into Morva's face, which was full of varying expressions.

At first, there was the pleasurable excitement of unfolding and tasting the wedding cake, but it quickly gave way to a look of pensive sadness, which somehow had fallen over the girl rather frequently of late; the haunting thought of Gethin's absence, the cloud of suspicion which had so long hung over him, (it was cleared away now, but it had left its impress upon her life), her ignorance of his whereabouts, and above all, a longing, hidden deep down in her heart, to meet him face to face once more, to tell him that she was free, that no longer behind the broom bushes need she turn away from him, or wrest her hands from his warm clasp. All this weighed upon her mind, and cast a shadow over her path, which she could not entirely banish.

Sara saw the reflection of the sorrowful thought in the girl's tell-tale eyes, and her tender heart was troubled within her.

"A wedding cake is a beautiful thing," said Morva; "how do they make it, I wonder? Ann said I must sleep with a bit of it under my pillow to-night, and I would dream of my sweetheart, but that is nonsense."

"Yes, 'tis nonsense," said Sara, "but 'tis an old-time fable; thee canst try it, child," she added, smiling, and trying to chase away the girl's look of sadness.

"'Twould be folly indeed, for there is no sweetheart for me any more, mother, now that Will is married. Oh! indeed, I hope that sweet young lady will be happy, and Will too."

"He will be happy, child; but for thee I am grieving. Thou art hiding something from me; surely Will's marriage brings thee no bitterness?"

"No, no," said the girl, "I am glad, mother, so thankful to be free; I could sing with the birds for joy, and yet there is some shadow in my heart. 'Tis for Garthowen, I think, 'n'wncwl Ebben is so sad—Gethin has never come home, and that money, mother! who stole it and put it back again? We used to be so happy, but now it seems like the threatening of a stormy day."

"Sometimes those stormy days are the end of rough weather, lass. Through wind and cloud and lightning, God clears up the sky. Thee must not lose patience, 'merch i; by and by it will be bright weather again."

"Do you think, mother?"

"Yes, I think—I am sure."

"Well, indeed," said Morva, "you are always right; but oh! I am forgetting my cheese, I set the rennet before I came out. I must run."

And away she went, and in a short time had reached the dairy, where the curdled milk was ready for her. First she went to the spring in the yard to cool her hands and arms, and then with shining wooden saucer, she broke up the creamy curds, gradually compressing them into a solid mass, while the delicious whey was poured into a quaint brown earthen pitcher.

The clumsy door stood wide open, and the sunshine streamed in, and glistened on the bright brass pan in which Morva was crumbling her curds, her sleeves tucked up above her elbows, showing her dimpled arms. With her spotless white apron, her neatly shod feet, and her crown of golden hair, she looked like the presiding goddess of this temple of cleanliness and purity.

Round the walls stood shelves of the blue slaty stone of the neighbourhood, upon which were ranged the pans of golden cream, above them hanging the various dairy utensils of wood, polished black with long use and rubbing.

Morva's good spirits had returned, for she hummed as she rubbed her curds:

"Troodi! Troodi! come down from the mountain,
Troodi! Troodi! up from the dale!
Moelen and Trodwen, and Beauty and Blodwen,
I'll meet you all with my milking pail."

Meanwhile at home in the thatched cottage on the moor Sara seemed to have caught the mantle of sadness which had fallen from the girl's shoulders. She went about her household duties singing softly it is true, but there was a look of disquiet in her eyes not habitual to them, an air of restlessness very unlike her usual placid demeanour. For sixteen years her life and Morva's had been serene and uneventful, the limited circle which bound the plane of their existence had been complete and undisturbed by outward influences; but latterly unrest and anxiety had entered into their quiet lives, there was a veiling of the sun, there was a shadow on the path, a mysterious wind was ruffling the surface of the sea of life. No trouble had touched Sara personally, but what mattered that to one so sympathetic? She lived in the lives of those she loved; and as she moved about in the subdued light of the cottage, or in the broad sunshine of the garden, a thread of disquietude ran through the pattern of her thoughts. The cause of Morva's sadness she guessed at, but how to remove it, or how to bring back the peace and happiness that seemed to have deserted the old

Garthowen homestead, she saw not yet.

Suddenly she started, and standing still crossed her hands on her bosom with a look of pleased expectancy; her lips moved as if in prayer, she passed out into the garden, and gathering a bunch of rue, tied it together and hung it to the frame of the doorway so that no one could enter the house without noticing it. Then returning to the quiet chimney corner, she sat down in the round-backed oak chair, and clasping her hands on her lap, waited, while over her came the curious trance-like sleep to which she had been subject at intervals all her life. She was accustomed to these trances, and even welcomed their coming for the sake of the clear insight and even the clairvoyance which followed them. They were seasons of refreshing to this strange woman's soul—seasons during which the connecting thread between spirit and body was strained to the utmost, when a rude awakening might easily sever that attenuated thread, when Morva knew that tender handling and shielding care were required of her. In the evening when she returned from the farm she came singing into the little court, where the gilly flowers and daffodils were once more swaying in the wind, and the much treasured ribes was hanging out its scented pink tassels. She stopped to gather a spray, and then turning to the door, was confronted by the bunch of rue, at sight of which she instantly ceased her singing and a look of seriousness almost of solemnity came over her face, for the herb had long been a pre-concerted signal between Sara and herself.

She gently pulled the string which lifted the latch, and entered the cottage, treading softly as one does where death has already entered. The stillness was profound, for it was a calm day and the sea was silent, the fire only crackling on the hearth. The old cat slept on the spinning bench, and Sara lay there unconscious and dead to all outward surroundings. Morva approached her softly, and pressed a kiss on the marble forehead; she felt her hands, they were supple though cold; the eyes were closed and the breathing was scarcely perceptible, but Morva had no fear for Sara's safety. She gently raised her feet upon the rush stool, and rested her head more comfortably; then bolting the door and making up the fire, she took her supper and prepared for a long night's vigil.

And now came one of those seasons of contemplation and of wondering awe which Sara's trances brought into Morva's simple life, which made her somewhat different from the other girls of the neighbourhood, yet in no way detracted from the brightness and cheerfulness of her character. Magw, the house servant, was often out under the stars, but she paid more attention to the stubble in the farmyard than to the glittering spangled sky above her. Dyc "pigstye" often passed over the cliffs and up the moor, but his own whistle, the bleat of the sheep, the lowing of the herds, were more to him than the whispers of the sea or the singing of the larks. Ebben Owens was out from morning to night, in the brilliant sunshine, and under the mellow moon, but they taught no tale to him, and brought no messages to his soul, save of crops, of work, of harvests. But to Morva, every tint of broom or heather, every shade of sea or sky, every flower that unfolded in the sunshine spoke and stirred within her sentiments of love and wonder which she had no words to express, but which left their impress upon her spirit.

Sitting by the fire on her low stool, she kept a careful watch over the still figure on the other side of the hearth. The night wind sighed in the chimney, the owls hooted, and the sea whispered its mysterious secrets on the shore below. The candle burnt low in its socket, and Morva replaced it with another, for she would not be left in the dark with this silent unconscious being, much as she loved her.

Sometimes she ventured upon a gentle appeal, "Mother

fach!" but no answer came from the closed lips, and again she waited while the night hours passed on.

"Where is her spirit wandering, I wonder?" thought the girl, setting her untaught and inexperienced mind to work upon the fathomless mystery. "Perhaps in the land which we roam in our dreams. 'Tis pity she cannot remember; 'tis pity she cannot tell me about it, for, oh, I would like to know."

But to-night, at all events, it seemed there was to be no elucidation of this enigma of life. The night hours dragged on slowly, and still Sara slept on, until in the pale dawn Morva gently opened the door and looked out towards the east, where a rosy light was beginning to flush the clear blue of a cloudless sky. Already the sun was rising over the grey slopes, the cottage walls caught the rosy tints, and the ribes tree, which alone was tall enough to catch his beams over the high turf wall of the court, glowed under his morning kiss. Morva looked round the fair scene with eyes and heart that took in all its beauty. A cool sea breeze, brine-laden, swept over the moor, refreshing and invigorating her, and she turned again to the cottage with renewed longing for Sara's awakening.

When she entered, she found that the rays of the rising sun shone full upon the quiet face, on the placid brow, and the closed eyes, imparting to them a look of unearthly spirituality. Moved by the sight, and by the events of the night, the girl knelt down, and, leaning her face on her foster-mother's lap, said her prayers, with the same simple faith as she had in the days of childhood. The sunlight pouring in through the little window bathed her in a stream of rosy light, and rested on her bent head like a blessing. As she rose from her knees a quiver passed over Sara's eyelids, a smile came on her lips, and opening her eyes she looked long at Morva before she spoke, as though recalling her surroundings.

"Mother," said the girl, kissing her cheek, which was beginning to show again the hue of health. "Mother fach, you've come back to me again."

"Yes," said Sara, "I am come back again, child," and she attempted to rise, but Morva pushed her gently back.

"Breakfast first, mother fach."

And quickly and deftly she set the little brown teapot on the embers, and spread her mother's breakfast before her.

"Now, mother, a new-laid egg and some brown bread and butter."

And Sara smilingly complied with the girl's wishes, and partook of the simple fare.

"Mother, try and remember where you have been. Oh, I want to know so much."

"I cannot, 'merch i, already it is slipping away from me as usual; but never mind, it will all come back by and by, and I hope I will be a wiser and a better woman after my long sleep. It is always so, I think, Morva."

"Yes," said the girl, "you are always wiser, and better, and kinder after your long sleeps, if that is possible, mother fach."

Sara's ordinary cheerful and placid manner had already returned to her, and in an hour or two she was quite herself again, and moving about her cottage as if nothing had happened; and when Morva left her for the morning milking she felt no uneasiness about her.

Allen Raine

"She's in the angels' keeping, I know, and God is over all," she murmured, as she ran over the cliffs to Garthowen.

She said nothing at the farm of the events of the past night, knowing how reticent Sara was upon the subject herself. Moreover, it was one of too sacred a character in the eyes of these two lonely women to be discussed with the outside and unbelieving world.

In the evening, when Morva returned from the farm, a little earlier than usual, she was full of tender inquiries.

"Are you well, mother fach? I have been uneasy about you."

"Quite well, child, and very happy. 'Twill all be right soon, Morva. Canst take my word for it? For I cannot explain how I know, but I tell thee thy trouble will soon be over. How are they at Garthowen to-night?"

"Oh, well," said the girl; "only 'n'wncwl Ebben is always very sad. Not even Will's marriage will make him happy. 'Tis breaking his heart he is for the old close companionship. Will ought to come and see him oftener. Poor 'n'wncwl Ebben! 'Tis sad to lose his two sons."

"Gethin will come home," said Sara; "and Ebben Owens will be happy again."

Morva made no answer, but watched the sparks from the crackling furze, as they flew up the chimney, and thought of the night when she had stamped them out with her wooden shoe, and had dared the uncertainties of the future. She was wiser now, and knew that life had its shadows as well as its glowing sunshine. She had experienced the former, but the sunshine was returning to her heart to-night in a full tide of joy, for she had implicit confidence in her foster-mother's keen intuitions.

"Mother, what did you see, what did you hear, in that long trance? I would like to know so much. Your body was here, but where was your spirit?"

"I cannot tell, 'merch i. To me it was a dreamless sleep, but now that I am awake I seem to know a great many things which were dark to me before. You know it is always so with me when I have had my long sleeps. They seem to brighten me up, and it appears quite natural to me when the things that have been dark become plain."

She felt no surprise as the scenes and events of the recent past were unfolded to her. She understood now why Gethin had gone away so suddenly and mysteriously. Morva's love for him she saw with clear insight, and, above all, the cause of Ebben Owens's increasing gloom. How simple all was now, and how happy was she in the prospect of helping them all.

"Mother," asked Morva again one evening, as they walked in the garden together, "there is one question I would like to ask you again, but somehow I am afraid. Who stole the money at Garthowen?"

"Don't ask me that question, 'merch i. Time will unfold it all. 'Tis very plain who took it, and I wonder we didn't see it before; but leave it now, child. I don't know how, but soon it will be cleared up, and the sun will shine again. Ask me no more questions, Morva, and every day will bring its own revealment."

"I will ask nothing more, mother. Let us go in and boil the bwdran for supper."

At the early milking next morning Ebben Owens himself came into the farmyard. He stooped a good deal, and, when Morva rallied him on his sober looks, sighed heavily, as he stood watching the frothing milk in her pail.

"See what a pailful of milk Daisy has, 'n'wncwl Ebben! Yesterday Roberts the drover from Castell On passed through the yard when I was milking, and oh, there's praising her he was! 'Would Ebben Owens sell her, d'ye think?' he asked, and he patted her side; but Daisy didn't like it, and she nearly kicked my pail over. 'Sell her!' I said. 'What for would 'n'wncwl Ebben sell the best cow in his herd? No, no,' said I. 'Show us one as good as her, and 'tis buying he'll be, and not selling.'"

"Lol! lol!" said the old man; "thee mustn't be too sure, girl. I am getting old and not fit to manage the farm. I wouldn't care much if I sold everything and went to live in a cottage."

"'Twt, twt," said Morva, "you will never leave old Garthowen, and 'twill be long before Roberts the drover takes Daisy away. Go and see mother, 'n'wncwl Ebben; she is full of good news for you. She says there is brightness coming for you, and indeed, indeed *she knows*."

"Yes, she knows a good deal, but she doesn't know everything, Morva. No, no," he said, turning away, "she doesn't know everything."

CHAPTER XIX

THE "SCIET"

"Art going to chapel to-night, Morva?" said Ebben Owens on the following Sunday afternoon, as he sat smoking in the chimney-corner, Tudor beside him gazing rather mournfully into the fire. He was looking ill and worn, and spoke in a low, husky voice. He had sat there lost in thought ever since he had pushed away his almost untasted dinner.

"Yes," said Morva, "I am going; but mother is not coming to-night; she doesn't like the Sciet, you know."

"She is an odd woman," said Ann. "Not like the Sciet indeed! If I didn't love her so much I would be very angry with her."

Morva flushed.

"She is very different to other people, I know; but she is a good woman whatever."

"Yes, yes, yes," said Ebben Owens emphatically; "but why doesn't she like the Sciet?"

"Oh! that's what she is saying," answered the girl, "that she doesn't see the use of people standing up to confess half their sins and keeping back the other and the worst half. She has been talking to Gwilym Morris about it, and he is agreeing with her."

"Och fi!" sighed the old man, relapsing into his moody silence, from which not even little Gwyl's chatter was able to rouse him.

At last when the cheerful sound of the tea-things, and Ann's oft-repeated summons, recalled him to outward surroundings, he rose as if wearily, and drew his chair to the table, where, stooping more and more over his tea, Ann detected a tear furtively wiped away.

"You won't take little Gwyl to chapel to-night, will you? 'tis rather damp," he said, though it was really a clear twilight.

"No, no," said Ann, "Magw will take care of him at home."

Gwilym helped the old man to change his coat.

"Where are his gloves, Ann, and his best hat? There's grand he'll be!"

But there was no answering smile on his father-in-law's face.

"Twt, twt," he said, "there is no need of gloves for me, and I won't wear my best hat, give me my old one."

He sighed heavily as with bent head, and hands buried deep in his coat pockets, he followed Ann and her husband down the stony road to the valley where Penmorien Chapel lay. It was one of the unlovely square buildings so much affected by the Welsh Dissenters, its walls of grey stone differing little in appearance and colour from the rocky bed of the hill which had been quarried out for its site.

As the Garthowen family entered, led by the preacher hat in hand, there was a little movement of interest in the thronging congregation, and a settling down to their prospective enjoyment, for an eloquent sermon possesses for the Welsh the intense charm of a good drama. The familiar pictures of every-day life with which the sermon is frequently illustrated, the vivid word-painting, the tender but firm touch which plays upon the chords of their strongest emotions, all combine to awaken within them those feelings of pleasurable excitement, denied to them through the medium of the forbidden theatre.

Gwilym Morris was heart and soul a preacher, full of burning zeal for his mission, and, moreover, at this period of his ministry he was passing through a crisis in his spiritual life—a crisis which left him with a broader field of vision, and more enlightened views of God's Providence than he had hitherto dared to adopt. As he passed up the pulpit stairs and saw the thronging mass of eager faces upraised to his, a subtle influence reached him, a fervour of spirit which he knew was the answer to the expectancy depicted on his people's faces. It was as though that waiting throng had formed itself into one collective being, for whose soul he bore a message, and to whom he must unburden himself, and there was a depth of meaning in his voice as he gave out the words of an old familiar hymn which fixed his hearers' attention at once. Ebben Owens had always led the hymns, but latterly he had dropped that custom, and to-night he stood silent with eyes fixed upon the evening sky, visible through the long chapel window. The hymn was sung with fervour, and in that volume of sound his voice was not missed. The old grey walls reverberated to the rich tones, which filled the chapel, and pouring out through the open doors, flooded the narrow valley with harmony. It was followed by a prayer, and another hymn, after which the candles were lighted, one on each iron pillar supporting the crowded gallery, one on each side of the "big seat" under the pulpit, and one on each side of the preacher, who, leaning his arms on the open Bible before him, began in low impressive tones to deliver himself of the message which he bore to his people. Only the old familiar words, "Come unto Me all ye that are weary and heavy laden and I will give you rest." Only the message of a greater Preacher than he—only the theme of a love unchanging and unfathomable, but told in such vivid though simple language, that the sensitive Celtic hearts of his audience, were enthralled and subdued, and there were few in that large crowd who did not gaze at the preacher through eyes blurred with tears. Sometimes his voice rose in indignant protest, and sometimes fell in tender appeal, and when at last the sermon was over and the last hymn had been sung, there was an evident feeling of regret and a furtive drying of eyes.

In curious almost ludicrous contrast to the preacher's mellow tones, Jos Hughes's cracked voice broke the solemn silence, with the information that there would be an "experience" meeting after the service. One third of the congregation therefore, remained seated while the rest poured out through the narrow doorways into the stony road, up which the sea wind was blowing. Then the doors were closed and the preacher came down and sat among the deacons in the "big seat." Ebben Owens was asked for his usual opening prayer, but he declined the request with a shake of his head. Jos Hughes gladly took his place, and after a long-winded prayer from him, a hymn was sung again, and then the business of the meeting commenced.

From a dark corner pew a weak voice broke the silence, and every eye turned to the speaker, a little shrivelled woman who was a frequent confessor of sins, and was correspondingly respected.

"I wish to say," said the quavering voice, "that I am daily and hourly becoming less sure of my salvation, my past sins weigh heavily upon me, and neither prayer nor reading bring a gleam of comfort into my heart. I should be glad to see the preacher or one of the deacons if they will trouble to come to Ffoshelig."

"I will certainly," said the preacher; and again there was a pause, till Jos Hughes stood up, and with great unction delivered his soul of its burden.

"My dear brethren," he said, with eyes upturned to the ceiling, his stubby fingers interlaced over his waistcoat of fawn kerseymere, "I am much perplexed and disheartened! I have been deacon of this chapel for thirty years, and I am not aware that I have ever failed in my duty as a member of this 'body.' I neglect no opportunity of prayer, or hymn singing, or warning my neighbour. I teach in the Sunday School, and I fulfil every duty as far as I am able—and yet, my friends, for two whole days in the week that is past, I was as dry as— a paper bag! I felt no fervour of spirit, no uplifting of soul; in fact, dear people, it was low tide with me, the rocks were bare, the sands were dry, and I was almost despairing. But thank the Lord! the tide turned, grace and praise and joy flowed in upon me once more; I have received the 'Invoice' of good things to come, and I am filled with the peace and content I generally enjoy."

A few words of congratulation and sympathy were spoken by another grey-headed deacon, after which a silence fell upon the meeting, the preacher making no comment upon what he had heard. The tick of the clock on the gallery, the distant swish of the waves, and the soft sighing of the evening breeze alone were audible.

At length another voice broke the silence. It was Ebben

Owens, who was standing up, and for a moment looking round at the old familiar faces of his fellow worshippers.

It had been a frequent custom of his to relate his religious experiences at the "Sciets," so neither Ann nor her husband were surprised; but Morva detected something unusual in the old man's manner. At many a meeting he had confessed to the frailties of human nature, with platitudes, and expressions of repentance, which had lost all reality from constant repetition. But he had satisfied the meeting, and at the end of it he had taken up his hat, smoothed his hair down over his forehead, and walked out of the chapel in the odour of sanctity. To-night it was a very different man who stood there. At first his voice was low and trembling, but as he proceeded it gathered strength, so that his words were audible even in the corner pew, whose little shrivelled occupant was eagerly listening, in the hopes that another person's experience—and he a good man—might throw some light upon her own difficulties.

"Good people all!" said the old man, "will you bear with me for a few moments, while I unburden my mind of a weight that is pressing sore upon me? and God grant that none of you may suffer what I have suffered lately! but justly— remember justly am I punished.

"You think you know me well, my dear friends. 'There is Ebben Owens Garthowen,' you say, 'our deacon,' and perhaps you say 'an upright man and honest!' But I am here to-night to tell you what I am in truth. I have stood before you dozens of times, and told you of want of faith—of cold prayers—and lack of interest in holy things. I have asked for your prayers many times, and have gone home and forgotten to pray myself! Yes, I have been your deacon for thirty years, and all that time I have deceived you, and deceived myself. I never told you about my real sins, but you shall know to-night what Ebben Owens is. I have been weak and yielding in money matters—have lent and given my money, not out of real charity, but because it brought me the praise of man. I have lied and cheated in the market, and still my soul was asleep, and you all thought well of me. I have pretended to be a temperate man, but I have often drunk until my brain was dull, and my eyes were heavy, and have flung myself down on my bed in a drunken sleep, without thought and without prayer."

He paused a moment, and the sea wind, coming in at the window, blew a stray lock of his grey hair over his forehead. His tongue seemed parched and dry, his voice husky and uncertain, but with a fresh effort he continued:

"Are you beginning to know me, my friends? Not yet, not yet, listen! God gave me two brave boys, and how did I take his gift? I made an idol of one, and was unjust, and often harsh, to the other. As the years went on I continued in that sinful path, and in my old age the Lord is punishing me. The boy I idolised and loved—God knows with a love that effaced the image of the Almighty from my heart—has deserted me, has grown ashamed of me, and my punishment is just and righteous. The other—whom I treated harshly and thrust from me—has also deserted me in my old age; this, too, is just and righteous. The sting of it is sharp and hard to bear, for God has made me love that boy, and long for his presence; and this, too, is just and righteous. Let no one pity me, or think I am punished more than I deserve. And now, do you think you know me? Not yet, my friends, for listen, your deacon, Ebben Owens of Garthowen, is a thief! Do you hear it, all of you? A thief!" and he looked round the chapel inquiringly.

The men looked at him with flushed, excited faces, the women stooped forward to hide theirs, some of them crying silently, but all moved as by a sudden storm. Ann had bent lower and lower in her pew, and was weeping bitter tears of shame, clasping Morva's hand, who stood looking in frightened amazement from one to another.

"A thief!" continued the old man, "and a cowardly thief! One who sacrificed honour and truth and common honesty that he might gratify his foolish pride. But to come nearer, my friends, hear what I have done. By careless spendthrift ways I had wasted my money so that I had not sufficient to send my son to college. This galled my pride, and I stole from my son-in-law's drawer the sum of 40 pounds which I knew he had placed there. I was too proud to borrow from a Methodist preacher the money I required to get my son into the Church. When the theft was discovered," and the old man held up his finger to enforce his words—"are you listening?—when the theft was discovered I tried at first to throw the blame upon a member of this congregation, whom, of course, I knew to be innocent; later on, when circumstances seemed to point more directly to my dear eldest son, I gladly let the suspicion rest upon him, and I did everything in my power to give colour to the idea of his guilt. There I am, dear friends. That is Ebben Owens. You know him now as what he is—a liar—a sot—a thief! You will turn me out of your 'Sciet.' You are right; I am not worthy to be a member of it. I don't want anyone's pity, I only want you to know me as I am, and may God forgive me."

And he sat down amidst breathless silence, his hands sunk deep into his pockets, his chin resting on his chest. Shame, repentance, and sorrow filled his heart, and it required all the strength of his manhood to keep back the tears which would well up into his eyes. It was all so still in the chapel, not a word of sympathy; even a word of reproach would have been acceptable to the miserable man, who could not read beneath the surface, the tumult of varied feelings which were surging through the hearts of the congregation.

Suddenly two heavy paws were resting on his knee, and Tudor's warm breath was on his face as he tried to lick the old man's bare forehead. The touch of sympathy was more than he could bear, he rose hastily to his feet, and, followed by the dog, passed out of the chapel, leaving Gwilym Morris, with a tremble in his voice, to bring the meeting to a close.

Although he had sometimes strayed into the chapel Tudor had never before been known to invade the sanctity of the "big seat," and what brought him there on this particular evening was one of those mysteries which enshroud the possibilities of animal instinct. Perhaps he had been struck by the dejected attitude of his master, as he followed his daughter and son-in-law through the farmyard; at all events the loving and loyal heart had felt that over that bent head and stooping figure a cloud of trouble hung low, and as he followed his master through the silent congregation he hung his head and drooped his tail as though he himself were the delinquent.

"Come, Ann, let us follow him," whispered Morva.

"No," answered Ann, withdrawing her hand from Morva's warm clasp, "I cannot. Go thou and comfort him. I will wait for Gwilym."

And Morva did not hesitate, though it required some courage to make her way through that shocked and scandalised throng.

Gaining the door, where the fresh night air met her with refreshing coolness, she saw the tall, stooping figure moving slowly up the stony road, followed by the dejected Tudor, and in a moment was at his side. Taking his hard, rough hand in both her warm palms she lifted it to her cheek and pressed it to her neck.

"'N'wncwl Ebben dear, and dear, and very dear! my heart is breaking for you! To think that while we knew nothing about it you were bearing all the burden of your repentance alone. But there is plenty of love in all our hearts to sink every sin you ever committed in its depths, for the sake of all the good you have done and all the kindness you have shown to me and to every one who came near you, and you know God's forgiveness is waiting for every sinner who repents."

The old man said nothing for some time, but trudged heavily beside her.

"*Thou* art tender and forgiving, whatever," he said at last; "but Ann, where is she? Will she ever forgive me?"

"She is waiting for Gwilym," answered Morva.

"She is right; but come thou with me, lass; thou must help me to-night, for I have only done half my task," and as they passed under the elder tree at the back door he hurried before her into the house.

"Now, 'merch i, bring me pen and ink and some paper."

Now was the time, he felt, when he must make a clean breast of all his guilt, and drink his bitter draught of expiation to the dregs. He seized the pen eagerly and with trembling hands began to write, "My beloved son." The letter was to Will, of course. A clergyman! a gentleman! with a lady to wife! What would he say when he heard that his father was a thief?

He made a full and ample confession, adding no extenuating circumstances and making no excuses. He wrote slowly and laboriously, Morva meanwhile rifling Ann's work-box for a seal.

"There's beautiful writing for an old man," she said at last, as Ebben Owens toiled through the address, his tongue following every movement of the pen. "Now, here's the seal, and I will put the letter in the post at once, and then your mind will be easy."

"Easy!" he said, leaning his head on his folded arms; "'tis my son, girl, my beloved son, whose love and respect I am cutting off from me for ever. Tell thy mother, too; let them all know what I am. Here come Ann and Gwilym; perhaps they will be as hard upon me as I deserve."

Here Tudor again laid his soft head on the table beside his master's, and the old man passed his arm round the dog's neck.

"Yes—yes, 'machgen i, I know I have thee still. Go, Morva, post my letter at Pont-y-fro, though 'tis Sunday night. Good-night, girl, thou hast an old man's blessing. For what it is worth," he added, under his breath, as the girl passed out of one door, while Gwilym and Ann entered at the other.

On their way home through the clear starlight, Gwilym had endeavoured to soothe Ann's distress, to point out to her how real a proof of repentance was her father's confession. He reminded her of the joy amongst the angelic host over one sinner that repenteth! but his words failed to make their usual impression upon her. Shame, and contempt for her father's weakness were uppermost in her heart, and expressed upon her countenance, when she entered the kitchen. One glance, however, at the bowed grey head and the dejected attitude, banished every feeling of anger to the winds; with a bound she was at her father's side, her arms round his neck, her head leaning with his on the table, Tudor laying his own beside them.

Ebben Owens's departure from the chapel had been followed by a few moments of breathless silence. No more experiences were told, no hymn was sung, but a short and fervid prayer from the preacher alone preceded the dismissal which sent the astonished and deeply-moved congregation pouring out into the roadway.

Jos Hughes had trembled with fright when Ebben Owens had alluded to his want of money at the time of Will's entering college, and had expected nothing less than an exposure of his oft broken promises and the long delayed payment of his debt; but as the old man proceeded without allusion to his shortcomings, he had regained his courage, and his usual smug appearance of righteous peace and content.

"Well!" he said to his fellow-deacons, as they followed the rough road to Pont-y-fro, "did you ever think we had such a fool for a deacon?"

"'Ts—'ts! never indeed," said John Jones of the "Blue Bell."

"Well, indeed," said old Thomas Morgan, the weaver, "I didn't know we had such a sinner amongst us; but fool! perhaps it would be better if we were all such fools."

But no one took any notice of his remark, for he was never considered to have been endowed with his full complement of sense, though his pure and unblemished life had caused him to be chosen deacon.

"Well," said Jos again, as he reached his own shop door, "I always knew Garthowen's pride would come down some day; but I never, never thought he was such a fool!"

CHAPTER XX

LOVE'S PILGRIMAGE

It was nearly midnight, and still Sara and Morva sat over the fire in earnest conversation. The March wind roared in the chimney, the sound of the sea came up the valley. Outside, under the night sky, the furze and broom bushes waved and bowed to each other, and in the sheltered cwrt the daffodils under the hedge nodded and swayed in the wind; but the two women inside the cottage were too much engrossed in their conversation, and with their thoughts, to notice the wildness of the night. Often they sat in silence, broken by occasional words of sorrow.

"Oh, poor 'n'wncwl Ebben! No wonder he was sitting thinking and thinking in the chimney-corner!"

"No, no wonder indeed, och i! och i! But now he has done the best thing for his own peace of mind."

"Peace of mind!" said Morva. "I am afraid he will never have that, mother. He said when we were walking home together that he wished he could die; and I'm afraid he will before long. He is breaking his heart for his two sons."

Sara did not answer; she was gazing at the glowing fire,

Allen Raine

whose flames and sparks chased each other up the chimney. At last she straightened herself.

"Garthowen shall not die while I can help him, Morva," she said. "I have seen all this coming, 'merch i, and I know now what my dreams have meant lately. *They* are calling me, Morva; *they* have been calling me since the turn of the year, and I have closed my ears. But now"—and she stood up, though still leaning on her stick—"but now I must go."

Morva looked at her in astonishment, for the aged form seemed to grow young again with the strength of purpose within it. The gentle face appeared to lose the wrinkles of age. In the fitful light of the fire, it took again the lines of beauty and youth which had once belonged to it.

"Thou must not be surprised, child," she added, "if some evening when thou com'st home from the farm thou shalt find the house empty. The key will be on the lintel, and thou must come in and wait in patience till I return. I thought there was nothing more for me to do, but I see it now," and with her stick she pointed into the dark corner where the spinning-wheel stood, and the red earthen pitcher which went so often to the well. "I see it, 'merch i; 'tis a journey for me. I don't see quite where it ends, but I will be safe, Morva, for God is everywhere. *They* are calling me, and they will bring me safe home again. Let me go, child; 'tis to fetch a blessing for Garthowen and for thee, so don't thee fret, lass. Then my work will be done; there will be only one more journey for me—the last! and from that thou wilt not see me return. But I will be with thee, and thee must not sorrow for me."

"Oh, mother," said the girl, burying her face in her apron, "are you going to die? How can I live in this world without you?" And swaying backwards and forwards, she cried bitterly.

"Not yet, my child, not yet; I have work to do and there are happy days in store for us both; but some day, Morva, it must come, and when it comes thou must not grieve for me. Come, 'merch i, 'tis late; let us go to bed."

And the girl, somewhat comforted, dried her eyes and closed the rickety door. She slept heavily after her late watching, so heavily that she did not hear when Sara rose in the grey of the dawn. At her usual time Morva rose too, and immediately missed her mother. A wild fear throbbed through her heart as she searched in and out of the cottage.

"Mother!" she called up the step ladder which led to the loft, out in the cwrt and in the garden. "Mother fach! where are you?" But there was no answer, and she realised that Sara had gone, and that she was alone!

After the first pang of fright, a calmness and even happiness entered her heart; she had learnt to put implicit trust in her strange foster-mother, and a feeling of complete reassurance and content began to take possession of her mind.

It would be well with Sara, for whatever she attempted she never failed to accomplish, and it would be well with Garthowen too! "Her ways are blessed," said the girl, clasping her hands, and returning to her solitary breakfast. "The spirits have her in their keeping, that I know, and she will come back and bring us joy and happiness!"

Whether in the depths of her heart it was dawning upon her what blessing she expected from Sara's pilgrimage is difficult to know; perhaps unconsciously she already nourished the hope which was to grow with every day of her mother's absence, until it gilded her whole life with a rapturous expectancy; at all events, it was a very blithe and joyous maiden who brushed the dew off the sheep path to

Allen Raine

Garthowen in time for the milking that morning. She would have sung one of Sara's old Nature songs, had not the remembrance of the sorrow at the farm kept her silent. The March wind blew keen and crisp around her, the air was filled with the quivering songs of the larks, the furze was bursting into bloom, even the bare blackthorn put on its speckled mantle of white; what wonder was it in a world so fair, that Morva's heart sang for joy? But as she turned round the Cribserth, a sudden shadow came upon her, for here was Ebben Owens coming towards her, with bent head and slow dragging step. She hurried forward to meet him.

"I thought thee wouldst turn back, lass, or make an excuse to pass me by," he said.

"But no! no! no!" said the girl, linking her arm into the old man's, and turning back with him, "'tis closer and closer we must cling together, 'n'wncwl Ebben, dear, the further we go on the path of life. Did you think that Morva could pass you by? Ach y fi! no indeed! But where are you going so early?"

"To see Sara," said the old man—"to see if she will still be my friend when she knows how bad I am."

"She knows it all," said Morva; "I told her last night, and her heart was torn with sorrow and love for you; and now turn back with me to Garthowen, for Sara is gone; the cottage is empty!"

"Gone!" said the old man, with a gasp, "Sara gone!"

"Yes—gone! 'Garthowen shall not die of grief while I can help him,' she said; 'I am going a long journey, child, and ye must not grieve for me; I will come back and bring joy and comfort with me.' That's what she said," and Morva nodded her head emphatically. "Oh, she will come, she will come, as she has promised, and bring you comfort; what it will be I cannot tell," and leaning her head coaxingly on the old man's arm she asked, in a playful tone of mystery, "now what can it be, this great blessing she is going to bring you?"

"I don't know," said the old man, taking scant interest in her surmises; he was thinking how he would bear this fresh loss!

"But what do you think?"

"A Bible, perhaps."

"A Bible!" said Morva impatiently, "no—no, not a Bible; Sara knows you have plenty of them at Garthowen, and she has too much sense to bring you another—no! 'tisn't that! but oh, what will it be, I wonder?"

And day after day this was the question that ran through her thoughts, "What will it be, I wonder?"

Sitting down to her milking she sang with full voice once more the old song which Daisy loved. Of late her voice had been very low, and the song scarcely reached beyond Daisy's sleek sides, but to-day it came back, and the farmyard was filled with happy melody.

Everything went on as usual in the farm. Ann tried to let no difference be seen in her manner to her father, unless indeed she was a little more tender and loving. The farm servants, who, if they had not been at the Sciet, had yet heard the tale of disgrace, were unanimous in their endeavours to comfort the old mishteer whom they loved with so much loyalty.

"Pwr fellow bach!" they said to each other, "'twas for his son after all, and if he had kept it to himself nobody would have known anything about it!"

Allen Raine

He alone was altered, going about with a saddened mien and gentler voice than of old, and apparently finding his chief solace in the company of his little grandson, who followed him about as closely and untiringly as Tudor did.

"Ah, we are brave companions, aren't we, Gwil?" he would sometimes ask with a tremble in his voice.

"Odin (Yes, we are)," said the child.

"And thou lov'st thine old grandfather with all thine heart, eh?"

"Odw (Yes, I do!)," said the child, impatient to be gone.

They were sitting under the elder tree in the farmyard.

"Stop a minute," said the old man, in a husky, anxious voice, "if da-cu (grandfather) had done anything wrong, wouldst love him still the same?"

"Oh, more!" said the boy, "because then we'd be two naughty boys!"

And while they sat under the elder tree, and Morva helped Ann with her churning, five miles away, on the wind-swept high road, a bent figure was trudging along, with slow but steady footsteps, with the thought of them all in her mind, and the sweet memory of home in her heart, but with an earnest purpose in her eyes; to bring happiness and hope to her old friend, to the man who in the days gone by had jilted her, and torn her heart strings, who had won her love, but had married another woman, and regretted it ever after.

It was Sara, who had risen with the first streak of dawn, and snatching a hurried breakfast had left her foster-daughter asleep. She had lifted the lid of the coffer and had taken out the best half of her scarlet mantle, leaving the worn and faded half hanging Over the spinning wheel. "Morva would understand," she thought, "and would wash it and lay it away in the coffer until her return." A gown too she wore, instead of her peasant dress, a gown of red and black homespun, which had been her best when she was first married. On her head a black felt hat, with low crown, and slouching brim over her full bordered cap of frilled muslin. Strong shoes with bows on the instep, her crutch stick in her hand, and a little bundle of clothes tied up in a cotton handkerchief completed her outfit, and thus equipped she stole silently to the bedside where Morva lay, flushed with the heavy sleep of youth and health.

"My little daughter!" was all she said, but her eyes were full of tears as she passed through the cwrt and took the sheep path which led to the top of the moor. Reaching the brow of the hill she turned into a narrow lane, over which the thorn bushes, just showing signs of their budding greenery, almost met together. Under their branches she made her way, to where the lane opened out to a grassy square, on which stood a tiny whitewashed cottage. The thatch reached low over the door, and its one window no bigger than a child's slate. There were no signs of life, but Sara did not hesitate to raise the wooden latch and open the door, which she found unbolted.

In the murky gloom of the cottage it was difficult at first to see where the bed lay, but as space was circumscribed she had not far to look; in fact, one curtained side of the bed made the wall of the passage, and she had but to turn round this to see an old and wrinkled face asleep on the pillow.

"I must wake her, pwr thing," said Sara, and she began to call softly, "Nani, Nani fach!"

The sleep of age is easily put to flight, and Nani opened her eyes.

"Sara "spridion'!" she said, in astonishment. "Sara Lloyd, I mean, but I was dreaming, Sara dear. What is it?" and she sat up not a little disturbed, for Sara's name alone sufficed to arouse the latent fear of the "hysbis" or occult, always lurking in the Celtic mind.

Sara only smiled as the word "'spridion" escaped the frightened woman's lips.

"Is it time to get up?" she said, beginning to rub her eyes.

"No, no," said Sara, taking a seat by the bedside, and leaning upon her stick. "Lie still, Nani fach, and forgive me for awaking you, but I am going a journey, and a journey that won't wait."

"Oh, dear!" said Nani, "are you going by the old tren, then? As for me, I'm too frightened of it to go and see my own daughter. She's asked me many times, and I would have good living there, but I wouldn't venture in the tren for the whole world!"

"I'm not afraid of it," said Sara, "but I have never seen it. 'Twould be strange to me, and the shipping comes more natural, so I'm going to Caer-Madoc, for I know the steamer sails from there to Cardiff every Tuesday. I hope I will be there in time; but tell me, Nani, about Kitty your daughter."

"She is married again, and such a good husband she has. John Parry nearly killed her, pwr thing, and then he died, and she married this man—his name is Jones."

"But I want to know," said Sara, "did she say anything about

Gethin Owens when she was here?"

"She said she was never seeing him, and she didn't know why he was keeping away from her, and the sailors were often seeing him about the docks, but she didn't know where he was lodging now. There's glad I was to see her; but indeed, Sara fach, it cost me a lot of money, 'cos she's got a good appetite, whatever. 'Tis a great waste to come all that long way by the tren. She wants to come again, and if it wasn't for the money—"

Sara, who had no sympathy with the parsimony of many of her class, rose to go.

"Well, I won't stop longer, Nani fach; good-bye and thank you."

When she saw her visitor was really going, Nani was profuse in her offers of hospitality.

"Going! Caton pawb! not without breakfast?"

But Sara was gone, and already making her way to the high road which led along the brow of the hill to Caer-Madoc. It was twenty years since she had last been in the town, and even in this remote place twenty years had brought changes —the busy streets, the shops, the cries of the vendors of herrings and cockles, would have bewildered and puzzled her had she not been possessed by a strong purpose and sustained by that faith which can move mountains. Aided by old memories she found her way to the quay and to the small steamer with the long English name, which plied twice a week between the ports of Caer-Madoc and Cardiff.

"Are you going to Cardiff?" she asked the master, who stood on the quay.

"Why, yes, of course this is the day, and we are starting in a quarter of an hour. Who are you?" he said, looking with amused curiosity at the quaint figure with her crutch stick and black bundle.

"I am Sara Lloyd of Garthowen Moor, and I want to go with you to Cardiff. Will you take me?"

"Of course, little woman, if you can pay."

"Oh, yes," said Sara, undoing the corner of her pocket-handkerchief, "how much is it?" and she held out a half-sovereign.

"Eight shillings—you pay in there," and he pointed to a red painted shed, "but look you here, little woman, that big pocket doesn't suit such a place as Cardiff, 'tis too easily got at; tie your money up tight and put it inside the breast of your gown."

"Yes," said Sara, obeying, "and thank you."

"Look alive, then, and I will take you on board."

Sara found a seat near the prow of the ship.

"We'll have to tie a few weights to you by and by, I'm thinking, or you'll be blown away," said the captain, as he kindly arranged some boxes and baskets so as to shelter her a little from the strong March wind.

"Am I the only passenger?"

"Yes. 'Tis mostly goods we carry, but sometimes we have a stray passenger. And where would you be going now so far from Garthowen Moor in your old age?"

Welsh curiosity is a quantity that has to be taken into account.

"I am going to Cardiff."

"Yes, yes; but when you get there?"

"I don't know for sure."

The captain looked grave.

"You have a daughter, perhaps, or a son at Cardiff?"

"No, neither," said Sara. "'Tis the oldest son of Garthowen I am seeking for—Gethin Owens, have you ever seen him?"

"Gethin Owens!" said the captain, in a tone of surprise. "What? the dark brown chap with the white teeth and the bright eyes like a starling's?"—Sara nodded—"and gold rings in his ears?"

"That's him," said Sara. "Do you know him?"

"Caton pawb! as well as if he was my own son. He's mate of the *Gwenllian*, trading to Monte Video and other foreign parts. The *Gwenllian* sailed about four months ago and would be back about now. Is that what you are expecting?"

"Yes," said Sara, "Ebben Owens Garthowen is wearing his heart away longing for his son, and I think if I can see him I have news for him that will bring him to the old home."

"Well, well," said the captain, "little did I think the mate of the *Gwenllian* was the son of my old friend Ebben Owens Garthowen! Why! long ago I have been stopping with him, when he was a young man and I the same. I remember he was courting a handsome girl there, the finest lass you ever set your eyes upon, straight she was, and tall, with brown hair and dark blue eyes, like the night sky with the stars in it; oh! she was a fine lass, and she carried her pail on her head as straight as a willow wand," and the old captain clasped his own waist above the hips, and strutted about with an imaginary pail on his head. "Well, I heard afterwards that Ebben Owens treated her shocking bad, and married another girl, with money, but they say he never cared for her, and was never happy with her; and serve him right, say I. Dear! dear! how the time slips by!"

"Yes," said Sara, "he is an old man now, and in sore trouble. I live on his land, and I want to bring happiness back to Garthowen."

"Of course, of course!" said the captain, "but indeed; little woman, I'm afraid you'll have hard work, for there's something strange about that lad lately; he's keeping with the English sailors when he's in port and avoiding all his old companions. I have heard my son tell of him too, and how altered he is, and how angry the Welsh sailors are with him, but I believe he is stiddy and upright."

"Well," said Sara, "if I can only have a word with him 'twill be all right."

"Jar-i! you have pluck, little woman, and 'tis well to have a friend like you. Well, I'll do my best for you. I'll find you a night's lodging and somebody to show you the way about next day. Mrs. Jones, Bryn Street, would take you in; it's where I go myself when I do spend a night ashore."

"A hundred thanks. That's where I'd like to go because I know her and her mother."

When the captain left her she fell into a reverie, her sweet, patient face, with its delicate complexion, lighted up by the images of retrospection; the dark blue eyes, which held so much insight and purpose in their depths, were still beautiful under their arched eyebrows, the soft, straight fringe of hair combed down over her forehead like a little child's showed the iron-grey of age, and the mouth, a little sunken, told the same tale, but the spirit of love and peace within preserved to Sara a beauty that was not dependent upon outward form. It was felt by all who came in contact with her, and perhaps was the cause of the curious feeling of awe with which her neighbours regarded her.

As the little puffing steamer ploughed her way through the clear, green water, the ever-changing sky of a March day overhead, the snow-white wreaths of spray, the clear white line of the horizon, the soft grey, receding shore, all unheeded by the captain and his three subordinates, aroused in Sara's mind the intense pleasure that only a heart at peace with itself and with Nature can feel, and as she leant her soft veined hands on her crutched stick, resting her chin upon them, a little picturesque figure on the commonplace, modern steamer, the romance of life which we are apt to associate only with the young, added its charm to the thoughts of the woman of many years. The beauty of the world, the joy of it, the great hopes of it, all filled her soul to overflowing, for she believed her journey would bring light and happiness to Ebben Owens. This had been the desire of her young life, and would now be granted to her in her old age. Yes! Sara's heart was full of joy and gratitude, for she knew neither doubt nor fear.

CHAPTER XXI

THE MATE OF THE "GWENLLIAN"

"There!" said Mrs. Jones next morning, as she gave Sara's toilet a finishing touch, consisting of sundry tugs of adjustment to the red mantle and an encouraging pat on the shoulders; "there! go 'long with you now and find your precious Gethin, and give him a good scolding from me. Tell him he is the last man in the world I would expect to desert an old friend as he has done lately. There! the sight of such a tidy, fresh-looking little country woman will do our pale-faced town people good. Oh, anwl! I wish my Tom was alive; he'd have piloted you straight to the *Gwenllian*. He knew every ship that came into the docks. His heart was with the shipping though he could do nothing but look at them, poor boy!" and drying her eyes with her apron she dismissed Sara, who started with a brave heart.

Up the grimy, uninteresting Bryn Street, which the bright morning sunlight scarcely improved, and soon into a wide, busy thoroughfare where hurrying footsteps and jostling crowds somewhat disconcerted her.

The gay shops, especially the fruit shops, interested her greatly, as well as the vehicles of every description, from the humble costermonger's to the handsome broughams bearing their wealthy owners to their offices for the day; the prettily-dressed children who toddled beside their busy mothers to their early shopping; and, above all, the strains of a brass band which was enlivening the morning hours with its familiar *repertoire*. Each and all were a revelation of delight to the simple peasant. Straight from the gorse and heather, a woman exceptionally endowed with the instincts of a refined nature, one whose only glimpses of the world had been gathered from the street of a small provincial town, was it to be wondered at that to her the varied sights and sounds around her seemed like the pageantry of a dream?

"'Tis a blue and gold world," she murmured, "and I'm glad I have seen it before I die, but I can't think why the people look so dull and cross."

Although she was unconscious of it, she was herself an object of interest to the hurrying passers-by. Many of them turned round to look at the picturesque peasant woman, with her country gown and quaint headgear.

"A woman come down from the hills," said a lady to her companion, as Sara passed them, for a moment raising her eyes to theirs.

"And what a sweet face, and what wonderful eyes, so dark and blue. There is something touching in that smooth fringe of grey hair."

But Sara passed on unheeding. She was now in a quieter street, and as she passed under the high grey walls of the jail, the prison van crossed her path. The heavy iron doors opened and it passed out of her sight; the doors closed with a soft click and a turn of the key, and Sara went on her way with a sigh.

Allen Raine

"There are grey and black shadows in the making of it, too," she said, and hurried on.

Once or twice she stopped to ask her way of a passer-by.

"The docks this way? Yes, go on, and turn to the left."

At the end of the road she came upon a crowd of boys who were playing some street game with loud shouts and laughter, and Sara, who had hitherto braved all dangers, shrank a little.

"Hello, mother! where are you going? There's a penny to pay for passing through this way," and they crowded clamorously around her.

She looked at them calmly, disregarding their begging.

"Iss one of you will show me the docks, then shall he have a penny. You," she said, pointing to one with a round pale face, and honest black eyes.

"Yes 'll I," said the boy, and he turned down a corner, beckoning to her to follow.

"Go on, old witch!" cried the disappointed ones; "where's your broom?"

"Can't you speak Welsh?" she asked, as she came abreast with her guide.

"Yes, that can I," said the boy in his native tongue.

"Oh, very good, then. 'Tis the *Gwenllian* I am wanting— Captain Price—can you find her?"

"Oh, yes, come on," said the boy. "I was on board of her yesterday morning, but she was about sailing for Toulon with a cargo of coal. Most like she's gone."

Sara's heart sank, and as they came in sight of the forests of masts, the bales of goods, the piles of boards, of pig iron, of bricks and all the other impedimenta of a wharf, for the first time her heart was full of misgivings.

"Stop you there," said the boy, "and I will go and see," and he darted away, leaving Sara somewhat forlorn amongst the rough crowd of sailors and dockmen.

"Hullo, mother!" said a jolly-looking red-faced man who had nearly toppled over the little frail figure; "what you doing so far from home? They are missing you shocking in some chapel away in the hills somewhere, I'm sure."

"Well, indeed, 'tis there I would like to go as soon as my business is ended. 'Tis Gethin Owens I am looking for, mate of the *Gwenllian*."

"Oh, ho," said the man, "you may go back to chapel at once, little woman; you won't find him, for he sailed yesterday for France."

At this moment the boy returned with the same information, and Sara turned her face sorrowfully away from the shipping.

"I will give you two pennies if you will take me back to Bryn Street."

"Come on," said the boy.

He did not tell her that his home lay in that identical street, and that he was already due there.

Once more the little red mantle passed through the busy crowd. Not for years had Sara felt so sad and disappointed, the heavy air of the town probably added to her dejection.

Mrs. Jones was loud in her sympathy as Sara, faint and weary, seated herself on the settle.

"Oh, Kitty Jones fach!" she said, leaning on her stick and swaying backwards and forwards. "I am more sorry than I can say. To go back without comfort for Garthowen or my little Morva. He's gone to France, and I suppose he won't be back for a year or six months, whatever, and I have no money to stop here all that time."

"Six months!" said Mrs. Jones; "there's ignorant you are in the country. Why, he'll be back in a fortnight, perhaps a week. What's the woman talking about?"

"Yes, indeed?" said Sara, in delighted astonishment. "Yes, I am a very ignorant woman, I know, but a week or a fortnight, or even three weeks, I will stop," and the usual look of happy content once more beamed in her eyes.

Every day little Tom Jenkins, upon whom Sara's two pennies had made a favourable impression, went down to the docks to see if the *Gwenllian* had arrived. When a week, a fortnight, and nearly three weeks had passed away, and still she was not in port, Mrs. Jones suggested that probably she had extended her voyage to some other port, or was perhaps waiting for repairs.

At last one sunny morning Tom Jenkins came in with a whoop.

"The *Gwenllian* is in the docks!" he cried, and Sara prepared at once for another expedition in that direction.

"Wait a bit," said Mrs. Jones. "You can write, Sara?"

"Yes, in Welsh," said the old woman.

"Well, then, send a letter, and Tom will take it for you."

Sara took her advice, and, putting on her spectacles, wrote as follows:

"Sara Lloyd, Garthowen Moor, is writing to thee, Gethin Owens, to say she is here at Mrs. Jones's, No. 2 Bryn Street, with good news for thee. All the way from Garthowen to fetch thee, my boy, so come as soon as thou canst."

The writing was large and sprawly, it was addressed to "Gethin Owens, mate of the *Gwenllian*,—Captain Price," and when Tom had departed, with the letter safe in his jacket pocket, the two women set themselves to wait as patiently as they could; but the hours dragged on heavily until tea-time.

"Gethin was fond of his tea," said Mrs. Jones, "and I wouldn't wonder if he'd be here before long."

The tea table was laid, the cakes were toasted the tea brewing was delayed for some time. It was Mrs. Jones's turn now to be anxious, and even irritable; but Sara had quite regained her composure.

"He'll come," she said. "I know he'll come. I know my work is nearly over."

"There's missing you I'll be," said Mrs. Jones. "I wish my poor old mother was as easy to live with as you, Sara; but 'tis being alone so long has made her cranky. And the money—oh, she loves it dearly. Indeed, if I can get Davy to agree, we will give up this house and go home and live near her; 'tis pity the old woman should grow harder in her old age."

"Yes," said Sara. "'Tis riper and softer we ought to be growing in our old age, more ready to be gathered. I will go and see her sometimes; oftener than I have."

Their conversation was interrupted by a shadow passing the window, and a firm footstep in the passage.

"Hoi, hoi!" said a loud, breezy voice, "Mrs. Jones!—how is she here?" and Gethin Owens clasped her hand with a resounding clap.

"Much you care how I am, Gethin Owens. Never been to see me for so long."

"Well, you look all the better for my absence, I think. But what you want with me? Tom Jenkins said an old woman wanted to see me shocking, and I gave him a clatch on his ear, to teach him not to call a young woman like you an old woman. Why, you look ten years younger than when I saw you last."

"Go 'long, Gethin Owens," said Mrs. Jones. "Didn't you have the letter?"

"No. Tom said the boys in the streets had torn it in a scrimmage they had; but he gave me your message."

"Well, come in and look on the settle then."

In the shadow of the settle, Sara sat listening to the conversation, with a look of amusement in her eyes.

Gethin looked a moment into the dark corner, and, recognising her, took two steps in advance, with extended hands and a smiling greeting on his lips; but suddenly the whole expression of his face changed to one of anxiety and distrust.

"What is it," he said, "has brought you so far, Sara? Is the old man dead?"

"Nonsense, no!" said Sara.

"Well, you wouldn't come so far to tell me Will was married."

"Indeed I would, then," she said, rising. "Come, thou foolish boy, didn't I say it was good news? Oh! but thou hasn't had my letter."

Gethin took both her hands between his own.

"'Tis very kind of thee, Sara fach, but a letter would have brought me the news quite as safely. Well! I wish him joy. 'Tisn't Gethin Owens is going to turn against his brother, because he has been a fortunate man, while I have been unfortunate. Yes, I wish him joy, and sweet Morva every blessing under the sun."

"Twt, twt!" said Sara, "thee art all wrong, my boy. 'Tisn't Morva he has married at all! and that's how I thought a letter could not explain everything to thee as I could myself, and bring thee home to the old country again."

Gethin shook his head.

"No, no; I have said good-bye to Garthowen, I will never go there again."

"Well! why?" said Sara, still holding his hands, and looking into his face with those compelling eyes of hers.

"There is no need to tell thee, Sara," said the sailor, a dogged, defiant look coming into his eyes. "I have said good-bye to Garthowen, and will never darken its doors again."

"And yet thou hast been very happy there?"

"Ah! yes," said Gethin, a tender smile chasing away the angry look on his face. "I was very happy there indeed, when I whistled at my plough, with the song of the larks in my ears, and the smell of the furze filling the air. But now— no—no! I must never turn my face there again."

"Wilt not, indeed?" asked Sara. "Wait till I've told thee all, my lad. And now I have a strange story to tell thee, 'tis of thy poor old father, Gethin."

"My father? what's the matter with him? Thou hast said he's alive, what then? Is he ill? Not ill? What then, Sara?" and his face took a frightened expression; "what evil has come upon the old man?"

His voice sank very low as he clutched the old woman's hand and wrung it unconsciously.

"What is it? not shame, Sara—say, woman, 'tis not shame that has come upon him in his old age!"

Sara was embarrassed for the first time.

"Shame," she said, "in the eyes of men, is sometimes honour in the eyes of God! Listen, Gethin—Dost remember the night of thy going from Garthowen?"

He nodded with a serious look in his eyes.

"That night I had a dream; only, I was awake when I saw it. I was at Garthowen in my dream, and I saw a dark figure entering Gwilym Morris's room; he stooped down and opened a drawer, and took something out of it. I could not see the man's face, but it was not *thee*, Gethin, though thy sudden disappearance made them think at first, that thou wert the thief; only Morva and I knew better. She heard a footstep that night, and when she went out to the passage, she saw thee coming out of that room. But she and I knew that it was not thou who took the money. What dreadful sight met thee in that room, Gethin bach, we did not know, but it was something that made thee reel out like a drunken man."

"It was, it was," he answered, shuddering and covering his eyes with his hands, as though he saw it still.

"'Twas a sight that shadowed the whole world to me, and has altered my life ever since. Dei anwl! 'twas a sight I would give my whole life not to have seen."

"I know it all now, my boy, and I know what thou must have suffered. *'Twas thy father who took Gwilym Morris's money.* Sorrow and bitter repentance have been his companions by day, and have sat by his pillow at night, ever since he was tempted to commit that sin. He has become thin, and haggard, and old. He confessed it all at the Sciet. And think how hard it must have been for him to bring himself to tell it all before the men who had thought so highly of him. 'Twas for Will's sake, but 'twas you that he wronged, Gethin, and that is what is breaking his heart."

"Me!" said Gethin. "Me? He is not grieving for me, is he? Poor old man! he did me no wrong; 'twas I by going away, brought the dishonour upon myself. And he confessed it all!"

"Yes," said Sara, "and made it all as black as he could. Canst forgive him, Gethin?"

"Forgive him? Fancy Gethin Owens *forgiving* anyone! as if he was such a good man himself! especially his own father! I have nothing to forgive; he did me no harm, poor old man. And if all the world is going to turn against him because his love for his son did prove stronger than his honesty, why! it's home to Garthowen I'll go, to cheer him and to love him, and to show the world that I for one will stick to him, weak or strong, upright or sinful!"

"Gethin bach! thou know'st what real love is! Love that no folly or weakness, or even sin, in the dear one can alter. That is what I have come to fetch; a son to support and comfort my old friend in his latter days. Gwilym Morris is good and kind to him, and Ann—thou know'st they are married these four years?"

"Yes, Jim Brown told me, and I was very glad."

"But 'tis his own son he is longing for. "Tis my boy Gethin I want to see,' he says; 'he was so kind to me.'"

"Did he say that?"

"That did he."

"Diwss anwl! I never knew he cared a button for me."

He was longing to ask for Morva.

"Thee hasn't asked for Morva yet," said Sara.

"Is she well?"

"Oh! well—quite well, and as happy as a bird since Will is married."

"Since Will is married! How can that be if he has deserted her and married another woman? I never thought Will would do that! And who has he married?

"A lady, Gethin! Miss Gwenda Vaughan of Nantmyny—didst ever hear such a thing?—and as sweet a girl as ever lived!"

"Well, well, and so Will has married a lady? Well, that's his choice, mine would never lie that way; a simple country lass for me, or else none at all, and most likely 'twill be that. Well, we may say good-bye to Will. I suppose we sha'n't see much more of him."

"Perhaps not."

"But 'tis Morva I'm thinking of, Sara; how does she bear it? She is hiding her grief from you—she loved him, I know she loved him! and for him to turn from her and give his love to another must have been a cruel grief to her."

"Gethin," said the old woman, "she never loved him. She promised to marry him when she was a child, before she knew what love meant, but since she has grown up her heart has been refusing to keep the promise which bound her to Will. She has tried over and over again to get her freedom; like those poor birds we see caught in the net sometimes, she has fluttered and fluttered, but all in vain; and when the letter came from Will to Garthowen telling his father of the wonderful marriage that was coming so near, 'twas as if someone had broken the net and let the bird go free. And there's Morva now, happy and bright like she was before she found out that her promise to Will was galling her sore. 'Tis only one thing she wants now, Gethin. 'Tis for Garthowen to be happy, and that will never be till thou art home once more. Come, Gethin bach, come home with me; our hearts are all set upon thee."

"Halt!" said Gethin, and he pushed his fingers through his hair until it stood on end. "Phew! Mrs. Jones was never stinting with her fire; 'tis stifling hot here," and he turned away to the doorway, and stood a moment looking out into the street. "Will married—and not to Morva!" What wild hopes were rising again within him? but he crushed them down, and turned on his heel with a laugh. "How you women can live day after day with a roaring fire I can't think—but come, Sara, on with your story."

"Well!" she said, "all the way from Garthowen I have come to fetch thee, Gethin, and thou must come home with me."

"Would Morva like to see me?" he said, in a low, uncertain voice.

"Oh! Gethin, thou art a foolish man, and a blind man! Morva does not know what I have come here for; but if thou ask'st me the question, 'Would Morva be glad to see me?' I answer 'Yes.'"

"D'ye think that—that—"

"Never mind what I think, come home and find out for thyself."

"Sara, woman," said Gethin, bringing his fist down with a thump on the table, "take care what you are doing. I tell you it has taken me three long years to smother the hopes which awoke in my heart when I was last at home. Don't awake them again, lest they should master me; unless you have some gleam of hope to give me."

Sara laughed joyfully.

"Well, now, how much will satisfy thee?"

"D'ye think, Sara, she could ever be brought to love me?"

"Well," she said mischievously, "thee canst try, Gethin. Come home and try, man!"

"What day is it to-day? 'Tis Tuesday; I'll only stop to settle with Captain Price, and I'll come home, Sara. Wilt stop for me?"

"No, no, I have been too long from home. Tomorrow the *Fairy Queen* is going back, and I will go with her. I can trust thee, my boy, to follow me soon."

"Dei anwl! Yes! the ship's hawser wouldn't keep me back! I'll be down there one of these next days. I'll cheer the old man up—and Sara, woman, I have money to lay out on the farm. 'Tis too long a story to tell thee now, how a man I helped a bit in the hospital at Montevideo died, and left me all his money, 500 pounds! I didn't care a cockleshell for it, but to-day I am beginning to be glad of it. There's glad I'll be to see the old place again! Mrs. Jones," he shouted, "come here and hear the good news. Didn't I tell you years ago I was going home to Garthowen, to the cows and the sheep and the cawl! and so I am then, and it is this good little woman who has brought it about!" and clasping his arms round Sara, he drew her from the settle, and twisted her round in a wild dance of delight, Sara entreating, laughing, and scolding in turns.

"Caton pawb! the boy will kill me!" but he seated her gently on the settle before he went away.

"I'll be on the wharf to meet you to-morrow, Sara, and see you safe on board the *Fairy Queen*. Good-night, woman, 'tis a merry heart you are sending away to-night!" and as he passed up the street they heard his cheerful whistle until he had turned the corner.

CHAPTER XXII

GETHIN'S STORY

True to his promise, Gethin was early at the docks, and as he sat dangling his legs over a coil of rope, he laughed and slapped his knee, when amongst the crowd of loiterers on the wharf-side he saw Sara's red mantle appear.

"Didn't I say so?" he exclaimed, crossing to meet her, "didn't I say you'd be here an hour and a half too soon? Just like a country woman! why, the ship must wait for the tide, Sara fach. But I'm glad you're come, we shall have time for a chat; there's some things I want you to know before I see you again."

"Afraid I was, 'machgen i," said Sara, "that the steamer would start without me, and I will be quite happy to sit here and wait. Dear, dear! how full the world is of wonders that we never know of down there in the gorse and heather! all these strange people, different faces, different languages. Gethin bach, those who roam away from home see much to open their minds."

"Yes," said Gethin, "and much to make them sick of it all; 'tis glad I'll be to say good-bye to it, and to settle down in the old home again. But the time is passing, Sara fach, and I

Allen Raine

wanted to tell thee what I have never told any one else, why I left Garthowen so suddenly. I can tell you now, since my father has let every one know of it; but I couldn't talk about it before Kitty Jones last night, for 'tis a bitter thing to know your father has been dishonourable, and has lost the respect of his neighbours. Well—'twas a night I never will forget—that night when Gwilym Morris lost his bag of gold; 'twas a night, Sara, that made a deep mark on me, a blow it was that nearly drove me to destruction and ruin. I may as well tell thee everything, Sara, and make a clean breast of it all. I had grown so fond of Morva, Diwss anwl! she was in my thoughts morning, noon, and night, and I thought she cared for me a little; but there I was mistaken, I suppose, for when I asked her, she told me she was promised to Will. 'Here behind this very bush,' she said, 'only two nights ago, I met him, and I promised him again that I would be true to him.' I have been in foreign lands when an earthquake shook the world under my feet, and at those words of Morva's I felt the same, as if the world was going to pieces; but I had to bear it; 'tis wonderful how much a man can bear!"

"And a woman too, 'machgen i," said Sara, laying her soft hand upon his, "'twas a bitter time for Morva too."

"I didn't know that," said Gethin, "or 'twould have been worse to bear. Well, when I went to bed that night, there was no sleep for me, no more sleep than if I was steering a ship through a stormy sea. Well, that dreadful night, the old house was very quiet, no sound but the clock ticking very loud, and the owls crying to the moon; there was something wrong with Tudor too, he was howling shocking all night, and 'twas a thing I never heard him do before, perhaps because I slept too sound. I tossed and turned till the clock struck twelve, and then I began to feel drowsy; but all of a sudden I was as wide awake as I am now. I thought I could hear a soft footstep in the passage, as if someone was walking without shoes; I listened so hard I could hear my heart beating. I thought 'twas a thief, or perhaps a murderer, and I determined to rush upon him, but somehow I could not move, for I heard a hand rubbing over the wall; 'tis whitewashed and rough you know, Sara, and the hand was a rough hand—I could hear that; then somebody passed my door, and in to Gwilym Morris's room. I was out of bed in a minute, and across the passage in the dark, for there were black clouds that night, and the moon was hidden sometimes. Just as I reached the door of Gwilym's room, whatever, she came out and lighted up the whole place, and there, Sara, I saw a sight that made my heart leap up in my throat. Indeed, indeed, 'twas a sight that I would give my life never to have seen, but I did see it, Sara, plain enough, and now you know what it was, and I can't bring my lips to put it into words. I turned back to my bed with my hands over my eyes, as if I could tear away the horrid sight. And if 'twas like an earthquake when Morva refused me, 'twas worse—oh, much worse—when I saw what I did. My old father had always been so dear to me—so much I loved him, so highly I thought of him, although, I knew he was over fond of a drop sometimes; but caton pawb! I would have staked my life on his honour, and more upon his honesty. I lay awake of course that night—yes, and many a night after, going over my troubles—worse than that, my shame; and through all my tossing and turning, one thought was clear before me, 'twould be better for me to bear the blame than for old Ebben Owens Garthowen to be known as a thief. I thought I would be far away in foreign lands or on distant seas, and so I would not hear the whispering, nor see the pointing of the fingers. What did it matter what people said about me? Morva would not have me, so what was the use of a good name to me?"

"I got up before the sun rose, and I pushed a few things into my canvas bag, and went quiet down the stairs. I stopped a minute outside Ann and Morva's room. I could hear them breathing soft and regular, and so I hoped they had slept all night. Then I went into the dairy and cut enough bread and cheese to last for the day, and before anyone was up at Garthowen, I was far on my way towards Caer-Madoc.

"I sailed from there to Cardiff, and there on the docks I saw many of my old friends—Tom Powell and Jim Bowen, and many others; but diwss anwl! I was ashamed to look them in the face, so I avoided them all, and went amongst the English and the foreign sailors; and in every port I was avoiding the Welsh sailors, and when I came to Cardiff I never went to Kitty Jones's any more.

"Well, then, I took ship for South America, and I didn't come home for two years. All that time I led a wild and reckless life, Sara fach. Wasn't a fight but I was in it—wasn't a row but Gethin Owens was there, drinking and swearing and rioting. I didn't care a cockle-shell what became of me; and if ever a man was on the brink of destruction, it was Gethin Owens of Garthowen during those two years. I tried everything to drown my sorrows.

"'Twas just then in Monte Video I caught a fever—the yellow fever they call it—and I was in the hospital there for many weeks. They told me afterwards that I had a very bad turn of it. The doctors said they'd never seen a man so ill and yet recover. I took their word for it. But I knew nothing about it myself, for I was as happy as a king those weeks, roaming about Garthowen slopes, dancing in the mill, and whistling at the plough, and Morva at my side always. Dei anwl! When I came to myself, and saw the bare, whitewashed walls of the hospital, the foreign nurses moving about—very kind and tender they were, too, but 'twasn't Morva—Garthowen slopes, Morva, the mill and the moor had all gone, and when I saw where I was, what will you think of me, Sara, when I tell you I cried like a little child, like I did the day when I tore myself away from little Morva long ago, when I ran away from home, and heard her calling after me, 'Gethin! Gethin!'"

"The nurse was very kind to me. She saw my tears were falling like the rain. "'Tis weak you are, poor fellow,' says she, for she could speak English. God bless her! I will never forget her. And she did her best to strengthen me with good food and cheering words; and in time I got well, but 'twas many months before I felt like myself again.

"Well, in the next bed to mine was a man, brought in when I was at my worst, or my best, having that jolly time on Garthowen slopes with Morva. When I came to myself, he was there, poor fellow, as yellow as a guinea, with black shadows under his eyes, and the parched lips that showed he was having a hard fight for his life. But singing he was all through the long nights in that strange place, though his voice was so weak and husky you could scarcely hear him; but the words, Sara fach! I almost rose up in my bed when I heard them. What d'ye think they were but, 'Yn y dyfroedd mawr a'r tonau'?[1] My heart leapt out to him at once, and I tried hard to speak to him, but he couldn't hear me; and when I was getting better he was getting worse, till one day the black vomit came on, and then I thought 'twas all over with him. But instead of that, it seemed to do him good, for he got better after that, and very soon I was able to sit a bit by his bedside, and to talk to him about the old country. His name was Jacob Ellis, and he had been captain of the *Albatross* trading between Swansea and Cardiff and Monte Video. He hadn't a relation in the world that he knew of. He had got on well, and had saved five hundred pounds. They were safe in the bank at Cardiff, and when he found he was not going to get better after all—for he hadn't the same healthy constitution that I had—well, nothing would do for him but he

Allen Raine

must make his will and leave all he had to me. 'Twas all right and proper, Sara, and the nurse and the doctor witnessed it.

"Caton pawb! he thought I had done a lot for him, poor fellow; when, if he only knew, the Welsh hymns and the talks about Wales had helped me to get well. I had my hand on his, just like you have yours on mine now, when he died. He said a few serious words to me before he went, Sara. I will keep them to myself, but I can tell you they often come back to my memory. Well, he died and I got well, and as soon as I was strong enough I hired on board a ship bound for Cardiff. I went at once to a lawyer to see about my 500 pounds, and I felt a rich man, I can tell you, but there was no pleasure in it, Sara.

"I would willingly have thrown it over the docks, if that would blot out one evening behind the broom bushes at Garthowen, and one night when I saw a sight which spoilt my life. It's twenty minutes to the starting time yet, Sara. Art tired, or will I tell the rest of my story?"

"Go on, 'machgen i," said Sara, "tell it me all today, and there will be no need for us ever to have any more talk about it."

"No; that is what I wish," said Gethin. "Well, with my pay in my pocket, and 500 pounds at my back, I thought I would enjoy myself as much as I could, and smother the hiraeth[2] that was so strong upon me, the longing to go home to see Morva, and you, and the moor, Sara; my father, Ann, and Will, and all of them were dragging sore at my heart, so I threw myself in with a lot of roystering fellows, who were bent upon having as many sprees as they could while their money lasted. I was keeping away from the Welsh sailors entirely, and my friend, Ben Barlow, and I were having what they call in English a jolly time. We went together to a low place near the docks, where there was singing and dancing every night for sailors. I saw many of my old companions there and amongst them was a girl called Bella Lewis, who used to come often to see Kitty Jones in Bryn Street. She wasn't a bad sort altogether, very kind-hearted and merry. She was altered a good deal since I saw her last, she looked older and thinner, but she was laughing and dancing as lively as ever. As soon as she caught sight of me, she came to me, and I think she was real glad to see me, because she thought I had been kind to her once when she was ill and very poor.

"'Gethin Owens, I do believe,' she says, 'where have you been all this long time? Kitty Jones will be glad to see you, whatever.'"

"I saw the foreign sailor she had been dancing with looking very black at me, and I began to laugh, and talk, and joke with Bella, just to plague him, and we danced and drank together, and I soon saw that the two years I had been away had not improved her. She was more noisy, and her talk was more coarse, and many an oath was on her lips. I saw it, but I didn't care, because I had become quite reckless, and my laugh and my jokes were louder than anyone's in the room.

"'Well, wherever you have been,' says Bella, 'you're very much improved, Gethin.'"

"'Am I that?' says I. 'And how, then?'"

"'Oh, well, you are not afraid of a joke, and you've not got that hard look on your mouth when you hear a light word. Oh, anwl! I was afraid of you those days; but I will say you had a kind heart, Gethin Owens.'"

"'Well,' I says, 'that's alright still, whatever.'"

"'Well then,' she says, 'if it is, you'll take me to the Vampire Theatre to-night. Come on, Gethin Owens, for the sake of old times,' she says; and I was glad to see her, certainly, 'twas so long since I had met an old friend, and the brandy had got in my head a little, though I hadn't had so much as Bella.

"'Come on, then,' sez I, for I couldn't refuse her when she said 'for the sake of old times'; and I looked round for Ben Barlow to tell him I was going, but I couldn't see him anywhere. Well, off we went together, and when we got out in the street, in spite of the flaring gas-lamps, you could see 'twas a beautiful night. The moon was shining round and clear above us, and I never could see the full moon, Sara, even far away in foreign countries, without thinking of Garthowen slopes and the moor. Well, this night they came before me very plain, but I shut them out from my thoughts, with the music from The Vampire sounding loud in nay ears, and Bella Lewis hanging on my arm."

"All of a sudden, when we reached the door of the theatre, Bella turned round, and something glittered on her neck in the moonlight."

"'What is that?' I said, pointing to it."

"''Tis my necklace that you gave me,' she said; 'twas in my pocket at the dancing. I was so afraid it would drop off.'"

"And there it was hanging row under row, and the shells showing all their colours in the bright moonlight. I don't know how can such things be, Sara, but as sure as I'm here I saw Morva standing there, just as I saw her that night when I gave her her necklace, standing under the elder-tree, with the round moon shining full on her face. Sara, woman, I nearly lost my breath, and had to lay my hand on the doorpost to steady myself. Bella had hold of my arm, and I felt as if a snake was hanging there that I wanted to throw off. The music came full and loud into the street, and I hated it all. I cannot tell what came over me, but my knees trembled and my hands—mine, remember, Gethin Owens, the big, strong sailor!—my hands were shaking like a leaf when I took the tickets. I tried to throw it off, and to laugh and talk again with Bella.

"'What's the matter?' she said; but I couldn't answer, for whenever I looked at her that glittering necklace brought Morva's face before me so plain as if she had been there herself; and when we sat down in the theatre I couldn't hear the music and I couldn't see the stage, because soft in my ears was Morva's voice calling me, like she called me that day on the slopes when I tore myself from her little clinging arms: 'Gethin! Gethin! come back!' was plain in my ears."

"I looked round me quite moidered. Lots of Bella's friends were there, and lots of mine; but I could not stop. I stood up, determined to go out, whatever the others might think of me, for all the time Morva's voice was in my ears calling 'Gethin! Gethin!'"

"'I am going,' said I to Bella; 'somebody is calling me.' And there, close to me, who should I see but Ben Barlow sitting alone. I pushed the play bill in his hand. 'Look after Bella,' I said; 'I am going,' and I went towards the door. I could hear Bella's friends laughing and shouting, and the last thing I heard as I went out was a shower of bad names and foul words that Bella was flinging after me."

"The tide is nearly full, I see; she'll be starting directly, but I have almost told you everything now."

"I shipped for another long voyage after that, and only now I have come back; but indeed, Sara fach, whether 'twas a dream or vision, or what, I don't know, but never, in storms or wrecks or fine weather, on land or sea, will I forget the strong hand that laid hold of me that night, and turned my face away from the music, the lights, the sin and the folly of the town. I have told thee all, Sarah fach. Wilt still be my friend?"

"For ever, 'machgen i!"

"Then it is to the old country I'm going, Sara, back to the sea wind, the song of the lark, and the call of the seagulls on the bay. I'll be home one of these days; as soon as I can get things settled here. Diwss anwl! I must make haste or the steamer will start with me aboard. All right, captain, take care of her. She's a good friend to me."

"Don't I know it?" said the old captain, shaking hands warmly with both. "Didn't she come up with me about a month ago, and didn't I direct her to safe lodgings? 'Fraid I was, man, that with her innocent face and her wide tick pocket, she would be robbed or murdered or something. But here you are safe again, little woman. Going home to the old countryside?"

"Yes," said Sara, laughing. "I am quite safe, and I have spent a pleasant time with Kitty Jones, but I am not sorry to leave your big smoky town. Ach y fi! 'tis pity to think so many people live and die there without sight of the sea and the cliffs and the moor. Poor things! poor things!"

"Well! 'tis well to be contented with one's lot," said the old man, "but I don't know how I would be now without a sight of the docks and the shipping, and a yarn with my old comrades on the waterside sometimes, but I am going to try it, whatever. Marged is grumbling shockin' because I don't stop at home in our little cottage. It's a purty place, too, just a mile outside Carmarthen, but quiet it is, shockin' quiet! And you, Gethin Owens, little did I think these two years I bin meeting you about the docks and the shipping, that you wass the son of my old friend, Ebben Owens of Garthowen! Why din you tell me, man?"

Gethin coloured with embarrassment, while he pretended to arrange a sheltered seat for Sara, who came bravely to his assistance.

"And how could he know, captain, that you were the friend of his father?" she said in Welsh, for she had gathered the sense of the English talk between the two sailors.

"Well! that's true indeed," said the captain, scratching his head; "we were both in the dark. But there's the bell! You must go, my lad, if you won't come with us."

"Not to-day," replied Gethin, "but one of these next days I'll be following that good little woman."

And when, from the edge of the wharf, he watched the little steamer making her way between the river craft, Sara's red mantle making a bright spot in the grey of the fog and smoke, his heart went with her to the old homestead, his old haunts, and his old friends.

[1] "In the deep waters and the waves," a well-known and favourite hymn.

[2] Home sickness.

CHAPTER XXIII

TURNED OUT!

The first few days following the Sciet were days of anxious waiting for Ebben Owens. He had laid his soul bare before his son, the idol of his life, and he waited for the answer to his letter, with as intense an anxiety as does a prisoner for the sentence of the judge. He rose with the dawn as was always his custom, but now, instead of the active supervision of barn or stable or cowshed, which had filled up the early morning hours, his time was spent in roaming over the moor or the lonely shore, his hands clasped behind his back, his eyes bent on the ground. Morva watched him from the door of her cottage, and often, as the morning mists evaporated in curling wisps before the rising sun, the sad, gaunt figure would emerge from the shadows and pass over the moorland path. Then would Morva waylay him with a cheerful greeting.

"There's a braf day we are going to have, 'n'wncwl Ebben!—"

"Yes, I think," the old man would answer, looking round him as if just awakening to the fact.

"Yes, look at the mist now rolling away from Moel Hiraethog, and look at those rocks on Traeth y daran which looked so grey ten minutes ago; see them, all tipped with gold, and, oh, anwl, look at those blue shadows behind them, and the bay all blue and silver!"

"Yes," answered her companion, looking round with sad eyes, "'tis all beautiful."

"Well, now," said Morva, "I am only an ignorant girl, I know, and I have many foolish thoughts passing through my mind, but this, 'n'wncwl Ebben, isn't it a wise and a true one? 'Tis Sara has told me, whatever."

"What is it?" he asked. "If Sara told thee 'tis sure to be right."

"Yes, of course," said Morva.

The sun was gradually lighting up the moor with golden radiance. The old man stood with his back to the light, the girl facing him, bathed in the bright effulgence of the sunrise, her hair in threads of gold blown by the sea breeze like a halo round her face, her blue eyes earnest with the light of an inner conviction which she desired to convey to her companion.

"Look, now," she said, "how everything is bathed in light and beauty! Where are the grey shadows and the curling mists? All gone! 'Tis the same world, 'n'wncwl Ebben, dear, but the sun has come and chased away the darkness. 'Tis like the grace of God, so mother says, if we will open our hearts and let it in, it shines upon us like the sunlight. His love spreads through our whole being, He blots out our sins if we are sorry for them, He smiles upon us and holds out His loving arms to us, and yet we turn our backs upon Him, and walk about in the shadows with our heads bent down, and our eyes fixed upon the ground. Every morning, mother says, when the sun rises, God is telling us, 'This is how I love you, this is how I will fill your hearts with warmth and light and joy.' Now, isn't that true, 'n'wncwl Ebben?"

"What about the mornings when the mist does not clear away, lass, but turns to driving rain?"

"Oh, well, then," said Morva, not a whit daunted, "the rain and the clouds are wanted sometimes for the good of the earth, and, remember, 'tis only a thin veil they make; the sunshine is behind them all the time, filling up the blue air, and ready to shine through the least break in the clouds. And, after all, 'n'wncwl Ebben," she added, in a coaxing tone, "'tis very seldom the mornings do turn to rain and fog. You and I, who are out on the mountains so early, know that better than the townspeople, who lie in bed till nine o'clock, they say, and often by that time the glory of the morning is shaded over."

"Well, perhaps," he said. "Thou art more apt to count the clear dawns, while I count the grey ones."

"Twt, twt, you must leave off counting the grey ones. There's a verse in mother's Bible that says, 'Forgetting the things which are behind, and reaching forth unto those things which are before.'"

"Yes, indeed, 'merch i, I've read it many times, but I never thought much of the meaning of it before. 'Tis a comforting verse, whatever, and I will look for it in my Bible."

"Yes, I suppose 'tis in every Bible," said Morva, with a merry laugh; "but, indeed, I feel as if mother's brown Bible was the best in the world, and was full of messages to brighten our lives. Didn't I say I was a foolish girl?"

"Thee't a good girl, whatever; but 'tis time to milk the cows."

"Yes, indeed. Let me shut the door and I will come back with you." And as she ran over the dewy grass, he looked after her with a smile.

"She's got the sea wind in her heels, I think," he said.

He chatted cheerfully as they walked home together, and gladdened Ann's heart by making a good breakfast.

In the course of the morning Morva entered the best kitchen, bearing a letter which Dyc "pigstye" had just brought from Pont-y-fro.

"Tis from Will, 'n'wncwl Ebben," said the girl; "here are your glasses, or will I call Ann to read it to you?"

"Let me see, is it English or Welsh?" said Ebben Owens, opening it with trembling fingers. "Oh! 'tis Welsh, so read thou to me. My glasses are not suiting me so well as they were."

The truth was, he was too nervous to read the letter himself, a fact which Morva quite comprehended.

"MY DEAR FATHER," began Will, "I daresay you are expecting to hear from me, but I have had a good deal to do since we returned from our wedding tour. The contents of this letter will surprise you, I am sure, but I hope they will please you too. We are very happy in our new home, and my uncle, though living under the same roof with us, is very kind and considerate, and never interferes with our plans. He seems very fond of Gwenda, and it would be strange if he were not, for she is as good as she is beautiful. The church here is filled with a large congregation, and they seem to appreciate my ministrations thoroughly. There is, I am glad to say, very little dissent in the parish. You know I never liked dissent, but Gwenda is broader in her views, and wants to convert me to her way of thinking. Now this letter is really more a message from her than from me. She wants to know if you will have us at the farm for a week or a fortnight, when the spring is a little more advanced. She wants to see the moor when the gorse is in blossom. She would like to know you more intimately, she says, and would enjoy nothing more than a taste of real farm life; she therefore begs, that if you can have us you will not make any alteration in your ways of living. She sends her love to Ann, and hopes she will put up with her for a little while. If you will let us know when it will be convenient to you, we will fix a time to come to Garthowen. I remain, dear father,

"Your affectionate son,
"WILLIAM OWEN."

Ebben Owens had been gradually growing more excited, and at the last word said with a gasp:

"He has forgotten my confession, Morva; I am of no consequence to him!"

"Yes—yes," said the girl, "here's another half sheet with 'P.S.' at the top," and she continued to read:

"Dear father, Gwenda was looking over my shoulder, so I could not add what I say now. Please ask Ann to put the best knives and forks on the table, and to bring out mother's silver teapot when we come. I forgot to refer to the contents of your last letter. You make too much of your fault, dear father, you have made a cornstack of a barleymow. I am only sorry you have published it abroad as you have done. You need only have confessed to God, or if you wanted to do more, I am an ordained priest. I can't imagine why you did not ask Gwilym to lend you the money; at all events you returned it as soon as you could. Ask Jacob the Mill to keep one of Fan's pups for me."

Ebben Owens was too excited by the rest of the letter to notice the callousness of the postscript, and thought only of the kindness which so easily forgave his sin.

"Call Ann," he said, and Morva went joyfully.

"Come, Ann fach!" she cried, at the foot of the stairs, "here's good news for you. Will and his wife are coming to see you."

Ann came down in a flurry, half of pleasure and half of fright.

"Oh, anwl!" she said, as she entered the kitchen, "there's a happy time it will be for us all. Oh! mustn't we bustle about and get everything nice for them. I must rub up the furniture in the best bedroom and get the silver teapot out and the silver spoons!"

"Yes," said her father, rubbing his knees, "'twill be a grand time indeed! When will they come, I wonder? Perhaps we have not quite lost Will after all."

"Twt, twt, no," said Morva; "didn't mother always say that they would come back to you?"

"Yes, indeed—do you think she meant Gethin too?"

"I think she meant him too," said Morva, blushing.

"When will the gorse and the heather be in full bloom, I wonder? Caton pawb! I have never noticed it much," asked the old man.

"Oh! in another month," answered Morva, "'twill be gold and purple all over, with soft blue and brown shadows in the mornings, and in the evenings grey and copper in all the little hollows. Oh, 'tis beautiful! and I can show her where the plovers lay their eggs, and I will take her to listen for the curlew's note coming out of the mist like a spirit whistler, and I can take her down to the rocks by Ogo Wylofen, too, where the seals are making their home. But, indeed, Will knows it all as well as I do, and he will like to show them all to her himself, I think."

From that day light seemed to dawn upon the old man's soul; his step grew firmer, he stooped less in the shoulders, he looked less on the ground and more bravely on his fellow travellers on the road of life. He did not flinch from the consequences of his confession, but seemed to find some inward peace, which more than recompensed him for the discredit which he had brought upon himself. From this time forward a great change was observable in him, a change for which we can find no better name than *conversion*. It is an old-fashioned word, all but tabooed in modern polite society, but where will be found another which so well expresses the complete transformation in the life and character of a man who awakes from the sleep of selfish worldliness, to the better and higher principles of spiritual life? To every human being this awakening comes sooner or later. To some, gradually and naturally as the dawning of morning, and the bright effulgence of its rays is not recognised until the darkness and clouds have already rolled away, and, lo, it is day. Upon others it bursts with the suddenness of a thunderstorm, and the soul cowers under the threatening peals, and is riven by the lightning flashes of conscience before it reaches the haven of calm and peace. To some, alas, the awakening comes not at all, until through the open door of death the soul escapes from the veil of flesh which has hidden from it the true life.

"Is there a 'Sciet' next Sunday?" asked Ebben Owens, as they all sat at tea together one evening.

"No—not till the Sunday after," said Gwilym, reddening.

Ann's hand shook as she poured out the tea.

"Father bach!" she said tenderly, looking at him with eyes in which the tears welled up.

"Oh! don't you vex about me," said the old man. "I must bear my punishment like everyone else; 'twill not be so hard as I deserve."

"I must not let my feelings influence me in this matter," said Gwilym, "though you know, father, how it breaks my heart."

And he held his shapely hand across the table and grasped the old man's warmly.

"Yes, yes, 'tis all right; you must do your duty, only I would like it to be over soon. Gwae fi! that it could be next Sunday."

"Well, I will give it out at the prayer-meeting tonight if you like, and have a special meeting next Sunday."

"Yes," said Ebben Owens, "the sooner I am turned out the better. I am quite prepared. Perhaps they will take me back again some day, though I was pretty hard upon Gryffy Lewis when he got drunk, and would not agree to his being taken back again for months, when the other deacons were quite ready to forgive him. Well, well! I must live a good many years yet to repent of all my bad ways, and you must have patience with me, my little children."

"Well, next Sunday it shall be then," answered the preacher; "and may God turn the bitter to sweet for you, father bach."

"Oh, it will be all right for me!" said the old man again, and sitting under the big chimney after tea, Tudor and Gwil both leaning on his knees, the old peace and content seemed in some measure to have returned to him.

The following market day was a trying ordeal to him, but one from which he did not flinch.

At breakfast no one suggested the usual journey into Castell On, until Ebben himself called to Magw as she passed through the kitchen.

"Tell them to harness Bowler, and put the two pigs in the car. I'll sell them to-day if I can."

"I will come too," said Ann, "and take little Gwil to have a new cap. He wants one shocking."

She chatted volubly as they drove under the leafy ash branches which bordered the road, her father answering only in monosyllables.

When the pigs had been carried shrieking, in the usual unceremonious ear-and-tail fashion into their pens, and Bowler had been led into the "Lamb" yard, the old man looked rather forlorn and desolate as he gazed after Ann, who was making her way with little Gwil down the busy street.

"'Twill be hard to bear to-day," he thought. "They are all talking about me; but 'tis not so hard as I deserve."

Suddenly a hand was laid on his arm, and a kindly greeting

reached his ears. Mr. Price the vicar, standing at his window, had observed the Garthowen car pass into the market, and had startled his housekeeper by turning round suddenly with the question.

"Didn't you say we wanted a pig, Jinny?"

"That I did about six months ago, sare, but you never got one. We wanted one then because we had so much milk to spare, but now Corwen is drying up very much, and Beauty is not so good as she was."

Mr. Price took snuff vigorously.

"I think a little pig would look well in that stye, and he would be company for you, Jinny and we could buy a little bran or mash or something for him," he added, hunting for his stick and hat, and hurrying to the front door, Jinny looking after him with a smile of amused disdain.

"'Ts-ts!" she said; "Mistheer, pwr fellow, is very ignorant, though he is so learned. 'Tis a wonder, indeed, he didn't want to buy hay for the pig!"

But she went out pleased, nevertheless, and spread a bed of yellow straw in readiness for her expected "company."

"I wonder who is wanting to sell a pig now," she soliloquised. "I daresay Mishteer saw an old 'bare bones' passing that nobody else would buy, and is going to take pity on him."

"Poor old Ebben Owens. 'Twill be hard for him to-day," thought the vicar, as he made his way to the pig market, and in another moment he was gladdening the heart of the lonely old man by his kindly greeting.

Allen Raine

"Well, well, Mr. Price, sir! Is it you indeed so early in the market?"

"Yes, I have come to buy a pig," said the vicar, holding out his hand.

Embarrassment and shame suffused Ebben Owens's face with a burning glow, and he hesitated to place his own hand in the vicar's.

"Have you heard about me, sir?" he asked,

"I have heard everything," answered the vicar, grasping the timid hand and pressing it warmly.

"And yet you shake hands with me, sir? Well, indeed."

"Yes, with more respect than I have ever done before. Not condoning your sin, remember that, Ebben Owens; but honouring you for having the courage to confess it. That is sufficient proof of your repentance."

There were tears in the old man's eyes as he tried to answer; but Mr. Price, seeing his emotion, hastened to change the subject.

"Now let us see the pigs," he said, holding out his snuff box, from which Ebben Owens helped himself with more cheerfulness than he had felt since the meeting at which he had made his confession.

They bent over the pen in conclave, during which the vicar exhibited such lamentable ignorance of the points of a pig that, had it not been for his previous kindness, he would have fallen considerably in the old farmer's estimation.

"This is the fattest," he said, prodding one with his stick, and trying to look like a connoisseur.

"Oh! he's too fat for you, sir; this is the one that would look well on your table."

"Poor thing," said the vicar, a shadow falling on his face, as he realised that there would come a morning when the air would be rent with shrieks, and he would wish himself in the next parish. "No doubt, you're right, you're right, he looks a nice little pig; there's a nice curl in his tail, and I like his ears; he'll do very nicely. And here's Dyc 'pigstye.' Well, Dyc, how are you? Will you drive the pig home to my yard, and tell Jinny to give him a good meal, and a glass of beer for you, Dyc. And now we have settled that matter," he said, turning to the farmer with a business-like air, "I want you to come home with me, Owens, I won't keep you long, just that you may see a very nice letter I have had from your brother, Dr. Owen; 'tis all about your son and his bride, and the home they are coming to."

"But, Mr. Price, sir, you haven't asked the price of the pig," said the farmer, with a gasp.

"Bless me! no!" said the vicar, "I quite forgot that," and he laughed heartily at his own want of thought. "But I'm sure it won't be much. Two or three pounds, I suppose!"

"Two pounds I thought of getting for this one, and two pound ten for the other."

"Very cheap, too," said the vicar, drawing out the two sovereigns from his waistcoat pocket.

Leaving the pen in charge of a friend, Ebben Owens accompanied Mr. Price in a state of joyful bewilderment. To walk up the street, in friendly converse with the vicar, he felt would do more than anything else to reinstate him in the good opinion of his neighbours, and as they passed through the crowded market in animated and confidential conversation, the hard verdict which many a man had passed on his conduct was changed into one of pitying sympathy.

"Well," they thought, "the vicar has forgiven him, whatever, and he is a good man."

Sitting in the vicarage dining-room, listening to the praises of his beloved son, Ebben Owens became less depressed, and felt braver to meet the consequences of his confession.

Although he never discovered that the purchase of the pig was but a blind of the vicar's to hide his plans for helping him to regain, in some degree, the respect of his neighbours, Ebben Owens never forgot the strengthening sympathy held out to him on that much dreaded morning, and Price the vicar became to him ever after, the exemplar of all Christian graces.

"There's a man now," he would say, rubbing his knees as he sat under the big chimney at home; "there's a man now, is fit to help you in this world, and to guide you to the next; and there's the truth! But he does not know much about pigs."

The prospect of seeing Will once more in his old home shed a radiance over everything, and in spite of the humiliation and contrition which overshadowed him, a new-born calmness and peace gradually filled his heart.

To Morva too had come a season of content and joy—why, she could not tell, for she was not free from anxiety concerning Sara's prolonged absence. Certainly the longing for Gethin's return increased every day, but in spite of this, life seemed to hold for her a cup brimming over with happiness. Going home through the gloaming one evening, singing the refrain of her milking song, she broke off suddenly and began to run towards the cottage, for lo! against the brown hill across the valley she saw the blue smoke rise from Sara's thatched chimney, and in another moment a patch of scarlet showed bright against the golden furze.

"Mother anwl! Dear mother! you have come!"

And she was folded in the tender loving arms.

"My little daughter! I have missed thee!" said Sara, and together they entered the cottage.

Supper was on the table, and the crock of porridge hung over the blazing furze fire on the hearth.

"They called me into Penlau," said Sara, "as I passed through the yard, and made me bring this oatmeal, 'for thee'lt want something quick for thy supper,' they said; and there's asking questions they were about what I had seen in Cardiff. Let us have our bwdran, child, for oh! I am tired of the white bread, and the meat, and the puddings they have in the towns. Kitty Jones was very kind, making all sorts of dainties for me, but 'tis bwdran and porridge and cawl and bacon is the fittest food for human beings after all, and the nicest."

"Oh, mother, tell me what you have seen?"

"My little girl, 'twill take many days to tell thee all. Ladies in silks and satins—carriages and horses sparkling in the sun— men playing such beautiful music through shining brass horns—little children dressed up like the dolls you see at the fairs—fruit of every kind—grand houses and gay streets— but oh, Morva, nothing like the moor when the gorse and heather are in blossom, nothing like the sea and the rocks and the beautiful sky at night when the stars are shining; you couldn't see it, Morva, because of the lamps and the smoke."

"And the moon, mother, did you see her there?"

"Well, yes, indeed, she was there, but she was not looking so clear and so silvery as she is here. No, no, Morva, I thank God I have lived on the moor, and I pray Him to let me die here."

Morva was longing to ask whether success had crowned her mother's mysterious journey, but refrained from doing so with a nervous shyness which did not generally mark her intercourse with Sara.

"'Twas a long journey; mother; are you glad you took it?"

"Why, yes, child, of course, since I've gained my object. Gethin Owens will be home before long."

A crimson tide of joy rushed up into Morva's face, and an embarrassment which she turned away to hide, but which was not lost upon Sara.

"Well, indeed, then," said the girl, "there's glad 'n'wncwl Ebben will be. Will I go and tell him when I have finished my bwdran?"

"No, no, better not tell him anything till Gethin arrives. Lads are so odd; he may not come for a week, and that would seem long waiting to his father."

It was long waiting for Morva too, but she hid the secret in her heart, and flooded the moor with happy songs.

On the following Sunday evening a special Sciet was held in the gaunt grey chapel in the valley; an event of small importance to the outside world, but to Ebben Owens and every member of his family one of momentous interest. To them every event of life was brightened or shaded by its connection with their religious life, and Penmorien Chapel was almost as sacred in their eyes as the Temple of old was to the Jews.

The members dropping in one by one from moor, or village, or shore, looked with sympathising curiosity as the Garthowen family entered, and took their places in the corner pew, Ebben Owens sitting with them, and for the first time for many years vacating his place amongst the deacons in the square seat under the pulpit.

A formal admission of sin is of frequent occurrence at an "experience meeting," but the real confession of a sinful action is very rare. Therefore the Garthowen family required strong moral courage to enable them to pass through the trying ordeal of the Sciet, and its fiat of excommunication, with dignified firmness.

The doors were closed, the soft sea wind blew up the valley, and the breaking of the waves on the shore below was distinctly audible.

Sara and Morva did not attend the Sciet, but shut themselves up in their cottage, cowering over the fire as if it had been winter. Sara particularly, appeared to suffer acutely as the evening hours passed on.

"There's the sun going, mother, 'tis seven o'clock, the Sciet is over. Will I go and meet them? Oh! mother, I long to comfort 'n'wncwl Ebben."

"No, child, leave him alone to-night; he has better help than thou canst give him. To-night he will feel God's presence as he has never felt it before, and what else will he want, Morva? Come and read our chapter, 'merch i."

And while they read by the light of their tiny candle, and the furze crackled and sparkled up the open chimney, a bronzed and stalwart man was tramping down the stony road towards the chapel. Looking down the narrow valley, he saw the broad grey sea, its ripples tipped with the crimson of the setting sun. To the left towered the high cliffs which closed in the valley, and on the right stretched away the furze-covered slopes leading to Garthowen and the moor, and the rough sailor heart throbbed with the happiness of home-coming and the re-awakening of long deferred hopes. His brown face lighted up with pleasure, as he waved his hand towards the sunlit side of the scene, but he turned his face and his footsteps into the grey shadowed court-yard of the chapel. It was Gethin! He had sailed into Caer-Madoc harbour in the afternoon, the ships being the only things considered free to come and go during the Sabbath hours. He had met an Abersethin man in the town, who had promised to bring his luggage home in his cart next day, and had supplemented the promise by the information that on this particular evening, Ebben Owens would be turned out from the Penmorien Sciet.

"Jar-i! it's time for me to start, then," said Gethin; "will I be there in time, d'ye think?"

"Yes, if you walk sharp; but what will you do? You can't stop them turning him out! There's a pity!"

"No, no," said Gethin, "that's all right, I suppose; but I want to be there to meet the old man at the door. He'll find he's got one son that'll stick to him, whatever. God bless him!" and he started bravely along the old familiar road.

There were lights in the chapel windows as he approached, and outside the closed doors one solitary friend already waited. It was Tudor, who had sat there during the service, his eyes fixed on the blank closed door, doggedly resisting the inviting barks of a collie who had caught sight of him from the opposite hill. But when his long absent friend appeared on the scene his self-restraint was thrown to the winds, and Gethin in vain tried to check the joyous barks which accompanied his frantic gambols of greeting.

"Art come to guard the poor old man, lad?" whispered Gethin, holding up a reproving finger.

"Yes," said Tudor, as plainly as bark could speak.

"Then hush-sh-sh," said Gethin, pointing to the closed door, and Tudor smothered his barks.

The murmur of voices inside the chapel was distinctly audible, blending with the soft murmur of the sea. In a few moments the doors were opened, and the congregation filed out with a more than usually solemn look in their faces; some of the women dried their eyes, and actually refrained from even a whispered remark until they had got fairly outside the "cwrt."

Gethin kept out of sight until he saw his father leave the chapel, followed closely by Ann and Gwilym. The bent head and subdued appearance of the old man went straight to the sailor's warm, impulsive heart. With a single step he was at his father's side, taking his arm and linking it in his own.

"Who is it?" said Ebben Owens, his eyes blinded by tears and the darkening twilight.

"Gethin it is, father bach! come home to ask your forgiveness for all his foolish ways, and to stick to you and to old Garthowen for ever and ever."

"Is it Gethin?" asked the old man, in a tone of awed astonishment; "is it Gethin indeed? Then God has forgiven me. I said to myself: 'When I see my boy Gethin at home again, then will I believe that God has forgiven me.' Now I will be happy though I'm turned out of the Sciet. God will not turn me out of heaven, now that Gethin my son has forgiven me. Hast heard all my bad ways, lad?"

"Yes," said Gethin, "and I will confess, father, it nearly broke my heart. It made me feel there was no good in the world, if my old father was not good. But when I heard how brave you were in telling the whole world how you had fallen, and how you repented, my heart was leaping for joy. 'Now there's a man,' says I to myself, 'a man worth calling my father!' Any man may fall before temptation, but 'tisn't every man is brave enough to confess his sins before the world!"

Arm was already hanging on her brother's arm and pressing it occasionally to her side.

"Oh, Gethin!" she said, "Garthowen has been sad and sorrowful, but to-night it seems as if you had brought back all the sunshine. There's happy we'll be now."

"'Tisn't my doing," said her brother, "'tis Sara Lloyd who has done it all. God bless her! She came all the way to Cardiff to fetch me home. And where is she to-night? I thought she and Morva would surely be at chapel."

"She has kept away for my sake, I think," said his father. "They call her Sara "spridion,' and they mean no good by it, but I think 'tis a good name for her, whatever, for I believe the good spirits are always around her, helping her and blessing her just as she is always helping and blessing everybody around her."

"To be sure they are," said Gethin; "I always knew it from a little boy. Whether living or dying 'twould be well to be in Sara's shoes!"

When they reached the old farmyard, and passed under the elder tree where the fowls and turkeys were already roosting in rows on the branches, little Gwil bounded out to meet them, Gwilym Morris at the same moment caught them up from behind, and Ebben Owens felt that his cup of earthly happiness was refilled almost to overflowing. Gethin alone missed Morva.

CHAPTER XXIV

A DANCE ON THE CLIFFS

On the following morning Gethin was up with the dawn, and so was every one else at Garthowen, for the day seemed one of re-birth and renewal of the promise of life to all. Leading his son from cowhouse to barn, from barn to stable, Ebben Owens dilated with newly-awakened pleasure upon the romance of Will's marriage, and on his coming visit with his bride to his old home, Gethin listening with untiring patience, as he followed his father from place to place. The new harrow and pigstye were inspected, the two new cows and Malen's foal were interviewed, and then came Gethin's hour of triumph, when with pardonable pride he informed his father of his own savings, and of the legacy which had so unexpectedly increased his store; also of his plans for the future improvement of the farm. Ebben Owens sat down on the wheel-barrow on purpose to rub his knees, and Gethin's eyes sparkled with pleasure, but he looked round in vain for Morva. Some new-born shyness had overwhelmed her to-day; she could not make up her mind to meet Gethin. She had longed for the meeting so much, and now that it was within her reach, she put the joy away from her, with the nervous indecision of a child.

"Have the cows been milked?" asked Gethin, casting his eyes

again over the farmyard.

"Oh, yes," said Magw, "while you were in the barn, Morva helped me, and ran home directly; she said her mother wanted her."

All the morning she was absent, and nobody noticed it except Gethin, and Gwilym Morris, who, with his calm, observant eyes, had long discovered the secret of their love for each other. An amused smile hovered round his lips as, later in the forenoon, he entered the best kitchen bringing Gethin with him from the breezy hillside. Morva was tying Gwil's cap on when they entered, and could no longer avoid the meeting; but if Gwilym had expected a rapturous greeting, he was disappointed; for no shy schoolboy and girl ever met in a more undemonstrative manner than did these two, who for so long had hungered for each other's presence.

"Hello, Morva! How art, lass, this long time?" said Gethin, taking her hand in his big brown palm in an awkward, shame-faced manner, and dropping it at once as if it had scorched him.

"Well, indeed, Gethin. How art thou? There's glad we are to see thee. Stand still, Gwil," and she stooped to unfasten the knot which she had just tied.

Apparently there was nothing more to be said, and Gwilym saw with amusement how all day long they avoided each other, or met with feigned indifference.

"Ah, well," he thought, "'tis too much happiness for them to grasp at once. How well I remember when Ann and I, though we sought for each other continually, yet avoided each other like two shy fawns."

Allen Raine

In the evening, when the sun had set and given place to a soft round moon, he was not at all astonished to find that Gethin was missing: nor was he surprised, as he stood at the farm door, to see him rounding the Cribserth and disappear on the moonlit moor.

Reaching the broom bushes, Gethin waited in their shadows, recalling every word and every look of Morva's on that well-remembered night, when she had turned away from him so firmly, though so sorrowfully. Waiting, he paced the greensward, sometimes stopping to toss a pebble over the cliffs, and ever watching where on the grey moor a little spark of light shone from Sara's window.

Was he mistaken? Would she come to-night? Surely yes, for the broom bushes grew close to the path to Garthowen, and over that path she was constantly passing and repassing, whether in daylight or starlight or moonlight.

"'Tis very quiet here," he thought. "It makes me think of a night watch at sea."

The sea heaved gently down below, the waves breaking softly and regularly on the beach. He heard the rustling of the grasses as they trembled in the night breeze, the hoot of the owl in the ivied chimneys of Garthowen, the distant barking of a dog, the tinkle of a chain on some fishing boat rocking on the undulating waves; but no other sound broke the silence of the night.

"Jar-i! there's slow she is, if she's coming at all," said Gethin. "Will I go and see how Sara is after her journey? 'Tis what I ought to do, and no mistake, after all her kindness."

And leaving the shadow of the bushes, he stepped out into the full moonlight, only to meet Morva face to face.

"Well, indeed, Gethin!" she exclaimed, "I wasn't expecting to see you here so far from Garthowen."

"No; nor I, lass," said Gethin, taking her hand, and continuing to hold it. "I was so surprised to see thee out alone to-night; it gave me a start. I was not expecting to see thee."

"No, of course," said Morva, "and I wouldn't be here, only I was afraid I had not fastened the new calf up safely and—and—"

And they looked at each other and laughed.

"Well, now, 'tis no use telling stories about it," said Gethin; "I will confess, Morva, I came here to look for thee; but I can't expect thee to say the same—or didst expect to see me, too, lass? Say yes, now, da chi!"[1]

Morva hung her head, but answered mischievously:

"Well, if I did, I won't tell tales about myself, whatever; but, indeed, I mustn't stop long. Mother will be waiting for me."

"She will guess where thou art, and I cannot let thee go, lass. Dost remember the last time we were here?"

"Yes—yes, I remember."

"Dost remember I told thee what I would say if I were Will? Wilt listen to me now, lass, though I am only Gethin?"

Is it needful to tell that she did stay long—that Sara did guess where she was; and that there, in the moonlight, with the sea breeze whispering its own love messages in their ears, the words were spoken for which each had been thirsting ever since they had met there last?

Allen Raine

* * * * * *

In the early sunrise of the next morning Ebben Owens, too, was crossing the moor. He wanted to tell Sara of the happiness which his son's return had brought him, and to thank her for her share in bringing it to pass. He wanted, too, to tell her of the sorrow and repentance which filled his heart, and the deep gratitude he felt for all she had done for him.

She was already in her garden attending to her bees.

"Sara, woman," said the old man, standing straight before her with outstretched hands.

"Dear, dear, Ebben Owens, so early coming to see me! Sit thee down, then, here in the sun," and she placed her hand in his, endeavouring to draw him down beside her; but he resisted her gentle pressure and, still standing, bent his head like a guilty child.

"No, no," he said, with a tremble in his voice. "Tell me first, can'st forgive me my shameful sin? Everybody is forgiving me too easy, much too easy, I know. 'Tis only one will be always remembering, and that is me."

"I am not surprised at that, and I am glad to hear those words from thee," said Sara, "but my forgiveness, Ebben bach, is as full and free as I believe thy repentance is deep."

And gradually the old man ceased to resist her gentle persuasions, and, sitting down beside her, the bees humming round them, and the sun rising higher and higher in the sky, they conversed together in that perfect communion of soul which sometimes gilds the friendship of old age. Together they had experienced the joys of youth, in middle age both had tasted the bitterness of sorrow, and now in old age the calm and peace of evening was beginning to shine upon one as it had long shone upon the other.

"I have never thanked thee," he said at last, "for all thy loving-kindness to me; never in words, Sara, but I have felt it; and I thank God that thou art living here so near me, where I can come sometimes for refreshment of spirit, as my journey draws towards the end, for I am a weak man, as thou knowest, and often stumble in my path. Ever since that first mistake of my life I have suffered the punishment of it, Sara, and thou hast reaped the golden blessing."

"Yes," said Sara, looking dreamily over the garden hedge, "I have had more than compensation, my cup is full and running over. No one can understand how bright life is to me," and over her face there spread a light and rapture which Ebben Owens gazed at with a kind of wondering reverence.

"There's no doubt thou hast something within thee that few others have," he said, with a shake of his head.

Here Morva arrived from the milking, and finding them still sitting in the sunshine in earnest conversation, held her finger up reprovingly, and begged them to come in to breakfast.

"Oh, stop, 'n'wncwl Ebben, and have breakfast with us. Uwd it is, and fresh milk from Garthowen."

"No, no, child," said the old man, rising. "Ann will be waiting for me; I must go at once."

"Well indeed, she was laying the breakfast. She doesn't want me to-day, she says, so I am stopping at home with mother to weed the garden."

And as Ebben Owens trudged homewards, her happy voice followed him, breaking clear on the morning air as she sang in the joy other heart:

"Troodie! Troodie! come down from the mountain;
Troodie! Troodie! come up from the dale;
Moelen and Corwen, and Blodwen and Trodwen,
I'll meet you all with my milking-pail!"

The echo of it brought a pleased smile to the old man's lips, as he neared his home and left the clear singing behind him.

The day had broadened to noontide, and had passed into late afternoon, when Gethin Owens once more crept round the Cribserth. He crept, because he heard the sound of Morva's voice, and he would come upon her unawares—would see the sudden start, the shy surprise, the pink blush rising to the temples; so he stole from the pathway and crept along behind the broom bushes, watching through their interlacing branches while Morva approached from the cottage, singing in sheer lightness of heart, Tudor following with watchful eyes and waving tail, and a sober demeanour, which was soon to be laid aside for one of boisterous gambolling, for on the green sward Morva stopped, and with a bow to Tudor picked up her blue skirt in the thumb and finger of each hand, showing her little feet, which glanced in and out beneath her brick-red petticoat. She was within two yards of Gethin, where he stood still as a statue, scarcely breathing lest he should disturb the happy pair, his eyes and his mouth alone showing the merriment and fun which were brimming over in his heart.

"Now, 'machgen i," said Morva, "what dost think of me?" and she curtseyed again to Tudor, who did the same. "Dost like me? dost think I am grand to-day? See the new bows on my shoes, see the new caddis on my petticoat, and above all,

Tudor, see my beautiful necklace! Come, lad, let's have a dance, for Gethin's come home," and she began to imitate as well as she could the dance which Gethin had executed, with such fatal consequences to her heart, at the Garthowen cynos. Up and down, round and across, with uplifted gown, Tudor following with exuberant leaps and barks of delight, and catching at her flying skirts at every opportunity. As she danced she sang with unerring ear and precision, the tune that Reuben Davies had played in the dusty mill, setting to it the words of one refrain, "Gethin's come home, bachgen! Gethin's come home!"

Little did she know that Gethin's delighted ears missed not a note nor a word of her singing, or silence and dire confusion would have fallen upon that light-hearted couple who pranked so merrily upon the green.

But human nature has its limits, even of happy endurance; the temptation to join that dance was irresistible, and Gethin, suddenly succumbing to it, sprang out upon them. There was a little scream, a bark, and a flutter, and Morva, clasped in Gethin's arms, was wildly whirled in an impromptu dance, round and round the green sward, up and down, and round again, until, breathless and panting, they stopped from sheer exhaustion; and when Gethin at last led his laughing partner to rest under the golden broom bushes, he cared not a whit that she chided him with a reproving finger, for her voice was full of merriment and joy.

The sun was drawing near his setting, and still they sat and talked and laughed together, Tudor stretched at their feet, and looking from one to the other with an air of entire approval.

Allen Raine

Choose from Thousands of 1stWorldLibrary Classics By

A. M. Barnard
Ada Leverson
Adolphus William Ward
Aesop
Agatha Christie
Alexander Aaronsohn
Alexander Kielland
Alexandre Dumas
Alfred Gatty
Alfred Ollivant
Alice Duer Miller
Alice Turner Curtis
Alice Dunbar
Allen Chapman
Alleyne Ireland
Ambrose Bierce
Amelia E. Barr
Amory H. Bradford
Andrew Lang
Andrew McFarland Davis
Andy Adams
Angela Brazil
Anna Alice Chapin
Anna Sewell
Annie Besant
Annie Hamilton Donnell
Annie Payson Call
Annie Roe Carr
Annonaymous
Anton Chekhov
Archibald Lee Fletcher
Arnold Bennett
Arthur C. Benson
Arthur Conan Doyle
Arthur M. Winfield
Arthur Ransome
Arthur Schnitzler
Arthur Train
Atticus
B.H. Baden-Powell
B. M. Bower
B. C. Chatterjee
Baroness Emmuska Orczy
Baroness Orczy
Basil King
Bayard Taylor
Ben Macomber
Bertha Muzzy Bower
Bjornstjerne Bjornson

Booth Tarkington
Boyd Cable
Bram Stoker
C. Collodi
C. E. Orr
C. M. Ingleby
Carolyn Wells
Catherine Parr Traill
Charles A. Eastman
Charles Amory Beach
Charles Dickens
Charles Dudley Warner
Charles Farrar Browne
Charles Ives
Charles Kingsley
Charles Klein
Charles Hanson Towne
Charles Lathrop Pack
Charles Romyn Dake
Charles Whibley
Charles Willing Beale
Charlotte M. Braeme
Charlotte M. Yonge
Charlotte Perkins Stetson
Clair W. Hayes
Clarence Day Jr.
Clarence E. Mulford
Clemence Housman
Confucius
Coningsby Dawson
Cornelis DeWitt Wilcox
Cyril Burleigh
D. H. Lawrence
Daniel Defoe
David Garnett
Dinah Craik
Don Carlos Janes
Donald Keyhoe
Dorothy Kilner
Dougan Clark
Douglas Fairbanks
E. Nesbit
E. P. Roe
E. Phillips Oppenheim
E. S. Brooks
Earl Barnes
Edgar Rice Burroughs
Edith Van Dyne
Edith Wharton

Edward Everett Hale
Edward J. O'Biren
Edward S. Ellis
Edwin L. Arnold
Eleanor Atkins
Eleanor Hallowell Abbott
Eliot Gregory
Elizabeth Gaskell
Elizabeth McCracken
Elizabeth Von Arnim
Ellem Key
Emerson Hough
Emilie F. Carlen
Emily Bronte
Emily Dickinson
Enid Bagnold
Enilor Macartney Lane
Erasmus W. Jones
Ernie Howard Pie
Ethel May Dell
Ethel Turner
Ethel Watts Mumford
Eugene Sue
Eugenie Foa
Eugene Wood
Eustace Hale Ball
Evelyn Everett-green
Everard Cotes
F. H. Cheley
F. J. Cross
F. Marion Crawford
Fannie E. Newberry
Federick Austin Ogg
Ferdinand Ossendowski
Fergus Hume
Florence A. Kilpatrick
Fremont B. Deering
Francis Bacon
Francis Darwin
Frances Hodgson Burnett
Frances Parkinson Keyes
Frank Gee Patchin
Frank Harris
Frank Jewett Mather
Frank L. Packard
Frank V. Webster
Frederic Stewart Isham
Frederick Trevor Hill
Frederick Winslow Taylor

Friedrich Kerst
Friedrich Nietzsche
Fyodor Dostoyevsky
G.A. Henty
G.K. Chesterton
Gabrielle E. Jackson
Garrett P. Serviss
Gaston Leroux
George A. Warren
George Ade
Geroge Bernard Shaw
George Cary Eggleston
George Durston
George Ebers
George Eliot
George Gissing
George MacDonald
George Meredith
George Orwell
George Sylvester Viereck
George Tucker
George W. Cable
George Wharton James
Gertrude Atherton
Gordon Casserly
Grace E. King
Grace Gallatin
Grace Greenwood
Grant Allen
Guillermo A. Sherwell
Gulielma Zollinger
Gustav Flaubert
H. A. Cody
H. B. Irving
H. C. Bailey
H. G. Wells
H. H. Munro
H. Irving Hancock
H. R. Naylor
H. Rider Haggard
H. W. C. Davis
Haldeman Julius
Hall Caine
Hamilton Wright Mabie
Hans Christian Andersen
Harold Avery
Harold McGrath
Harriet Beecher Stowe
Harry Castlemon
Harry Coghill
Harry Houidini

Hayden Carruth
Helent Hunt Jackson
Helen Nicolay
Hendrik Conscience
Hendy David Thoreau
Henri Barbusse
Henrik Ibsen
Henry Adams
Henry Ford
Henry Frost
Henry James
Henry Jones Ford
Henry Seton Merriman
Henry W Longfellow
Herbert A. Giles
Herbert Carter
Herbert N. Casson
Herman Hesse
Hildegard G. Frey
Homer
Honore De Balzac
Horace B, Day
Horace Walpole
Horatio Alger Jr.
Howard Pyle
Howard R. Garis
Hugh Lofting
Hugh Walpole
Humphry Ward
Ian Maclaren
Inez Haynes Gillmore
Irving Bacheller
Isabel Cecilia Williams
Isabel Hornibrook
Israel Abrahams
Ivan Turgenev
J. G.Austin
J. Henri Fabre
J. M. Barrie
J. M. Walsh
J. Macdonald Oxley
J. R. Miller
J. S. Fletcher
J. S. Knowles
J. Storer Clouston
J. W. Duffield
Jack London
Jacob Abbott
James Allen
James Andrews
James Baldwin

James Branch Cabell
James DeMille
James Joyce
James Lane Allen
James Lane Allen
James Oliver Curwood
James Oppenheim
James Otis
James R. Driscoll
Jane Abbott
Jane Austen
Jane L. Stewart
Janet Aldridge
Jens Peter Jacobsen
Jerome K. Jerome
Jessie Graham Flower
John Buchan
John Burroughs
John Cournos
John F. Kennedy
John Gay
John Glasworthy
John Habberton
John Joy Bell
John Kendrick Bangs
John Milton
John Philip Sousa
John Taintor Foote
Jonas Lauritz Idemil Lie
Jonathan Swift
Joseph A. Altsheler
Joseph Carey
Joseph Conrad
Joseph E. Badger Jr
Joseph Hergesheimer
Joseph Jacobs
Jules Vernes
Julian Hawthrone
Julie A Lippmann
Justin Huntly McCarthy
Kakuzo Okakura
Karle Wilson Baker
Kate Chopin
Kenneth Grahame
Kenneth McGaffey
Kate Langley Bosher
Kate Langley Bosher
Katherine Cecil Thurston
Katherine Stokes
L. A. Abbot
L. T. Meade

L. Frank Baum
Latta Griswold
Laura Dent Crane
Laura Lee Hope
Laurence Housman
Lawrence Beasley
Leo Tolstoy
Leonid Andreyev
Lewis Carroll
Lewis Sperry Chafer
Lilian Bell
Lloyd Osbourne
Louis Hughes
Louis Joseph Vance
Louis Tracy
Louisa May Alcott
Lucy Fitch Perkins
Lucy Maud Montgomery
Luther Benson
Lydia Miller Middleton
Lyndon Orr
M. Corvus
M. H. Adams
Margaret E. Sangster
Margret Howth
Margaret Vandercook
Margaret W. Hungerford
Margret Penrose
Maria Edgeworth
Maria Thompson Daviess
Mariano Azuela
Marion Polk Angellotti
Mark Overton
Mark Twain
Mary Austin
Mary Catherine Crowley
Mary Cole
Mary Hastings Bradley
Mary Roberts Rinehart
Mary Rowlandson
M. Wollstonecraft Shelley
Maud Lindsay
Max Beerbohm
Myra Kelly
Nathaniel Hawthrone
Nicolo Machiavelli
O. F. Walton
Oscar Wilde
Owen Johnson
P.G. Wodehouse
Paul and Mabel Thorne

Paul G. Tomlinson
Paul Severing
Percy Brebner
Percy Keese Fitzhugh
Peter B. Kyne
Plato
Quincy Allen
R. Derby Holmes
R. L. Stevenson
R. S. Ball
Rabindranath Tagore
Rahul Alvares
Ralph Bonehill
Ralph Henry Barbour
Ralph Victor
Ralph Waldo Emmerson
Rene Descartes
Ray Cummings
Rex Beach
Rex E. Beach
Richard Harding Davis
Richard Jefferies
Richard Le Gallienne
Robert Barr
Robert Frost
Robert Gordon Anderson
Robert L. Drake
Robert Lansing
Robert Lynd
Robert Michael Ballantyne
Robert W. Chambers
Rosa Nouchette Carey
Rudyard Kipling
Saint Augustine
Samuel B. Allison
Samuel Hopkins Adams
Sarah Bernhardt
Sarah C. Hallowell
Selma Lagerlof
Sherwood Anderson
Sigmund Freud
Standish O'Grady
Stanley Weyman
Stella Benson
Stella M. Francis
Stephen Crane
Stewart Edward White
Stijn Streuvels
Swami Abhedananda
Swami Parmananda
T. S. Ackland

T. S. Arthur
The Princess Der Ling
Thomas A. Janvier
Thomas A Kempis
Thomas Anderton
Thomas Bailey Aldrich
Thomas Bulfinch
Thomas De Quincey
Thomas Dixon
Thomas H. Huxley
Thomas Hardy
Thomas More
Thornton W. Burgess
U. S. Grant
Upton Sinclair
Valentine Williams
Various Authors
Vaughan Kester
Victor Appleton
Victor G. Durham
Victoria Cross
Virginia Woolf
Wadsworth Camp
Walter Camp
Walter Scott
Washington Irving
Wilbur Lawton
Wilkie Collins
Willa Cather
Willard F. Baker
William Dean Howells
William le Queux
W. Makepeace Thackeray
William W. Walter
William Shakespeare
Winston Churchill
Yei Theodora Ozaki
Yogi Ramacharaka
Young E. Allison
Zane Grey